THE SCIE

The Science of the Stars

BY GUSTÁV REUSS

Translated from Slovak by David Short

JANTAR PUBLISHING

London 2023

First published in London, Great Britain in 2023 by
Jantar Publishing Ltd
www.jantarpublishing.com

Originally written in 1856.
This translation is based on the Slovak edition
first published in Bratislava in 2020 as
Hviezdoveda

HISTORICAL SCIENCE FICTION LIBRARY
Book 2

THE SCIENCE OF THE STARS
Gustáv Reuss
All rights reserved

Translation © David Short 2023
The right of David Short to be identified as translator of this work has been
asserted in accordance with the Copyright, Design and Patents Act 1988.

Introduction © Ľubica Schmarcová

Cover and book design © Davor Pukljak, Frontispis.hr
All illustrations made with the help of Midjourney AI

No part of this book may be reproduced or utilised in any form or by any
means electronic or mechanical, including photocopying, recording or by any
information storage or retrieval system without written permission.

A CIP record of this book is available from the British Library
ISBN 978-1-1914990-22-9

Printed and bound on paper sourced from sustainable forests by
Imprint Digital, Exeter, England

This book was published with the financial support of
the SLOLIA Board, Slovak Literary Centre.

Slovak
Literary
Centre

Contents

Editor's note from the Monokel edition of Reuss's
Hviezdoveda **(2020) by Ľubica Schmarcová** — 7

Translator's note for the present edition
by David Short — 8

THE SCIENCE OF THE STARS
BY GUSTÁV REUSS

Part One
The biography of Krutohlav, the things he discovered on Earth and around the Moon and Sun, and what he knew about the planets, comets and the birth and death of the world

17

Part Two
Contains Krutohlav's adventures and his memoirs regarding the rest of his journey and a detailed, but clear disquisition about the Sun

71

Part Three
Describes in detail the construction of the Dragon, flying aboard which Krutohlav explores Mercury, Venus, Jupiter, Saturn, Mars and other planets

101

Part Four

Contains an account of those bodies with tails called comets, of how Krutohlav and his companions were drawn into great peril and how they safely escaped the danger

159

Part Six

The Earth

209

Appendix

From the general geography of the world with which Reuss's book ends, appended here for the benefit/amusement of the Anglophone reader

255

Editor's note from the Monokel edition of Reuss's *Hviezdoveda* (2020)

This book is a selection made for the common reader from Gustáv Reuss's *The Science of the Stars, or the Life Story of Krutohlav, what he Discovered on Earth, around the Sun and the Moon, and what he Learned about Planets, Comets and the Origins and End of the World*. This is not a critical edition that would have reached for the original manuscript and copied the text therefrom, but an illustrated edition for the common reader, based on Viera Urbancová's 1984 edition (Gustáv Reuss: *Hviezdoveda*. Bratislava: Tatran, 1984; translated and with an Afterword and Explanatory Notes by Viera Urbancová).

From the original text we have taken only those sections that relate thematically to Krutohlav's astronomical explanations and expeditions, omitting several more tedious enumerations, explications and descriptions and the final 'geopolitical' section, which may be described as a period attempt to characterise nations, or as a Romantic psychology of the stock of races.

With a view to easing things for the contemporary reader and making the original more accessible, we decided to retain the historicisms in the text, providing explanatory notes on their meaning, but we have replaced archaisms with more readily comprehensible alternatives from modern Slovak. We took a similar approach, in the interest of comprehensibility, to period terminology. Abstract polysemic terms that could have any one of several meanings have been replaced by expressions adequate to the context in which they occur.

[Ľubica Schmarcová]

Translator's note for the present edition ...

I have kept the structure of the Monokel text, merely correcting a small number of editorial oversights therein and adding a range of notes that it lacks. Some overlap with, but develop as deemed necessary, the copious notes in Urbancová's 1984 edition, others fill gaps where, surprisingly, that edition has no note, while the majority are for the benefit of the 21st-century Anglophone reader. As for the text, the reader will be struck, above all, by the weights and measures employed: a rich assortment from various European systems alive in mid-19th-century Central Europe that it was deemed inappropriate to seek to convert into either the geographically inappropriate Imperial or anachronistic metric systems.

Some of the astronomical facts may have been corrected or re-interpreted by later *science*, but the whimsical humour of the *fictio*nal narrative skeleton is timeless.

As an aid to the reader, I should point out that the focal point of the narration is the hills around Gustáv Reuss's (1818–1861) small home town of Revúca in Gemer County, Central Slovakia, about 50 miles east of the country's geographical centre and only a little further east of the geographical centre of Europe. Among the many odd facts about the town I should at least make the point that it is home to the first Slovak *gymnázium* or grammar school (1862) in what was still Upper Hungary, one sign of how progressive it was.

Perhaps more remarkable than the place where this book came into being is its dating and the character of its author: completed in 1856, almost a decade *before* Jules Verne's *De la terre à la lune* appeared, and two decades before Verne's Capt. Hector Servadac made it to the planets, it was written by a man who was a doctor, a highly competent botanist, ethnographer, historian, archaeologist and astronomer and a man who was desperately keen to see the knowledge he had acquired made more widely available. The great pity is that *Hviezdoveda* had to wait almost 130 years before it first appeared in print. In this way, all the author's intentions were completely thwarted: the main concern was clearly to make a huge body of astronomical knowledge available, essentially in textbook form, more visible in the first, complete, modern edition of 1984. However, the present translation, like the Monokel edition on which it is based (v.s.), has kept only a tiny fraction of the geographical and geopolitical, i.e. non-astronomical, half of the work), retaining all of the whimsical fictional narrative of the book's first half that was doubtless meant to lure in a wider readership.

Even today, despite the two modern editions, Reuss remains unknown to many Slovaks. And this appears also to apply to his work as an ethnographer, in which he collaborated with his father Samuel (1783–1852) and brother Ľudovít (1822–1905), and that despite their vast collection of folk tales being a source for later work by the much better known Pavol Dobšinský (1826–85) and despite Gustáv's having even engaged in correspondence with his fellow-folklorist, the Czech Božena Němcová (1820–62), who had discovered the Reuss MS collection, *Codex revúcky*, on her travels. Even as a botanist he seems to have fallen into oblivion for a century, for all that his *Května Slovenska* (Flora of Slovakia, 1853), which describes over 2000 species of the 4000 he had collected, actually provided a large part of the botanical terminology of the still barely stabilised modern Slovak language. Reuss himself writes in what has been described as "incorrect Czech intermingled with a form of Slovak conspicuously influenced by his local dialect" (Viera Urbancová, in the end-notes to her 1984 modernised text, p.287).

It has been said (Wikipedia) that Reuss was possibly inspired to use the fantasy approach to his work on astronomy by the fantastical elements encountered in many of the folk tales he had collected. The outcome became, however, the first big step, for all that its actual appearance was so lamentably delayed, along Slovakia's quite modest road to science fiction. There have been those who would deny, from ignorance, that Slovak literature has any sci-fi thread at all, but a sterling attempt to jettison any such notion (and one which makes due note of the parallel history of fantasy literature in Czech, from Jakub Arbes [1840–1914] onwards) can be found in an article by Jozef Žarnay and Cyril Simsa: "Science Fiction from a Dusty Shelf: A Short History of the Fantastic in Slovak Literature to 1948" (*Science Fiction Studies*, Vol. 23, No. 1 [Mar., 1996], pp. 27–36; also at https://www.jstor.org/stable/4240477), which obviously takes Reuss as its starting point (and is the only source I have seen that gives his full name as Gustáv Maurícius Reuss). I was perhaps most taken by its conclusion: "... when someone asks us whether there is any SF in Slovakia, now at least we can reply in the same way that we reply when someone asks us whether there are any Slovak mountains: 'Yes, they're little – but they're ours!'"

... and acknowledgements

Despite the modernised language of the two printed Slovak editions, the text of the later one still contains certain expressions and geographical and historical references that are opaque, not to say mystifying, where Google, Wikipedia and online dictionaries failed to provide the answers I needed. In this respect I am extremely grateful to **Ľubica Balážová** of the Ľudovít Štúr Institute of Linguistics in Bratislava for assistance with some of the dialectisms and arcane terminology that occur in the text and are not covered by the glossaries in either of the Slovak editions, or by existing dictionaries, and to **Karin Kilíková**, Director of the Revúca Municipal Arts Centre, for the time and effort she put into finding answers to the local geographical and historical references that even many locals will not have understood. Karin is, incidentally, to be thanked – by others – for having seen to it that the edition used as the basis of this translation has also been turned into an audio book – quite an enterprise!

David Short, Windsor, June 2023

Gustáv Reuss

The Science of the Stars

OR

THE BIOGRAPHY OF KRUTOHLAV,
THE THINGS HE DISCOVERED ON EARTH
AND AROUND THE MOON AND SUN,
AND WHAT HE KNEW ABOUT
THE PLANETS, COMETS AND
THE BIRTH AND DEATH
OF THE WORLD

They called him Krutohlav[1] *because of the way he kept shaking his head. He came from Mníšany,*[2] *broad-shouldered, stout-hearted and level-headed. Those desirous of knowing him should take the trouble to acquaint themselves with his biography herein.*

---

[1] From *krútiť hlavou* 'twist *or* shake the head'. I originally called him Wryneck in English as the literal equivalent of Krutohlav, i.e. the bird name, which admirably captures in Slovak both the bird's curious faculty, and the motion of shaking – or, more literally in Slovak, 'twisting' – one's head in amazement or bewilderment, a major trait of the protagonist. Most of the time, the English version of the name did not appear particularly intrusive, merely jocular, but in certain sections of dialogue with alternating speakers, all of them having very Slovak names (many of them trisyllabic and ending in *-slav* or the essentially jocular *-oš*), *Wryneck* was distinctly incongruous.

[2] A village in south-central Slovakia, joined with neighbouring Kopráš in 1960 and renamed Magnetizovce. It lies about 10 km ESE of Revúca, the county town.

PART
ONE

A TRAVELOGUE BY THE CELEBRATED KRUTOHLAV, A SLOVAK FROM MNÍŠANY, RELATING HOW HE EMBARKED ON A TRIP TO THE MOON, WHAT HE DISCOVERED AND THE THINGS THAT BEFELL HIM.

This momentous story was copied from Krutohlav's manuscript by Eduard Hudáčik[3] during his sojourn at the Buda Observatory in 1855.

---

[3] The surname of this fictitious individual almost certainly contains a grateful nod in the direction of one of Reuss's grammar school teachers, Matej Hudáčik.

KRUTOHLAV'S PREAMBLE

Let us rise above the vanity of the world and let everything stay stuck in its same old rut so that we may, having borne ourselves aloft into the very heights of heaven, discern a new life and a new world. In our everyday life, all we ever see is duplicity, deception, iniquity, malignity and multitudinous transgressions against the Ten Commandments. What, then, is to keep us bound to such an inauspicious existence? Let us remove ourselves from Mother Earth the better to see our and her closest, ever-rotating companion and discover whether we might not feel better there, perhaps leading a peaceful and more benign existence and, in short, ending our brief life in blameless quietude and brotherly harmony.

Here, we Slovaks migrate to the Land of Canaan (he means the Lower Land or Hungary proper), over yonder, the Germanic tribes emigrate to various other lands, and, elsewhere, the English strain every sinew to make money, while the French would go to the ends of the earth just to stay in fashion. And why? All so that each might live more at ease within their own egotism. So why should not we, too, we who are more circumspect and infused with higher ideas, simply leave Earth to those peoples who just drift about and bicker among themselves, rise one rung higher and, sequestering ourselves against all such egotistical profit-seeking, take possession of domains like unto Paradise, since all that we crave is to live, move and have our being in peace, love and wholehearted goodwill? How vain is life, how short! So why should we not leave, or seek to leave, this Earth and the never-ending fight against misery and penury, cease seeking those parts of it that are so much better than our own, but seek instead higher, more benign spheres, more sublime than Earth? Let us then go there, to those faraway places, and even if we cannot be transported there immediately, be we mindful that nothing stands in our way, or in the way of our descendants, to prevent us from exploring the still inapprehensible ways by which we might arrive there, arrive...

... at the Moon!

I am, then, that person infused with higher ideas who shall blaze a trail for you, people, so that you may see, and not forget, the signs that I shall place before you. Hold on tight, and then, sometime in the future, you will be able easily to reach the new earth, where a new world, a new paradise will ensue.

Written in the vicinity of the Moon,

Krutohlav.

HOW KRUTOHLAV MEANT TO REACH THE MOON

Krutohlav never stopped thinking how he might find some way by which to reach the Moon, even if that meant moving at breakneck speed. Imbued as he was with grand ideas, it vexed him that he could not take a closer look at the Moon. So he picked up some mathematical instruments and began to investigate:

1. The distance of the Moon from Earth.

He ascertained that its mean distance from Earth was exactly 51,812 leagues. That brought him up short, because even hiking up to King's Ridge[4] left him gasping for breath, so what would it be like when he'd have to keep going uphill for thousands of leagues? Counting on his sound lungs and sturdy legs, he wasn't

---

4   Here translating Kráľova hoľa, a high point in the Low Tatras known for the vast panorama of Slovakia that it affords.

easily deterred from his resolve. With a sigh he took up a sheet of paper and a quill pen and calculated what 51,812 leagues meant. And he discovered that...

If he could head for the Moon as it were along a railway line and a steam engine could travel eight leagues in an hour, it would take only 270 days to get there, allowing for twenty-four hours per day. "Two hundred and seventy?" Krutohlav muttered, twisting his head this way and that. "That's a bit too long." So he abandoned the railway idea and looked for something else. And he found that...

If he took a post-chaise that could cover 24 leagues a day, it would take only five years and 247 days to reach the moon. He abandoned that idea as well, thinking that was too long a journey.

As he ruminated thus it suddenly dawned on him that he could hardly get there at all, with roads and railways being out of the question. So he cast aside all such silly ideas and hit on a better one: the only way to get there was through the air. Naturally, he resorted once again to his pen and paper. And he found that...

If he were to launch himself into the heavenly heights towards the Moon in a balloon made ready for the purpose, one which could rise at the rate of 15 feet per second, he might be able to get there in two years and 179 days. But travelling through the empty atmosphere, never to see a single little tree or anything else, struck our Krutohlav as terribly dreary over such a long period. So, pushing his spectacles up over his eyebrows and gripping his snuffbox, he took a jolly good pinch – and lo and behold! – another idea flashed through his mind and brain. This one resided in the possibility that the time could be shortened by some deliberately induced hurricane or windstorm; windstorms here have a speed of 60, at times as much as 100 feet per second, so that way he could reach the moon much faster, in 136 days.

This last calculation so spurred him to take a trip to the Moon that he would have boarded the balloon there and then and flown off to a new world. He remained in his musings, as if a huge balloon might be constructed at the drop of a hat, for weeks on end – having terrible thoughts that pursued him without letting up. In the course of his endless cogitation and complete immersion in his ideas it occurred to him that...

Balloonists surely don't know how to steer their balloon in a safe direction and the wind just takes it wheresoever it will. "What would become of me," he muttered inside himself, "if instead of travelling to the Moon I were to sink to the bottom of the briny deep?"

That a safe direction for a balloon to travel in can be set, of that Krutohlav had no doubt, trusting entirely that a compass would point him surely in the direction of the Moon and escort him there. In this respect he saw the kernel of the problem lying there cracked on his desk. Pursuing his thinking further, he appreciated that our Earth never stands still, but keeps spinning at a steep angle around itself, winging and zinging along at over 355,000 leagues a day, meaning that it defies comparison even with the flight of a cannon ball. This left Krutohlav in such a stupor that his pen fell from his hand. However, he was not to be put off and so went on to examine the Moon and where it stood in relation to Earth as it went on its way. Then he would see the light, he said, and the matter of whether he might or might not catch up with the Moon in his balloon and arrive there safely would be resolved of itself. So he taxed his mind further and discovered that the Moon – spinning around Earth at the same speed as it – did, firstly, travel at the same speed as Earth and so covered 355,000 leagues a day, and secondly, in addition, it whooshes past with a sinuous motion and at an uncertain speed. Having recalled that the Moon, circling Earth at a distance of 518,000 leagues and twisting past it 12.333 times a year without ever keeping to the same course, Krutohlav was quite distressed and remained in a daze for several weeks. He did finally come round and so even this matter seemed to have been dealt with. So with a merry mien he continued to ponder the many snags that might crop up on his way to the Moon.

He duly found that...

The gravitational pull of both our Earth and the Moon might well create impediments and complications for him. "What? Gravitational pull! That's just the piffle of astronomers and physicists," he exclaimed, flying into a rage. The more trivial the idea struck him, the more painful the brooding into which he sank. The more he ran his hand over his head, the more convinced he became that Earth's gravitational pull would not let go of the tiniest of poppyseeds, so it was even less likely that it would willingly let a huge balloon, which his mind's eye already saw constructed, leave its confines.

"This circumstance is ever more probable," Krutohlav mused on, "for Earth, as we know all too well, never gave anything to a third party, or let anything go. Selfishness – that's all it is," Krutohlav exclaimed, and this fact alone, that Earth itself exhibits selfishness, made him want to travel to the Moon as soon as possible. So agonisingly cross had he become with Earth! "But never mind, things look different with the Moon. Once I sneak across Earth's frontier – as I believe I will," he went on, "it will remove me from Earth's hold and embrace me gladly. True, the Moon also keeps a grip on what is its own, and it will grab and keep anything that arrives, but it can be forgiven for that as just a kind of antipathy that it's picked up from Earth." The now complacent Krutohlav let this idea mature for a long time before his cogitation took him another step forward.

He was imagining himself already flying somewhere in the region of the Moon when he also worked out that if he went any closer to it, it would want to pull him towards it with such a force of attraction that the balloon would face the risk of crashing and that his own life would be in the balance. Thinking that he might be able to help himself and cope with the problem in due course, his composure was restored.

It seemed, then, that he had surmounted all the preliminary obstacles, for he'd had all the craftsmen from the valleys of the Gran (Hron) and Muráň, and from as far away as Liptov, Zvolen and Šariš, brought along to start work on the gigantic balloon, which they were to haul first to the top of Kohút hill,[5] whence he would then travel to the Moon. Never before has the world seen so many workmen together! The entire valley of the Muráň was filled to bursting with carpenters, cabinet-makers, millers, leather workers and every kind of smith imaginable etc. etc. All round Veľká Revúca, from Bartová to Revúčka, he could see massive stocks of trees, panels, saws, axes, shingles, stringers, beams, nails etc. There was hammering here, there was sawing there, chopping here, cutting there, crushing here, sewing there, patching here, lopping there etc. etc. Here a bang, there a squeak, here a rattle, there some general commotion, all as if the Day of Judgement were nigh. There you might see some beams artfully assembled together and rearing higher than the Skalka hilltop redoubt, here you might

---

5 Kohút, at 1,409 metres above sea level, is the second highest of the Stolice Hills, some seven km NE of the town of Revúca, Reuss's birthplace, almost in the middle of today's Slovakia. His language carries with it some of the lexical features of the Revúca dialect.

see bladders like huge hollows, there bellows, belts, waxed threads and so forth. Not to mention axle grease and cobbler's glue, all so that even the smallest hole in the balloon was not missed beneath any grime, mud, stitching or planking. Thus, then, was created that celebrated balloon on which so many thousands had worked and aboard which Krutohlav hoped to abandon this selfish Earth and migrate to the more blissful dominion of the Moon.

WHAT KRUTOHLAV MEANT TO FILL HIS BALLOON WITH

At no time since the world began had anyone anywhere constructed a balloon like Krutohlav's. Even its smallest dome was 20 sections abeam. Following the constant taxing of his brain and the skilled workmanship of so many from far and wide, Krutohlav was brought up short by the matter of what would be best to fill the balloon with to ensure that it would rise steeply, comfortably and dependably up into the heavenly heights. Needless to say, such an important consideration would call for a gas that would be considerably less dense and lighter that what filled the space between Earth and Moon, otherwise it wouldn't be able to budge an inch or hold its own in the rarefied atmosphere of the heavens. So what to do about it? He knew very well that, filled with ordinary air, the balloon would easily rise three leagues above Earth, but thereafter, with the atmosphere growing ever thinner or disappearing altogether, how would it manage then? At that point, his mind, as the saying goes, went blank! For one last time he braced himself spiritually and rekindled his wits. The lines about his mouth were ample evidence that he would get the better of this problem as well! And his face flushed red-hot.

OTHER PROBLEMS
THAT KRUTOHLAV IDENTIFIED
BEFORE HIS TRIP TO THE MOON

Everything seemed set for the trip to the Moon when the prudent Krutohlav, still lost in contemplation of the whole enterprise, imagined yet more problems that stood in his way. "If," he said to himself, "I do manage to take off with my balloon and head for the Moon through lethal, unknown space, the gravitational pull of selfish Earth will still spoil everything because I lack the power to withstand it." But the keener he was to break free from Mother Earth, the more obstacles cropped up to stand in the way of his expedition. But in order shrewdly to get the better of them, too, he ordered yet more devices to be constructed, primed with gunpowder and capable of thrusting his balloon up and away into the heights and towards the Moon until it broke free of the gravitational pull of Earth and went into orbit round the Moon, which struck him as an ever more salubrious place to be. For a clearer idea of the gigantic contraptions that were to thrust the balloon to the Moon, let us look at Krutohlav's calculations, where he had written in the plainest terms:

"If the balloon is to break free from the gravitational pull of Earth, the force needed must be enough to hurl it 41,000 feet from Earth in the direction of the Moon within the first second. This awesome speed is 30 times faster than that of a cannon ball. Without it, it will be impossible to escape Earth's gravitational pull and go into orbit round the Moon."

Krutohlav almost literally ricked his neck, shaking his head as he puzzled away, and that despite believing unquestioningly all the true forces of physics. He meant to overcome the difficulty, which he often himself thought insoluble, by making monumental preparations and so reinforcing his balloon that it would withstand even the sixtyfold speed of a cannon ball.

A NEW DIFFICULTY STANDS IN KRUTOHLAV'S WAY

He even hit on the following idea: if he did rise up into the heavenly heights, he was going to need a supply of fresh air in order to stay alive, because there was none at all up there and above Earth it existed up to three leagues at most. What was to be done about that? It couldn't be sewn into a bladder, and a great deal of it gets exhaled over two years and 179 days. So he invented contraptions – huge ones – that would hold air and would be attached to the balloon like hideous tails.

He also took account of the absence of air on the Moon, and even if it did have air of a kind, it would be different from terrestrial air and deleterious to human lungs. That so annoyed him that he lashed out at all astrologers and said what he thought of them.

KRUTOHLAV'S NEXT INCONVENIENCE

He had now overcome all the difficulties that he might encounter in the course of his expedition, though there was still one that left him seriously depressed, and that resided in the fact that though he, Krutohlav, was tough, robust, of a fighting spirit and to the manner born where such voyages were concerned, he did enjoy living a life of ease. From this it follows naturally enough that he weighed just short of 40 stones. He wined and dined well, always kept his nose blown and insisted on a salutary nap after lunch, if not of the full six hours' duration, at least almost that long. He would rise at nine, take a good hour over his coffee and at two in the afternoon would consume several pounds of pork with sausages and black puddings. A pint of wine, invariably Tokay, was the necessary accompaniment. In a word, he lived like a knight aloof to the vanities of the world and, in his very eminence, delighting in his own capabilities. As an excellent mathematician he had computed his trip to the Moon, where he could live a life of yet greater ease! So how could our Krutohlav not be distressed at the discrepancy that, having set about this long journey to the Moon, he would see not a single tree, no other human soul, nor hills nor dales, not even a tavern wherein he would find his subsistence and sleep everything off in the quiet of his little room. How *was* he to part company with his table of delights? This distressed him no end and he might almost have abandoned his trip to the Moon, except that he had invested so much in the preparations, which had cost him millions: he had packed his balloon with binoculars, telescopes, microscopes, barometers, aero-colori-thermo- (etc.) -meters so that the world at large might be assured that he was a cut above all others, more majestic and given over not to earthly riches, but to God and mankind. Such amazing willpower on the part of Krutohlav, who, for all his maximum persuasion as to the rightness of the most minimal of his ideas, never stopped shaking his head in his perplexity.

THE TRIP
TO THE MOON

Anyone who doesn't know what travelling to the Moon means – such a long journey undertaken in such an arduous manner – can line up beside Krutohlav and fly up there, into the heavenly heights.

The only thing left for him to do was to haul his balloon, finally ready thanks to the endeavours of so many thousands of people, to the top of Kohút and take off thence for the Moon.

"Perfect job!" Krutohlav let slip. "Off to Kohút with it!"

Thousands of hands laid hold of the balloon. People even streamed in from Lower Hungary to watch and help haul the monster balloon up Parajka.[6] There's none can relate all the countless procedures by which the prodigious balloon was conveyed onward and upward. No mortal living had ever seen such huge herds of oxen, mules, horses, even rhinoceroses and elephants as Krutohlav had drafted in from sundry corners of selfish Earth to assist in the task. So thousands of beasts were hitched to the giant balloon by means of every kind of rope, chains from trip hammer forges, straps and whatever else might help on the ascent of Parajka.

It isn't hard to imagine that dragging the balloon from Skalka, on the outskirts of Revúca, to the top of Kohút took ten months, three weeks and five and a half hours. Or the shouting and screaming, the mooing and booing, the clinking and clanking, the banging and crashing that went with it. Or how many people departed this life here merely – as is brought home to us – as

---

6   The western slopes leading up to Kohút from Revúčka.

Mother Earth's bootless reward to them, meaning the carpenters, joiners, bootmakers, tanners, belt-makers and endless other -ers, even linen-weavers and quacksalvers! But no such reward has ever been enjoyed by anyone in Revúca since the beginning of time, as the dead among them now recalled all too well. From that time, the balloon having proved impossible to convey up the steep ascent in a straightforward manner, they hacked a way through to the top of Kohút that still remains visible below the summit.

With the application of the might and main of so many, the balloon was finally set up on the mountain's very peak and made ever more ready for take-off, and everything having been duly inflated, they waited with baited breath for it sail up into the atmosphere. And at the very moment when the Moon was full, so that the balloon wouldn't lose its way.

And rise it did, then flew off into the heavenly heights.

THE TRIBULATIONS THAT BESET A TRAVELLER TO THE MOON

"Farewell, my countrymen, I'm off to live an eternal life in yonder parts," he said, waving his hand as if he were never to return. He tightened the torsion spring, lit the fire and shot skywards so fast that the thousands of onlookers lost sight of him almost at once.

He flew higher and higher, but the Moon grew no bigger than as he'd seen it from Kohút. He'd been hurtling along for two weeks and each second brought him fifteen feet closer to the Moon, but it still remained the same size. It really is a long way away, and when Krutohlav recalled that he needed two years and 166 days more to get there, he became so distressed that he wanted to turn back. But his robust spirit stiffened his resolve even despite seeing naught but the Moon and the Sun and thousands of stars, not a rock, or tree, or even a little bush, nothing suggestive of either mankind or nature. So he just tightened up all his sails, air-bags and ropes, stoked up the fire and hurried on towards the Moon, if with his hopes subdued.

HOW KRUTOHLAV CONTINUED RUMINATING

Being of an exalted spirit, he intended to get to the bottom of every obscurity. The more complex things struck him, the more he endeavoured to simplify them. Small wonder, then, that he worked out that...

If the inhabitants of the Moon have eyes like ours, then they cannot fail to detect both every way in which light and colours mutate, and, with their naked eye, all the blotches showing on Earth just as we can see those on the Moon. So they must be able to make out islands, seas and dry land, and all in full colour. And since he wanted to be quite clear about everything, he averred that if, on Earth, a new moon rises around noon, they must be able to see Europe, Asia and Africa as a single whole, paler in colour, ringed by darker colour – that's to say the ocean – which surrounds them.

And more: after the passage of twelve hours, for them the blotches on Earth turn into America, where they'll see thousands of islands forming something like the shape of a horse's leg.

MORE OF
KRUTOHLAV'S VIEWS

The longer he mused over his discoveries, the more he liked them. He put his new ideas to the test time and time again so that, once he became a lunar resident, he could be an eye-witness to the future, or to the changes that would come about on Earth. This impelled him to more and more cogitation, and he hit on some quite magical things.

1. Our Earth – and this is a matter our astronomers have argued about since time immemorial – is oblate (flattened at its ends, the poles), which any inhabitant of the Moon could easily swear to; and indeed Krutohlav himself, the further removed he became from Earth, could indeed see it flatter at the poles. So he was astonished that Earthlings were still arguing over something of which any lunar peasant had not the slightest doubt.

2. Thriftless and mercenary Earthlings first learned of the existence of America and Australia in the days of Columbus, Amerigo Vespucci and Cook, whereas anyone local to the Moon could prove beyond doubt that America and Australia had definitely been there since the Creation.

3. They also know all about the route to the East Indies on the north side of Earth. We're told every year by the newspapers how many lives have been lost for the sake of profit and expanding our knowledge of geography. Moon-dwellers could have made a small fortune out of the government in London just by sending them a map with the route marked on it. Krutohlav was so beguiled by this idea that, if he were to face unforeseen problems during his sojourn on the Moon, he'd sell the route to the London government, or any other, for a tidy sum.

4. He was also propelled towards the Moon by the realisation that even if he were forced to turn back, he could, from this great distance investigate the landscape surrounding the South Pole, which had been familiar to the inhabitants of the Moon since goodness knows when, given that it presents itself to them almost thirty times a month.

5. Upon further enquiry he quite naturally realised that the inhabitants of the Moon must have looked on unfeelingly on both occasions when Earth suffered a great flood. How plain and simple must it have presented itself to them, while our own forebears were either completely flooded out or displaced in some other way! We only know of those deluges from legends, for instance the one about Atlas, but we also learn about them from the structure and stratification of the earth where marine creatures are found, even on mountain tops. Krutohlav was quite taken with the notion that he was going to be able to observe Earth's various future transformations from a safe height.

6. If a battle were to unfold on a plain, Krutohlav would be able to observe it from the Moon much better than any commander on the ground. "I wonder how they saw the Siege of Sevastopol,"[7] he mused, shaking his head with caution; they saw the city itself somewhat darker than Severnaya and the port was darkest of all. They would have seen the allies flying up and down like ants and, as the port was being taken, a tiny little cloud flaring up. "I do wonder what people thought of it all," he pondered, shaking his head all the while. "But for the inhabitants of the Moon," he thought, "it

---

[7] To Reuss, a recent (1854–55) event, in the Crimean War. I haven't been able to ascertain what he means by Severnaya (Rus. 'north'), hardly the river, which is the Chornaya. Possibly a reference to the north shore of Sevastopol Bay, to which the Russians had to evacuate across a pontoon bridge.

all looked different, because the attacks were carried out for no apparent reason, and furious they were, against Kamchatka,[8] Kornytov,[9] the Redan and Malakoff.[10] The Moon's inhabitants' blood must surely have run cold at the sight of so many two-legged flies massing to seize hold of some walls or other. Their amazement at such random murdering must have known no bounds," Krutohlav muttered, and he opened his snuffbox and took a pinch, because he was starting to get bored aboard his balloon.

7. Let's not be thinking, though, that Krutohlav hadn't travelled here and there on Earth, despite being a burgher of Revúca and dismissing all strangers as aliens, "goodness knows where from". No, he'd been as far away as Brno and Olomouc, and even Vienna, so it at once crossed his mind whether, once he'd reached the Moon, big cities like, say, Vienna, might not leap to the eye. He started to groan at his inability to work this problem out, but having gripped his pencil firmly, he discovered that if Vienna – as he found among his papers – measured 18,000 feet across, when he got up there, and using a telescope with 25× magnification, he'd see it the same size as we see Uranus. His eyes sparkled at the thought that his best telescopes would show him the Glacis[11] and all the famous streets of Vienna, and even, perhaps, his dear

---

8 Presumably an allusion to the Franco-British attack on Petropavlovsk in 1854,

9 The only reference to such a place turned up by an internet search is this very sentence from Reuss.

10 References to the Great Redan and the Malakoff (Malakhov) Redoubt, fortresses attacked by the British and French respectively in 1855 as part of the Siege of Sevastopol. The former presumably gave its name to the Redan Inn in Chilcompton.

11 The open field ramparts surrounding the walls that protected the inner city of Vienna. Later, they were to be replaced by the circular boulevard known as the Ringstraße. For a good map of what Krutohlav imagined he would see (with the Glacis marked), see the 'History' section of https://en.wikipedia.org/wiki/Vienna_Ring_Road (accessed on 11.11.2021).

friends, especially the girls he'd loved. And he was really looking forward to seeing Revúca town hall, Úkorová Hill and other local landmarks. He'd be able to make out the Danube, Tisza, Waag and Sajó,[12] and even the local River Muráň, etc.

8. Additionally, he was considering creating up there the best-ever map and sending it back down so that Earthlings might finally appreciate things that they'd never known since the start of time: what lay at the heart of Africa and New Holland;[13] whether it was all hills or whatever else. But let's not go thinking that he exhibited occasional signs of a profit motive, that he had no desire to evince his will as a scholar by being of service to Earthlings in all areas that had previously gone untouched and overlooked. His profound desire to be of benefit to Earth so spurred him on that he yanked on his ropes with such force that he almost fell out of his balloon. Small wonder that one who seeks the wellbeing of others risks destroying himself in the process, and there are very few who would appreciate that. But Krutohlav regained control of his balloon, wrenched it back into an upward direction and flew higher and higher. On the matter of such a disaster – as his tumbling back down – we merely note that his ideas, conceptions and the relationships between Moon and Earth would have remained forever lost in total darkness. It is thanks to his having been saved by being caught on a projecting spike that we are able to reproduce other, extremely useful things. So his indomitable spirit had no alternative but to draw his limp colours taut in order to reach the Moon as soon as possible. So on he flew, to the ends of the cosmos.

---

12 I.e. the major watercourses known in Slovak as Tisa, Váh and Šajava, the latter now known as the Slaná.

13 New Holland - Australia, a name that was just about dying out at the time Reuss was writing.

THE MOON'S CLIMATE

"That would never do, not to be able to ascertain what it's like," Krutohlav mumbled, "since I'm taking up residence there." So he quickly took up his pencil. He worked out that beneath the Moon's equator the Sun would always be burning the top of his head, but at its poles he would only get toasted horizontally. That he did not fancy, having been used, on Earth, to Spring, Summer, Autumn and Winter. But then it dawned that, beneath the equator, summer ruled eternal, while at the poles it was winter's turn. "Never mind," he told himself, "I'll go for the middle, and I'm sure the Moon won't disappoint me." Completely absorbed in his thoughts, he worked out that, if he took over some land between the equator and one of the poles with a view to settling there, it would have to be springtime all the time. He rejoiced at this truth and couldn't wait to reach a place where his days would constitute an endless spring.

NIGHT AND DAY ON THE MOON

Krutohlav, accustomed on Earth to resting well and sleeping long, was rather discomposed by the realisation that a day on the Moon was exactly as long as a night. But why, oh why should it be so? Shouldn't one be entitled to rest longer in wintertime? This irked him somewhat, but to no avail, for his calculations offered no other conclusion.

"I should have chosen a terrestrial pole instead, where it's either day or night for a long time, so I could get plenty of rest when it was night."

"It's a crying shame," he exploded right there in his balloon, "that at least a third of the time on the Moon isn't night; that way I'd get plenty of rest."

So enraged was he that he determined to check all the other properties of the Moon, including establishing how clement the air was (i.e. its temperature). And quite right, too, since he meant to take up residence there!

THE AIR ON THE MOON (TEMPERATURE)

"Eh?" Krutohlav muttered gloomily, "Could it be that the atmosphere on the Moon and on Earth isn't the same? Any dunderhead knows," he pursued his ruminations, "that the regions that lie close to one of the poles are steadfast in warming up during the summer, while, conversely, those about Earth's Equator cool down considerably just as things are at their hottest; so why couldn't I, on the Moon, cool down now and again during the lunar spring? And yet," he mused on, "when the Sun invariably shines determinedly horizontally at the poles, the air doesn't warm up, and, on the contrary, where the Sun beats down on the top of my head, I have to put up with the most blazing of heat. I shall yield to my fate and choose such a region where I shall be now cold, now hot, and even if not – since that just isn't possible – I shall make such regions mine as are dominated by a uniform, constant, moderate temperature. That way will be best for me, for I, accustomed to life on Earth, have often caught a chill or cold, especially on Kohút; and so in order to break free of any such indisposition, I have no other option. Even now, I can see the benign climes of my new world, where I shall be myself again!"

WHAT THE SKY IS LIKELY TO LOOK LIKE ON THE MOON

Another idea sprang into Krutohlav's head, one that had been bothering him much of the way already. Faced with such an important question, which he was keen to solve, he grabbed his spectacles from his pocket, set them upon his nose, extracted his snuffbox and took a good pinch so that the ideas going round inside his head would be the clearer for it, or so that fresh, smarter questions might emerge. And he ascertained that...

To moon-dwellers, as to him as a future new inhabitant, all stars, comets and even suns spin round and round the Moon in the same old way, or, actually, the Moon spins round them. The exception is our Earth, which plays no part in any form of rotation, but just shines happily away up there on the Moon's horizon. And that, to moon-dwellers, Earth appears much larger than the Sun, and larger than the Moon appears to us Earthlings, thirteen times larger. Krutohlav was quite taken with that idea, though this seeming falsehood and foolish notion troubled him enough for him to keep shaking his head in disbelief. So once again he took up his pencil and found that this really was the way things were. He rejoiced at the prospect of being able to observe and scrutinise Earth, invariably huge.

He didn't stop there, but wondered further about the regions of the Moon that would always offer him the best view of Earth. He discovered that if he wished to live at the centre of the Moon's disc, Earth would be towering vertically above his head the whole time. He didn't fancy that, because it would give him neck-ache if he had to keep straining upwards just for Earth's sake. So he went on to verify what Earth would look like if he took up residence at the Moon's poles, or endpoints of the disc. And he discovered that Earth would then present itself to him horizontally. He didn't fancy that much either, for if he settled in some valley or other, he'd never see his original Mother Earth ever again. So once more he resolved to take up residence somewhere in-between, twixt the centre and a lunar pole, so that he might observe that thirteen-times-larger Earth and relish it to the full.

Thus in the course of casting around for major truths regarding the world of the Moon he had become utterly engrossed in his thoughts and arrived at the facts that: from the Moon, Earth appeared thirteen times larger than the Moon as we know it, that Earth stood firmly and motionlessly in one spot, and that it could boast of a perpetual gleam. "What might moon-dwellers think of Earth, with so many millions of stars spinning round it, and even the Sun itself, while Earth alone stands firm and motionless on their horizon? Since they're pagans," he mused on, "it's natural that they should worship this Earth, as it stands idle before their gaze, create graven images and pray to it." Immersed in such thoughts, Krutohlav fell sound asleep!

THE INHABITANTS ON THE NEAR AND FAR SIDE OF THE MOON

Resurfacing out of his deep slumber, Krutohlav desired to know just how things were with the inhabitants of the Moon, and how they would be with him, its future inhabitant. First, he was curious about their everyday life, and he realised that...

Our Earth can only be observed by those moon-dwellers who live on the front face of the Moon's disc. The opposite, or rear, side of the Moon can know nothing of the kind. At best, the near-siders might write about it and report to the rear-siders about the appearance of an entirely new world, shining bright. "Might not some take it into their heads," Krutohlav said to himself, "or be impelled by such extraordinary aspects of the Moon-world, to gather in droves in order to witness the ineffability of the divine? I'm convinced that they arrive constantly in those favourable parts and marvel at the power of God!"

OTHER MERITS OF THE MOON'S INHABITANTS

Krutohlav, shaking his head as ever, determined to seek and find just which regions of the Moon would be best suited to him so that, having arrived, he might live there in the greatest comfort. Should that be the near or the far side of the Moon? – yet another question to occupy his mind and not leave him there just twiddling his thumbs. So he eagerly set about cracking this particular nut and clearing up the matter of his future abode.

"Settling on the facing side of the Moon's disc," he told himself, "will bring me the following benefits:

1. If ever my thoughts take me back to Earth and I want for more, I can just look up and see my homeland.

2. From the Moon, Earth will present itself to me with a fullness such as the Moon never presented itself to me from Earth. I shall see all the changes and alterations of colour on Earth – much as I observed from Earth those taking place on the Moon.

3. To suit themselves, Moon-dwellers have long since worked up a calendar from the Full Moon and the quarters, so he, too, would be able to adapt everything to accord with their time.

"And what would the far side of the Moon have to offer, were I minded to settle there?" Krutohlav's heart began to torment him. And he came up with something that he couldn't quite comprehend: that people on that side never saw the Sun or Earth. He frowned and decided that not for all the tea on the Moon would he ever go to live on its far side.

KRUTOHLAV SPOTS
HILLS ON THE MOON

The closer he drew to the Moon, the more the dark patches he could see on it changed into unevennesses of the terrain. At first he'd mistaken these patches for clouds, but that was wrong, because they grew ever more localised and unchanging than he had thought. So he picked up a more sharp-eyed telescope in order to discover more about how the Moon was moulded, a place where he, like Adam and Eve in Eden before him, was to dwell. And it was brought home to him that...

1. The Moon was a huge, gigantic sphere, for the closer he came, the larger it showed itself to be. He liked that, for he would not have wished to remain on a vertical lunar plane and risk falling off, as he saw it, into a boundless world at any moment.

2. The more he examined the surface of the Moon, the greater grew Krutohlav's conviction that it wasn't smooth and flat like a mirror, but that it was crisscrossed by valleys and hills. And that could scarcely fail to appeal, it having occurred to him that if the mood took him, he could go hunting to his heart's content and shoot goodness knows what kinds of animals.

3. That the Moon receives light from the Sun and as we on Earth get some light from the Moon, so he on the Moon would

receive some from Earth. That apart, the Moon was just as dark a body as Earth.

4. That Earth presents itself to Moon-dwellers as just as patchy as the Moon strikes us.

"So what do the light and dark patches mean?" he was keen to work out: straining his mind and eyes to the absolute limit, he discerned that the dark patches represented lower-lying, flatter parts, while light patches were elevations of considerable size. Let us not surmise, though, that he believed only his lens – their height and the depth of the valleys was brought home to him by the shadow falling on them from Earth, as from the Moon itself. This was, he now knew, the only real way to investigate the height of the Moon's hills and the depth of lunar valleys until he was actually on the spot. "When I reach the Moon," he told himself, "I can use chains to measure all these things. But out here, flying on my balloon, I have to make do with my telescope and mathematical calculations." So at increasingly closer quarters he went on observing the Moon with his telescope, the more so given that he had invented an even lighter gas, which sent him towards his goal by leaps and bounds.

KRUTOHLAV DESCRIBES THE HILLS THAT HE HAD SEEN ON THE MOON

The closer he drew to the Moon, the higher the mountains and the deeper the valleys revealed themselves to be – and as much more prodigious than those on Earth. To give himself a clearer idea of the matter, Krutohlav determined that the mountains on the Moon are four times higher relative to those on Earth. Obviously he liked that, because he promised himself that from such heights and using the best telescopes constructed by Herschel he would be able to observe the Sun and other heavenly bodies at closer quarters and, at some future date, write up a vast volume and offer it, especially to his new fellow-citizens, in a beautifully printed edition, or, time permitting, he might send these new things to Herr Littrow[14] in Vienna. Thrilled and laughing up his sleeve, Krutohlav rubbed his hands in glee.

KRUTOHLAV EAGERLY SETS ABOUT DISCOVERING WHAT THOSE ANNULAR ELEVATIONS ACTUALLY ARE

He turned his attention to the ring-like elevations that he'd seen, and it struck him as all the more likely that his first lodging on the Moon would, or could, be on some such elevation. Extending his telescope to the full, he discovered that they were too numerous to count and that not the slightest sign of any such thing could be found on Earth. He surmised that they were of volcanic origin, that is, they had come about in consequence of a huge conflagration that had raged goodness knows when and left them in the shape that Krutohlav was seeing. In the middle of their visible depression they are just like craters, with the difference that the Copernicus Crater has a diameter of seven leagues, while Etna's in Sicily measures only half a league. What a great fiery force can have raged here to rework an area seven leagues across and turn it

---

14 Joseph Johann Littrow (1781–1840), Bohemian-born Austrian astronomer, graduate of Charles University, Prague, professor of astronomy at Vienna University and director of the Vienna observatory (both posts held from 1819), and author of the tremendously popular and frequently reprinted *Wunder des Himmels* (Miracles of the Sky, 1835–36), which is held to be the inspiration behind Reuss's book (footnote on p.292 of the 1984 Tatran edition). Littrow has a lunar crater named after him.

into one gigantic pit! He took a closer look through his telescope into the hollows of many more craters and found that around the main interior embankments, in the middle, within the circular crater-like hollows themselves, there were entire lowlands and inclines often covering 4,000–5,000 square geographic leagues.

Krutohlav found this hard to fathom and he thought of Bohemia, likewise encircled by mountains. But the closer he looked, the more convinced he became that on the inside everything was desolate and arid, not at all like Bohemia, where you'll find many villages and towns etc. Then he set about measuring and working out the mean depths between the hills. Some came to 18,000 Paris feet and so were as deep as Chimborazo is high. Such an absolutely colossal depth must have surprised him – what on earth would he do in such an enclosed basin, so barren and arid? Whereupon he shook his head disconsolately.

KRUTOHLAV REFLECTS FURTHER ON THE MOUNTAINS OF THE MOON

At this stage in his investigations, these truths about the Moon were not nearly so solid as the next ones Krutohlav undertook to throw light on and investigate. First, his ingenuity told him that the matter (mass) of these annular elevations was exactly enough to fill in the basin or crater within them. In terms of matter, the ring, or annulus, of such an elevation was just like the surrounding mass. So, naturally enough, he deduced that all the surrounding elevations must have been upcast in some violent way and so the basins could not, as he'd first thought, have come about by mountain tops collapsing inwards.

He reminded himself that he'd observed no flow of lava-like deposits around the annuli, such as he'd seen in times past on Etna, Vesuvius or Thekla, and that what he was seeing could only have come about through some mechanical force. He wasn't pretending that a volcano hadn't been active here, but was ever more convinced by what his eyes could see, that it could and must only have all been piled up mechanically during a massive conflagration. "So what do these regular accumulations surrounding a vast basin mean? Would I not have seen signs of lava flows down the sides if it were otherwise?" Krutohlav mused. When, with his very best telescope, he saw their volcanic character, as in the depressions of Vesuvius and Etna, and the volcanic stratifications within them, he felt even more stout-hearted at the opportunity to investigate and find answers to such questions that would be especially important to his imminent residency on the Moon.

KRUTOHLAV OBSERVES VOLCANOES ERUPTING ON THE MOON

Krutohlav remained convinced that the annular elevations in particular had come into being through the power of fire and so he continued to subject them to proper observation. As he watched, he suddenly spotted some flashes of fire and, roaming about Plato[15] with his telescope, he saw a light disappearing through a fracture in it. And just as the Moon was presenting itself to him as dark, a sudden bright light caught his eye. That got him thinking that an erupting volcano gives out precisely such

---

15 *Plato*, a lava-filled impact crater on the Moon with a diameter of 63 miles.

a flash. Just as he was taking a second look at the area around Hevelius,[16] with which he was already familiar, he was brought up short by a volcanic cauldron one and a half leagues wide where previously he'd seen nothing. What's more, in the so-called Mare Crisium[17] (whether or not it was a sea would transpire in due course, but that's what Krutohlav baptised it, because he wanted to place English ships on it), he found the elongated elevation that he had often painted images of and measured; and suddenly, having examined it, he saw in the clearest light that it was perfectly circular and that at its peak there was a cauldron a quarter of a league wide, of which he'd had no previous knowledge and had never even seen. Meanwhile something extraordinary happened to Krutohlav: a month later, the same elevation presented itself to his telescope, still elongated but with no cauldron. Many more of Krutohlav's excellent notes could be added at this point, if only he'd set them down with greater clarity, but he only made jottings in his precious papers, meaning to work them up later before offering them to the world. So let us, too, stand back from them until the day dawns when we can see them verified.

The Moon's volcanic mountains brought him both joy and a measure of disquiet, for he had meant to investigate the cause of their vulcanicity, which is presently being so widely argued over, yet once again: given the great vulcanicity of the mountains, he could see in advance that his very life could be in danger; having taken up residence on such a rampaging Moon, he could be blown up and burn to death. So as we can see, Krutohlav was quite convinced about the burning mountains, for he never

---

16 *Hevelius* is a lunar impact crater at the western edge of the *Oceanus Procellarum*, named after the astronomer and mayor of Danzig, Johannes Hevelius (1611–87).

17 *Mare Crisium*, a lunar 'sea' located NE of the Sea of Tranquillity.

ceased to ponder how safe life was – if he ever did settle on the Moon. But he thought that, despite all that fire on the Moon, he might yet find a landscape where no volcanoes had ever raged, or one that had long been extinct. Exhausted, Krutohlav fell asleep!

KRUTOHLAV, MEDITATING ABOUT THE ATMOSPHERE AND WATER ON THE MOON, STARTS SPOUTING GIBBERISH

Krutohlav had been contending quite enough with the complex problems of the Moon, but when he got round to the atmosphere and water on the Moon, his mind, as the saying goes, went to pot, or at least he started maundering. For now let's listen to his views and maybe we'll learn a thing or two.

The closer he approached the Moon, the more untarnished it presented itself to him, and he could detect no rain or clouds or anything else. That disconcerted him greatly, for if Earth has an atmosphere, it also has clouds and must also have water, which is entirely natural and is indeed how things are on Earth. So, then, if the Moon has an atmosphere, why wouldn't it also have water?

So it did matter to him whether the Moon held on to some sort of air or not. "Without air, I can't live on the Moon," he told himself and strained his eyes until they began to water. "Since the Moon isn't as large a body as Earth, it can't sustain such a thick and dense layer of air," was his initial conclusion. "But precisely because it is a heavenly body affected by both Sun and Earth, it must have something akin to an atmosphere." That was all that Krutohlav let unfold from his mind.

He therefore extended his telescopes and found that the boundaries of light on the Moon are sharply defined, that the brightest light of one side of the Moon switched into the darkest dark on the other side. "In which case one ought not to find any atmosphere," he brooded, "and that would prove highly unfavourable to me."

Seeking to secure greater safety for himself on this journey, he turned his telescope towards Venus and observed that there the brightest light merged into the densest darkness only gradually. Turning to our Earth, he observed the same thing. In this respect, then, Earth was quite similar to Venus while the Moon *eo ipso* differed greatly from it. Having once theorised that the Moon must surely have an atmosphere of sorts, Krutohlav was moved to delve further into this important matter. A new moon had just started and Krutohlav turned all his attention to its so-called horns to see if he could detect any hint of the light fading, for if he found even the slightest sign of a transition from light into dark, that would show the presence of air. Finally he did find just the slightest degree of transition and calculated that the atmosphere on the Moon was one third of a geographic league thick. Turning then to Earth, he worked out that, by contrast, its atmosphere rose to between eight and ten leagues above it. He was filled with joy and consoled himself that even though the Moon afforded less of an atmosphere than Earth, it was, after all, possible to live there.

It wasn't just air that would enable Krutohlav to stay on the Moon, but water as well, which is entirely natural. So he scoured everywhere for rivers, streams, springs or seas, but failed to find any. "But how's that possible?" he yelped. "Where there's air, there has to be water as well," and he just stood there, lost in thought. Before long, however, he began rationalising thus: If air disappeared from Earth, all water courses and seas would be bound to dry up in short order, and the entire planet would perforce be totally dehydrated. Since the Moon does have air of a kind, it must also hold moisture of a kind within it. Despite failing, even with the aid of his telescope, to spot either river or sea or anything like what there is on Earth, he nevertheless braced his hopes that water would be found there. Again he surveyed what are called seas and found that most were pitted and gently undulating; elsewhere they were smoothly uniform, but nowhere could he descry even a glint of water or a hint of waves. At the same time he was still ruminating about actual fire-spouting volcanoes (of whose existence he had not the slightest doubt). After all, how could they burn without air, if there were none on the Moon? For it's a known fact that no fire can burn without air.

Despite Krutohlav's conviction that the Moon had no moisture and his impression of it as being as dry as something cast in gypsum or sulphur and spangled with countless bubbles and clefts, ups and downs, despite the appearance that its changing colours suggested it consisted of nothing but glassy debris, rocks without life, without plants or animals – where eternal repose and the grave held sway – and its appearance of having had its day and entering upon a new life, he – shaking his head in bewilderment as ever – could not apprehend that a body such as the Moon could be so wanting of everything. In view of its God-given purpose, it couldn't be lifeless, and why, besides air, should it not have water, too, and animals and plants and organisms, albeit different as to character and form from those on Earth?

Such conclusions stirred Krutohlav into probing further and opening the way to other sciences. He had been vexed at the thought of having to enter such an arena, though he cheered himself with the thought that the Moon, as it now struck him, would not be a completely soulless and impotent wasteland. So he cast his gloomy reflections aside and went on with his investigations in order to gain a glimpse of how Moon-dwellers lived and of his own future quarters. Feeling slightly giddy after his arduous deliberations, he had eased up for a while, but now he suddenly pulled himself together, ordered a new gas to be fired aboard the balloon so that it would hurtle even faster towards the Moon and so that he might the sooner convince himself of the truth of the conclusions that so mattered to him. After its brief respite, the balloon was now careering onward and upward at three times the speed, ever upward into the heavenly spheres.

KRUTOHLAV SEARCHES FOR ANIMALS AND PEOPLE ON THE MOON

Like never before, Krutohlav's puzzled head-shaking now went on for so long and with such vehemence that his face almost sank down to his neck as he wrestled with this problem. Having investigated every major corner of the Moon, he had failed to discover any kind of living creatures, buildings, castles or towns. To whichever point he turned his telescope, nothing of the kind was visible anywhere. "But that's not possible," he yelped, "I can see mountains and valleys, ridges and plains and so on, so how can an omniscient god have created the Moon for the sole purpose of its remaining an eternal desert? That's just not possible." He changed the lens in his telescope, set his spectacles on his nose for good measure and kept twisting the telescope hither and yon in the direction of the Moon so busily that he dislodged a number of sails from his balloon, which, having hit the ground near Constance and Neusiedl, caused Lake Constance and the Neusiedlersee to form. But his inflamed passion and zeal yielded nothing: all the elephants, horses, oxen and asses, even people, that he had conjured up in his imagination reverted the following day into impassive rocks and stones. He was quite cross with his lens for so deceiving him and grew thoroughly depressed and regretful that he was to arrive in such a disagreeable place where there'd be not a soul with whom he might have a chat.

So he tossed all his telescopes aside and began ruminating on the likely or most likely reasons for the moon-world to be.

KRUTOHLAV'S IDEAS ABOUT THE CREATURES WHO INHABIT THE MOON

Since he had failed to find any living thing on the Moon, Krutohlav began thinking along the following lines.

"If there are beings living up there," he told himself, "they must differ in every respect from people on Earth, because if there is some kind of air there, it is and has to be different from the air on Earth. And if there is water, which is probably not impossible, it will and must, because of the difference in the Moon's air, be quite different from the water on Earth. I've examined closely all the hills and dales, plains and tracks – or whatever they are – lakes and seas without finding a single trace of an actual river, stream or spring, let alone a true sea. So what kind of landscape can it be, atmosphere with no water, or even water with some air, but different from Earth's water and air?

"A lack of air and water – if there even is any of the latter – may be forejudged on the basis of the Moon's prevailing aridity, for I haven't spotted even the tiniest cloud. And if a little cloud were to be found, it would be so flimsy and so high up as to be imperceptible.

"And if we consider the same case that without water and air the Moon is almost completely without weather, how does it affect animal and plant life?" At this point Krutohlav seriously scratched his head, but that didn't arrest his speculations. "So there's no spring or summer, autumn or winter either!" he muttered. "What a mischievous fate! For a full fortnight the Sun blazes away at the Moon, then for another it's ruled by total darkness! That must be plenty for not just springs, but entire seas, to dry up. So what about those animals and plants? A plant can't take up water, for there won't be enough of it, or of air, and what's an animal to eat or drink? And with no plants growing, how is an animal to stay alive? It defies my imagination to accept that it could live on metals! So it is entirely natural that without air and water neither plants nor animals can live here at all. So much for my paradise!" We should not be surprised at such entirely natural ruminations on Krutohlav's part, for the greater part of his schooling had been Austro-German. His imagination led him yet further, as it might have been supposed to. In the end he did come to his senses and to other significant realisations that cast more light on things for him. But that's how things go anyway, with one thought chasing after another.

"All right," Krutohlav said to himself, "that's all true, but it must also be true of the Moon that, as is the relationship between an animal and man on Earth, so must be the Moon's relationship to Earth. That's how nature works." But he had sunk so deep into this idea that he barely wished to put such an utterly profound thought into words. The core of it was that a dog is a dog, or that no other animal can rise from its natural essence to some greater standing either, even it has reached the supreme degree of perfection. And just as an animal has its pre-defined purpose, so does man, and just as any individual has, so too any material entity. Duno is, surely, the wisest dog ever – beneath the church and wearing glasses, he has studied the whole of Kant, read Gesellschafter, behaved correctly, but on seeing a lady dog he reverts to his own, that is, canine realm. And are we to think that despite his celebrated book *Bonology*, in which he inveighs against all bones, might not the greatest bone of the many lash out and give him a nasty gash? Such is Nature's truth everywhere, and such will it be on the Moon, too, when I begin to compare it to Earth. Since the Moon is much smaller and has a much rarer and lower atmosphere, it may, nay must, have water, plants and animals commensurate with itself. That is its purpose, the way it has evolved! "The fact that I cannot see," Krutohlav went on, "or detect any plants and animals, that I cannot spy them with my big eye, does not mean that the Moon has been dispossessed of anything that lives and moves. Futile, nay crazy, is the thinking of anyone who believes in the death and not the life of such a body as the Moon appears to us."

Exhausted, Krutohlav would rather have undergone death than believed that the Moon is but a ghastly, lifeless wasteland. In the hope that he would soon discover that which he sought, he lay down and slept peacefully until the next day.

KRUTOHLAV MUSES ON THE DWELLINGS OF THE MOON'S INHABITANTS

Krutohlav, having thus arrived at an understanding of both air and dew, and thereby also figured out life on the Moon, thought it only natural to throw some light on the habitations of the animals there, as far as that were at all possible. "Since there is such blazing heat on the Moon as I have ascertained," he declaimed resolutely, "it is quite possible that its denizens have chosen as their dwelling places precisely those ravines, of which there are so many, so as to avoid being roasted by the Sun. And why wouldn't they indeed? We know that the deeper down they are in such lunar chasms, the denser the air must be there and the kindlier to their lungs. And why shouldn't these inhabitants live underground as terrestrial fish live under water, or like mice and moles? Why shouldn't they hide away in their caves, safe from the Sun during the 14-day heat, and only thereafter come out into the open? Or might they not have built castles and chateaux down in the depths the way our Slovak forebears built castles in the heights?

"Hm! This is all quite remarkable," he carried on musing, "why mightn't the Moon's inhabitants, the size of ants on Earth, be as fast-moving, agile, nimble, sprightly and quick off the mark as many of our beetles? Why mightn't they reside, like ants, in big heaps, digging, harrowing and finishing pathways and Lord knows what else just as they do in Revúca, Zdychava[18] or Vienna, Paris and London? And then, mightn't all the tracks and channels that I saw through my telescope prove to be genuine lines of communication between their towns and castles? And why should we who live on Earth and potter about on its surface not be able to concede that elsewhere, most notably on the Moon, living creatures might lodge underground?"

Krutohlav was entirely satisfied by these conjectures, convinced as he was that the Moon couldn't possibly be a gigantic, empty wasteland, despite the blazing sun that roasts and toasts it by turn so that little if anything can withstand it. He took into

---

18 Muránska Zdychava, a village in the hills 9 km north of Revúca and just west of Kohút hill, where it all began. It is renowned for its well-preserved folk architecture and sits astride a trout stream called Trout Brook.

consideration not only this, but all his previous conjectures and truths; he was also satisfied and gratified to be far removed from any kind of delusion. By turns his mind kept bringing up air of whatever kind, or dew, or the pathways that looked like roads, and so once again, with a clap of his hands, he exclaimed:

"The Moon's alive, it has air, and plants, and animals. It also has rain trapped in the dew." And with that he finished his note-taking for the day.

KRUTOHLAV FOUND CERTAIN SIGNS OF DWELLINGS ON THE MOON

Although Krutohlav could not have convinced anyone, or himself, that the Moon did show beyond doubt certain regular signs of having inhabitants and their enclosures, his conjecturing was perpetually brightened by the notion that the Moon could not be an utter wasteland without nature. So he unpacked his finest lenses and inserted them in his telescope to draw an extra sharp bead on the Moon, which suddenly seemed so much more convenient, given that the Moon was now considerably closer – or so it seemed – though that might have been just the lenses working. As he looked, he observed regular earthworks or embankments, artfully constructed and disposed in such a way that there was no concealing the fact that they had been constructed deliberately. Krutohlav went on to discover, at many points on the Moon, certain indications of roads, agglomerations (groupings) similar to our towns, and evident signs of husbandry.

KRUTOHLAV MEASURES THE SIZE AND WEIGHT OF THE MOON

Krutohlav set about a major task, having deduced that:

1. To the inhabitants of the Moon our Earth presents itself as 13 times larger than how the Moon appears to us and that all the alternating light patterns are the same as on Earth.

2. The Moon's mass is almost 70 times less than that of Earth. That's as much as if a loaf of bread were split into 70 pieces and one piece would represent the Moon, the rest Earth. Such then is the Moon, its valleys and hills. How could our Earth not appear gigantic by comparison?

3. The gravitational pull of the Moon is, compared to that of Earth, five times weaker, i.e. Earth attracts any solid body to it five times faster than the Moon does. If someone on the Moon fired a rifle shot, the bullet would travel five times further than on Earth.

KRUTOHLAV IMAGINES WHAT THE FAUNA AND FLORA ON THE MOON PROBABLY LOOK LIKE

Krutohlav was totally convinced that the Moon was home to buildings, plants, tillage and animals, and that there were even intelligent animals similar to humans. He was not going to have that called into question. "Since I have established the Moon's weight and size, what are they all going to be like?"

At which point he propped his head on his hand because it seemed impossible to discover anything on that score.

"Since it is true that all powers – except size – are the same on the Moon as on Earth, then the whole of nature: ground cover, animals etc., ought to be 70 times smaller than on Earth. And if there are people there, they ought to be 70 times smaller than any of us. The same goes for plants and animals."

"Yet as I see it," Krutohlav puzzled on, "and I've checked this properly, hills on the Moon, for example, are four times higher than on Earth. And why?" he asked himself, "Why? because of the five times weaker gravitational force of the Moon!" And this led him to the opposite of his previous surmise, to the conclusion, from the lower gravitational force of the Moon, that just as the Moon's hills are four times higher, so, too, people, animals and plants must be at least four, if not five times taller. That would make people, plants and animals huge. A man six feet tall on Earth would measure 18 feet there, and a dog standing at one foot would measure four or five feet, while a sparrow would be four to five times larger, that's to say the size of a crow. A briar would be like a linden tree and a violet like a briar.

If Jánošík[19] had lived on the Moon and if he could jump three feet in the air on Earth, there, with the same effort, he could leap upwards 24 to 28 feet. And if Clumsy-clot fell out of a loft six feet up, on the Moon he would bang himself four or five times harder and would surely die, if the ground on the Moon were as hard as that on Earth. If a boy shot a stone from a catapult, it would go five times further than on Earth at the same power. Everyone would be five times lighter, walk with a five times lighter tread, run five times faster, hit five times harder and jump five times as far as the same man on Earth. And Krutohlav was jubilant that he

---

19 Juraj Jánošík (1688–1713), the Slovak national highwayman, or Robin Hood figure.

was going to be able to chase hares and roe deer five times faster than on Earth, but he'd forgotten to allow for the same applying to every creature.

KRUTOHLAV APPLIES SOME MORE THOUGHT TO LUNAR MAN

Since lunar man is four times the size of an earthling, his individual parts must also be four times bigger. "If his eyes, ears, nose, hands etc. are four times the size of mine," Krutohlav mused, "what enormous optics and limbs a pretty girl must have! Could I find such a sweet creature truly appealing – with eyes four times as big as mine? No, that's impossible," he sighed, repeatedly blowing his nose to drive all such images right out of his head.

And on he went: "If the air on the surface of the Moon is at least five times thinner, what do such huge people breathe? What must their lungs be like! I for one couldn't inhale nearly enough and even in the deepest lunar gully my nose, throat and lungs would be flooded with blood, as has happened on Chimborazo in America. If their lungs are like humans', they must breathe very fast. Though the make-up of their lungs may be non-human, not terrestrial, but lunar. Their lungs must be more capacious, bigger, and their lobes wider in order for a greater volume of oxygen to enter the bloodstream in a short time. All the rest, veins, nerves, are thicker, more ample. In a word, all fibres and chambers throughout the body are structured five times more meagrely. So even the eye must be five times weaker, so their sight, hearing and sense of smell are all five times weaker, despite the body being five times larger.

"But if lunar man is 70 times smaller than us, then he must look no bigger than some kind of ant. In which case, what do his legs, arms, trunk and head, eyes, mouth, nose etc. look like? What young lady could ever fall for a freak like that? And what shall I do with such a tiny wife?"

Then he remembered the Lilliputians and grew really sullen at the prospect of coming among giants who would carry him in the palm of their hands, or among ants who would fire at him from cannon, which would be like being bitten by fleas. "In the one case I'll have to wrestle with a rat, in the other I'll kill an entire army at one fell swoop!"

KRUTOHLAV IMAGINES A SOLAR ECLIPSE, RELIGION ETC.

"Despite the fact that our Earth appears thirteen times bigger to them than the Moon does to us," Krutohlav thought, "here, too, there could be people whose sole concern is making a profit and who never once look at Earth. But those very ones who are afraid lest they lose their temporal mammon are brought up short all the more at the prospect that everything in the daily round might suddenly change, and if Earth comes to a halt between Moon and Sun, it will go into an eclipse. Krutohlav could well imagine the darkness that would reign and was well aware that, just as on Earth, not only fools and the common masses, but also so-called brighter people would be left wondering. Lunar inanity, just like human inanity on Earth, will send them all scampering into their holes and get them thinking that it's the work of vengeful gods. Earth being awash with selfishness, vanity and general stupidity, why shouldn't the people of the Moon, Earth's lackey, be five or even seventy times more gormless and have proportionately more prejudices. The Moon frightens earthlings, so why shouldn't Earth frighten them thirteen times as badly? Entire nations have already passed out of existence, on the other hand there are great populations who worship the Moon as their god, so why couldn't Moon people do likewise in reverse? And all the more so since Earth presents itself to them as a colossal giant. Or could it be that they, too, like Earthlings, think that they were created in the image of a god, that they are the wisest, most just, humblest etc., or might not their stupid pride and worldly vanity lead them to delusions and licentiousness? Are they, too, not filled with manias, and have they not spent their short life, just like Earthlings, on disgraceful acts and plans, do they not believe that they are learned, wise, while blathering on about the mischief they get up to and having about as much grit as would fit behind a finger nail; might not they, too, dream of liberty and in its name commit nothing but atrocities if enough sycophancy isn't forthcoming; they talk about being blessed, yet have no idea how to maintain that condition or enjoy it."

Krutohlav would have gone ranting on in the same vein if he hadn't remembered that the creatures he was sailing towards had to be different.

"The Moon's inhabitants," he deliberated further, feeling comfortable inside, "are compensated for the lack of rain in that their lands and fields are bedewed with dew, and they needn't be afraid of hailstones. Although they know nothing about night, they also know nothing about storms and clouds that would spoil their soil. Nor do they know anything about gales that might wreck their homes. They never see a rainbow, nor do they hear any thunder that would disturb their sleep. And while with us joy is often mixed with pain, they probably know nothing of the kind. And it could be that while Earthlings can be as hostile to one another as wolves, looking upon those nearby with disdain and animosity, seeking integrity and not finding it, it's possible," he told himself, "that people on the Moon know nothing of arrogance and pride and so have nothing to envy us for. And since they won't have invented printing, at least they're spared from reading untold numbers of trashy books; and since they have no knowledge of gunpowder, they won't be annihilating thousands of their confreres, destroying their busy towns and devastating their innocent landscapes."

Such were Krutohlav's thoughts as he continued to pursue what he was going to find on the Moon. There below him, on Earth, naught reigned but vanity, bad behaviour, pride, villainy, deceit and egotism, while now he might hope to find the everlasting peace for which he constantly yearned. – "Here," he assured himself, "I shall find a golden age, a morality without guile and I shall rediscover the common sense that has fled from Earth and perished. Here there'll be an end to all wrongdoing, and the deception and fraud, falsehood and malice that have thoroughly disgusted me on Earth will be quite alien to them; here, in blessed peace, I shall work my fields with a yoke of oxen, drink crystal-clear spring water; I shan't have to tussle with any niggardly, obstinate adversary and I shall dwell in eternal love, concord and peace, doing no-one any harm and without anyone wishing to harm me. This is going to be my eternal, everlasting paradise! Amen."

KRUTOHLAV HAS
A BAD TIME OF IT ABOARD
HIS BALLOON

Long before this, Krutohlav had observed that he was seeing Earth, and especially its higher mountains, as almost always the same, but in thinking that that was simply due to their height he forgot that he had been choosing ever stronger lenses and lost any sense of whether he was getting closer to the Moon or not. Now and again it did cross his mind that he still hadn't needed the air-filled bellows that the charcoal-burners had prepared for him on Kohút, though the time for that was ripe since by this stage he had been traversing God's universe for almost six months. His black puddings and sausages, water and wine were all gone, his sheep cheese had curdled, he'd spent so long ruminating that his pickled cabbage had leaked away, and his fairly solid Klenov cheeses had become seeded with maggots – goodness knows what other miseries he had to cope with before it finally dawned on him, on this important subject, that most of the comestibles he had brought with him were past it.

Krutohlav shook his head in annoyance. But how the colour drained from his features when, having got together his compasses, magnets, astrolabes and other instruments, he discovered that for all he had been travelling six months by then, he was floating barely six miles above Earth! He was almost prostrate with rage. He became even more convinced when he chose among his telescopes and saw a vast expanse of sea above him; he had never dreamed that after six months he was still to see a terrestrial sea. He was seized with a great fear and might well have yielded to his fate if his hopes and tenacity hadn't kept him going. What now – everything's slipped badly. However, since he had brought with him enough food for three years, he might, he thought, if he began to run out before reaching his lunar destination, compensate by making economies. So he stuck to his resolve and sailed on in order to arrive as soon as possible.

KRUTOHLAV FACES
YET MORE PROBLEMS ABOARD
HIS BALLOON

So he reissued the order to spread the sails, blew some extra gas into the balloon and had himself borne ever higher and higher into the heights in the direction of the Moon. Suddenly, he was surprised by a mighty windstorm which, far from driving him on towards the Moon, tossed him this way and that to all points on Earth. "Can't be helped," he thought, "I'm still in the grip of Earth, that's why I'm being treated like this, but once I rise beyond its confines I shan't be seized by any more windstorms." And so it came about, the hurricane passed and Krutohlav began to rise into the heights in greater comfort.

Thinking more about his predicament, he decided that it might have just been Mother Earth getting cross with him and that was why she had launched that storm against him. In the course of this discrepancy, when the high wind had dragged him a league and a half down closer to Earth, he saw with his own eyes that he was floating not far from Sidon in Syria and he worked out that during the six months he'd spent studying the Moon, Earth hadn't wanted to let go of him, so he had flown horizontally to a point above Palestine, whence the wind had driven him towards Sidon. Despite the excellent sails and oars that Krutohlav had invented by which he was to have been able to travel in safety whithersoever he would, not even all his oars together could stand up to a windstorm. Krutohlav abased himself before the higher power as all his balloon's ingeniously, meticulously designed oars and sails had had to.

KRUTOHLAV FAILS TO DISENGAGE HIMSELF FROM EARTH'S ORBIT

Krutohlav had never flown so fast, so briskly, towards the Moon as now, having overfilled the balloon's domes and drums, made of the finest leathers, with gas. He was just at the periphery of Earth's atmosphere, that's to say about seven leagues up, when he registered the unfavourable circumstance that the more rarefied the air became, the more his misshapen, stitched and hammered drums and domes burgeoned out. The fact of the matter was that the gas trapped in the balloon was trying to establish equilibrium with the surroundings, which was why everything was stretched tight to bursting point. Krutohlav was afraid that if that force remained, his balloon would be ripped apart with a noise like a hundred cannon shots, because all the gas locked inside the balloon would disperse in the endless, airless cosmos with such a bang that it would echo throughout Asia Minor. Down on Earth there is also a relative void into which air goes rushing with a bang. We see the same with rifles, cannon and other such equipment with the difference that on Earth the air strikes inwards (centripetal), while up there it seeks to break away from the balloon (centrifugal).

KRUTOHLAV TRIES HARD
TO BREAK FREE OF HIS ORBIT
ROUND EARTH

Although Krutohlav was in an ever more precarious situation, he never ceased having speedy recourse to everything that had been prepared for the expedition. The drums and domes were stretched ever tighter and eternal annihilation loomed. Having calculated that he'd done only seven leagues more, still within Earth's atmosphere, and having ascertained how many leagues he had left to reach the Moon (the space between being a perfect, absolute void), he was profoundly distressed at how long it would take him to reach the outer limits of the Moon and enter its gravitational field. "What's to become of me," he began to wail, "if I can't shed this burden that is Earth?"

So he sat down again at his little desk and calculated that he needed to fly from the edge of Earth's atmosphere at a speed of 41,000 feet per second. "Harrumph! Pretty damn' unlikely where there is no atmosphere! Never mind, I'll give it a go and we'll yet see me fly wherever I want!"

KRUTOHLAV STRAINED EVERY LAST
SINEW, HIS INTELLECT AND WIT IN ORDER
TO BREAK FREE FROM EARTH

Never was there anyone so determined, decisive and exasperated in his sentiments as Krutohlav was now. "We shall see whether I'm up to it or not." He strode briskly about his balloon, finally clapping his hand to his forehead and spitting. In the absence of any better idea, he blew his nose a few times. When he had a good idea, he rubbed his hands gleefully. If something bothered him, he scratched himself behind one ear. When a new idea popped up, he bent his nose with one finger. When nothing deigned to cross his mind, he tossed all his astrolabes and telescopes on the floor – in a word, and to keep things brief: nothing was going right inside Krutohlav's head, indeed he seemed close to lunacy. And if we didn't really want to concede that much, the eternal truth will be that, carried away by his ghastly plans to get to the Moon by any means whatsoever, he was still beating his brains out over them.

In his almost religious zeal he ordered everyone to untangle the balloon's gigantic tails, fill them with various gases and add some gunpowder on top so as to hurl it into space, in short, he had everything made ready for the balloon to be sent hurtling towards the Moon at a speed of at least 40,000 feet per second in order to escape Earth's gravitational pull as fast as possible. Never before had such a great mustering of forces been observed above Earth; the forces mustered for the capture of Sevastopol cannot be compared even remotely with the effort expended by Krutohlav.

As the astronomers observed it, Krutohlav's balloon made it to the vicinity of Berlin and Munich and it had the most enormous wings, a good league long. The papers were full of this wonder, a new, hitherto unseen kind of comet, one with wings. And so Krutohlav was being followed by the world's most brilliant astronomers, something he'd never imagined even in his wildest dreams.

Krutohlav began firing from the 2000 cannon made ready for the purpose, by turns, 1000 at a time. Each projectile was held by a 4000–foot-long platinum chain and after being fired and having reached that distance, always forwards, it jerked the balloon away from Earth's orbit. He kept firing like that for a fortnight and he did seem to be advancing his retreat.

But however much he advanced his retreat, he was jerked back again by the same amount, and so after a month he realised that with so little force per second he wasn't going to make it. As his calculations clearly demonstrated, the snag was that the longer the time he spent hurrying towards the Moon, the less successful was he at it, so he ended up not having progressed by a single step.

So there he was: Krutohlav was stuck at almost the same altitude as he had been a month and a few days earlier.

"Let's try one more thing," he shouted tetchily, seeing that he wasn't going to reach his destination.

He attached five thousand of the best trimmed beams that had been got ready back on Kohút to each wing of his balloon and to each he fixed an engine so artfully that he could count on each of them providing 500 hp. He commanded the engines to push the beams forwards towards the Moon and they, being firmly attached to the balloon, couldn't fail to thrust it forward at the fastest possible speed.

He linked the beams to his artillery batteries and so he did begin to get gradually closer to the Moon. Never had there been heard, above Earth or down on Earth, so much blaring and blasting, screeching and squawking, banging and crashing as Krutohlav produced in the vault of heaven.

KRUTOHLAV SEEMED TO HAVE PAID FOR HIS EXPEDITION TO THE MOON WITH HIS LIFE

In order for Krutohlav's excursion to acquire a little verisimilitude, I cannot omit to mention where I gleaned all these data, presenting them as exactly true as they are. One morning, just I was thinking about astronomy, someone had knocked at the door.

"Come in," I called.

Into my room came a man of average height, with regular features, bright eyes and a kind of magical air about him. I looked him over and realised that he was a quacksalver from Turiec.

"I am he," the quack began, "who makes the incomprehensible comprehensible. I see in your face a certain sadness and pallor, but I shall cure you of it for certain, as you shall see."

Gazing upon the soothsayer, I really did feel unwell.

"All right," I said, "if there is something wrong with me and you mean to put it right, tell me the causes of my indisposition!"

He began sniffing all round the room with his eyes in order to find confirmation of his theory. He must have been a great practical psychologist.

"Your ailment," he went on with his quiet presentation of the matter, "is rooted in a sickness of the spirit. It is from there that your disquiet proceeds, your fitfulness, sense of futility, your absentmindedness and even your frequent bouts of despair."

There was much else that he told me, all of it related to hypochondria, and I approved his natural insights and even gave him a little something.

"Now since I am dealing here with such a staunch Slovak as yourself and not some pinchbeck Deutsch-Böhmer, there is one thing that troubles me and I would like to bring it out into the open."

"What?" I asked him.

Whereupon he thrust his hand inside his tabard and fished out something with smudgy writing on it. I inspected it and discovered it was in Slovak written by an Englishman.

"Thing is, sir," said the quack, "I bought this for one guinea from an English merchant near Tyre (Tyre is in Africa, beside the sea, where the road to the Holy Land starts), and because he couldn't understand it he let me have it cheap. I am well-versed in Arabic, Turkish, Kalmyk, Mordvinian, Coptic and other oriental languages, so I spotted this would be Slovak, but because I couldn't get all the wishy-washy bits in German and especially English, I regretted paying a guinea for it."

I looked at the text and actually did find it was English writing labouring to convey the sounds of Slovak. I tool a closer look at it and gathered that a certain Krutohlav, a native of Mníšany, had taken it upon himself to give a true foretaste of a trip to the Moon that he had embarked on.

"So, what did the English merchant tell you," I asked him, "like where did he get the text from?"

"It was floating in the sea," he told me, "packed away inside a barrel. 'Since nobody could understand it, my captain had it copied out,' the merchant said. He'd then got hold of it and sold it to me."

"How much are you asking for it?" I asked the quack as he made to leave.

"Take it as a favour, as from one Slovak to another – nothing," he cried, and then he left. I never saw him again.

Here then are some of the bits about Krutohlav.

PART

TWO

CONTAINS KRUTOHLAV'S ADVENTURES AND HIS MEMOIRS REGARDING THE REST OF HIS JOURNEY AND A DETAILED, BUT CLEAR DISQUISITION ABOUT THE SUN.

As taken down by an eye witness, Benuš of Čierna Lehota[20] in 1855

---

20 This village lies a little to the east of the hill, Kohút, where the whole yarn began.

KRUTOHLAV'S ADVENTURES

It happened to be Epiphany, the day when several friends who got on really well together met up in Jaroslav's front room to while away the long evening by communing on various, especially scientific, subjects. There was a hailstorm outside and a mighty wind that made the chimneys howl and wail.

"What vile weather, the snow's knee-deep and the wind cuts you to the bone," said Benuš as he entered the room frozen stiff, the man the company had long been expecting.

"Krutohlav must have shot the gas out of his balloon all the way down here, we're almost done for, there's never been anything like it." That was Miloslav as he entered the room, his face bright red and frostbitten. "I could hardly stand up against the wind and falling snow. What I need now is a really good warm-up." He went across to the stove and rubbed his hands above the blazing fire. Around him the members of the little group gradually took their seats and finally he went and sat in his own, hitherto vacant, seat.

"No, he can't have," Benuš quickly responded to Miloslav. "Only today I was reading in *Svetozor* that Krutohlav is on his way back to Muráň." "What?" they chorused, leaping from their seats. "Krutòhlav's on his way back? That's impossible. That paper of his was found bobbing in a barrel in the sea off Tyre, and he himself must surely have drowned."

"Come in," Jaroslav called out to a knock on the door, and on the instant there stood Krutohlav himself, in the flesh. "I'm alive, I didn't drown, here you have me," he cried joyfully, letting his gaze run round the assembled company.

Not even at the time when the balloon was being got ready was there such a hurly-burly as broke out now, when they all, stupefied by the impossibility of Krutohlav's showing up like that, reached out to touch him to make certain.

"Is that you, Krutohlav?" said Jaroslav, pawing him in disbelief that this could be a human being. And so, turn and turn about, they all stared in wonder, then they became reassured and finally they hugged and kissed him.

Their peace of mind being restored all round, Benuš stepped forward and started explaining to Krutohlav how fragments of his writings had reached the observatory in Buda thanks to some quacksalver fellow, how they'd been copied and sent to Veľká Revúca and then reached Mníšany, and what they here, his kith and kin, thought about his jaunt to the Moon.

Krutohlav gave a long shake of his head, almost getting a crick in his neck, and then kept shaking it over and over again.

"How vain is human endeavour," he began to ruminate piously. "It was a close-run thing and my own sheer determination could have cost me my life."

"Oh dear, how so?" some of them enquired pityingly. Then Krutohlav removed his cape, hung it on a nail by the stove and tucked into some tasty cabbage and sausages. Having thus refreshed himself, he began to answer the question as follows:

"You, my friends and kinsmen, know all about how I made my balloon, how, in your presence, I rose from Kohút into the heavenly heights, and what I saw, found and went through up there; you will also know about all the problems I had to contend with in order to break free of Earth's gravity and fly onwards into the beneficent sphere of the Moon. But in vain was the toil of a mere man: the might and main of a mere man cannot prevail against the might of God, ever! When I gave the order for those devices to be tied to the ends of the beams and fired at full force, a lack of foresight on the part of my comrade, Kubo, led to the disaster whereby instead of the balloon being pushed out into cosmic space, the beams clipped the balloon and cut into it so mercilessly that soon all the ropes, cords, sails, belts, waxed threads and seams began to snap. And my balloon drifted down and down. Since the cannon and engines attached to the beams were to have kept firing for twenty-four hours – and fortunately this went wrong right at the start – the balloon would have been tossed this way and that and I'd have begun to have doubts about my very survival. I brought all my best efforts to bear, but to no avail, the din and racket went on and on, and, stupefied and terror-stricken, we made some even more perverse mistakes. The remaining hems and tucks kept splitting as well as the remaining belts and straps. I hastily calculated that I could hold out on the balloon for barely six hours and two minutes more, and lest all my discoveries be lost to mankind – even if I myself were to be lost – I hit on the idea of encasing all my writings in a barrel and tossing them into the sea. I did exactly that and it seems likely that they were netted in the sea by an Englishman, who sold them on to a quacksalver, for these people loath anything with even a whiff of Slavdom to it.

"As I had calculated, my balloon did begin to drift down. I crossed over to its right wing, because it was lighter and freer and was floating nicely in the air. I was also thinking that even if I did fall, Earth wouldn't drag me down with its fifteenfold force. And that's what happened: the last waxed thread snapped and my balloon crashed down into the sea with a wallop. I myself, hanging on its wing, had been flying about like an eagle, being tossed this way and that. I girded myself with a tough length of belt and latched on to the end of one sail; but then the belt snapped and I might well have been cast into the briny deep if I hadn't grabbed hold of the end of the sail in the nick of time. For six hours I was buffeted about like that and had begun to fear that my final hour was upon me.

"Whereas in fact... Descending through the clouds, that mighty storm was raging its fill of thunder and lighting. Then one great flash struck that part of the right wing of the balloon where it was held in place with ropes. Then I began to fall more gently, the more so the balloon itself, for that wing had held it upwards in the sky during flight. Then a great darkness descended, so great that I couldn't see where I was or whither I was flying. In a daze I could hear the opposite end of the wing shaking somewhere and then everything gave a crack like thunder. I was still falling fairly gently until I felt the ground, though even then I kept a firm grip on the wing.

"When I came to next morning after a very sound sleep, I saw I was perched on a smallish elevation. I took my small telescope, which I'd unconsciously kept in my hand, surveyed my surroundings and discovered an unfamiliar world. People in turbans were scurrying about, some barefoot, some naked, like people deranged. What's that there? I looked and saw the vast ruins of the sizable city of Bruffa in Asia Minor, lying not far from Scutari[21] and Constantinople. What could have happened to it? I puzzled.

"Earthquake, earthquake, the end, help," I heard through Stentor's trumpet. "Aha, I thought, "my wing clipping that hilltop – that's what brought on the earthquake. But wait awhile

---
21 Today's Üsküdar, on the East bank of the Bosphorus.

until it becomes a Jerusalem with not a stone left standing," Krutohlav sighed.

"The Slovak papers are saying right now that Bruffa, city of many sultans, has already been completely devastated by the earthquake," said Benuš. "Is it really to be blamed on your balloon's wing clipping the place?"

"Indeed so, not a stone will be left standing," Krutohlav crowned his narrative, and the whole company was left in amazement beyond comprehension at Krutohlav's conviction and at the power of a wing to reduce such a vast city to rubble.

"And can't anything be done to help?" Vratislav asked.

"No," replied Krutohlav, "until the cannon have shot their last, Bruffa will have to suffer." "And how long might that take?" asked Benuš. "It all depends on how and how soon the cannon and those engines complete the discharge; that's why the inhabitants can still hear the noise and see the flashes in the sky, caused by the cannon. Those people really are to be pitied," Krutohlav concluded. "It's more that there's no way to help them!"

"From there, having left the wing floating over Bruffa, I set off in search of the balloon," Krutohlav began ruminating. "I wandered up hill and down dale, tripped lightly through the heights, swam through marshes and across lakes, and saw people, both savage and amiable, who told me about a new comet that was hovering about with a wing attached to its left-hand side. Having asked the right questions, I learned from the local stargazers that my balloon had been flung further to the west by a westerly wind. As I approached the city of Abd al-Kurki I could hear and see my balloon, which the entire populace was admiring, and one after another they were snipping, ripping and cutting strips off, and bits of strapping and rope as souvenirs. If I hadn't got there in time, they'd have reduced it to shreds. None of them had a clue what it was or what it was for, which was a relief, because I could then take charge of it again while it was still in one piece.

"So I got hold of some craftsmen from the nearby town and began repairing it, at which I succeeded up to the point of being able to inflate it, stock it with food and other supplies and take off before the eyes of thousands and thousands. The locals made to drag me back down when they saw I might fly away and that they could be cheated out of the gigantic balloon. However, having aimed my cannon at them and sprayed the lot, I flew off towards Sevastopol.

"To cut a long story short, I floated away across the firmament and as I travelled on I made some very close observations of the Sun, quite unfamiliar to Earthlings, and took some hugely important notes down about it. Then I was flying above Sevastopol, where I spotted some funny little clouds and heard an odd kind of noise – as if it were a mouse squeaking. Having crossed Crimea, I flew to Transylvania, from where I began my descent. I dropped down into a dip beneath a grassy ridge at Gerlach in the Tatras, where I left my balloon, thinking that for as long as I was alive and travelling, it could survive there till eternity, given how inaccessible the mountains there are. Then I set off on foot over King's Ridge[22] and today I passed through Hron to join you here alive and well."

So much for Krutohlav's brief, but pithy confabulation, after which, being totally exhausted, and despite the assembled company, he lay himself down and slept peacefully for twenty-four hours.

---

22 See n. 4.

The day after, the company met up again and badgered him endlessly to be so kind as to tell them everything he knew about the Sun. Eventually he relented and, having filled his pipe with tobacco and taken a good pinch of snuff, he began:

ON THE SUN – KRUTOHLAV'S LECTURE ON THE SUN'S MASS

"Do not be misled into thinking, my good friends, that, as I traversed the heavenly heights, taking a good look at everything and making a close scrutiny of whatever I could, the Sun was just as small as it appears to us at first sight. That's only because of the immense distance. The Moon's close proximity to Earth makes it look bigger and no other cause need be considered.

"We all know what we owe to the Sun. There's light and heat, to mention but two of its many attributes. Where would we be without light and heat? Pause awhile and appreciate that we simply couldn't remain alive. Would there not be eternal darkness and cold? What could we do in the dark and cold?"

"We'd get light and warmth from the Moon," Jaroslav butted in.

"Oh no, we wouldn't," Miloslav rebutted. "If the Sun went out, the Moon would also go completely dark, because it, too, is fed by the Sun."

"Hear me out," Krutohlav went on "We'd all be dead on the spot if the Sun happened to go out. Miloslav's right about that. But just think of the Sun's great mass. It probably wouldn't occur to you that the Sun is 355,000 times greater than our Earth!"

"I wonder if you haven't you got something wrong there, Krutohlav," Benuš chipped in. "Didn't you mean to say only 355 times greater?"

"Three hundred and fifty-five *thousand* times *is* how much the Sun is greater than our Earth," Krutohlav responded frostily. "And if all the planets, such as Jupiter, Saturn, Mars etc., were lumped together, knocked into a single whole, the Sun would still be 700 times greater than the mass of all the planets."

"Gosh!" they all blurted, "That's some size, barely bears thinking about, let alone trying to get one's head around it."

"No two ways about it," Krutohlav continued, "it was proven long ago and my journey has convinced me that it is exactly right. That gigantic mass, meaning the Sun, gives out the orders to all the planets, makes them all spin round it and move in harmony and submission. The Sun is the centre of the entire planetary system and it dishes out the orders like some autocrat on a throne."

KRUTOHLAV DISCUSSES THE SIZE OF THE SUN

Hardly had Krutohlav dealt with all the probing questions about the Sun's mass when he was asked by the company to tell them more about what measurements he had taken of the Sun and what he had discovered.

"The size of the Sun," he continued, "is perhaps even harder to grasp. Its diameter, or the length of a line drawn right through it, comes to 180,000 German leagues, its surface measures 111,000 million Hungarian square leagues,[23] and so its volume comes to 3,500 billion cubic geographic leagues."

---

23   1 Hung. league = 8533.6 metres, or 5.3 miles.

"That's more than any of us can envisage," said Vratislav. "Put it better, so that with smaller numbers we can get a better grip on things."

"He's right," they all chimed in, "we just can't grasp it."

"All right, look at it this way," said Krutohlav, and they all strained hard in the hope of being enlightened.

"Vesta,[24] one of our planets encircling the Sun, is among the smallest, its diameter measuring a mere 60 leagues. So the Sun's diameter is 3,100 times greater than Vesta's. Likewise the volume of the Sun will be 30,000 million times greater."

"I don't get it," Benuš interrupted. "The numbers are still way too big for me to grasp. Make it more intelligible."

"All right, Benuš, listen. I do want you to understand. If you could become a huge giant and wanted to roll out the Sun like dough to make bread, then you could make 30,000 million Vesta-size baps out of it. And if you wanted them to be Earth-size, then you could make thirteen million. And if you wanted to make one big roll the size of all the planets lumped together, then it would be not quite one 560th the size of the Sun."

The whole company brooded over what Krutohlav had told them, quite astounded by the size of the Sun, which was so beyond comprehension.

"You trot out your examples like cracking a nut from its shell. So give us a different one to go by," some of them begged.

Krutohlav gave a troubled shake of his head and began again: "All right, if you insist: if we inserted Earth into the centre of the Sun, and with the moon still going round it 50,000 leagues away, half of the Sun's diameter would still be free. Got that?"

---

24 One of the four goddess asteroids (with Juno, Ceres and Pallas; Krutohlav will return to all four later), only discovered in the 19th century, Vesta being the last, not long, then, before Reuss was writing.

"Of course," some conceded. "But if someone wanted to travel all the way round it, as Cook did round Earth, how many days would it take him?" Vratislav pleaded to be told.

"A traveller doing ten German leagues a day until he'd gone full circle round Earth would need 540 days; but to go round the Sun he'd need 59,160 days, or 160 years!"

"My! The Sun must be some giant, and yet how small it seems to us, smaller than the Moon, and what's our poor little Earth like in comparison!"

"Nothing's going to change that," Krutohlav concluded and the company dispersed.

THE SUN'S DENSITY

The next day they were back to listen to Krutohlav's brilliant insights and learn yet more from him. So they huddled round the stove, stoked the glowing fire, lit up some fine Hungarian tobacco in their pipes and enjoyed a really good smoke. Krutohlav, on whom all further discussion depended, had another pinch of snuff, for he'd run out of tobacco aboard his balloon and had taken to snuff instead.

"Come on, man, don't keep us in suspense, we want to you to tell us more about the Sun." That was Svatovit speaking, a kinsman of his.

"Hear this then," and all eyes turned to Krutohlav. "What is so remarkable," he began, "is that the Sun, whose dimensions and mass far exceed all the planets knocked together, has, after all, to yield to them when it comes to density. The huge mass and matter of the Sun is four times as powdery as the soil on Earth."

HOW SOLID BODIES FALL ON THE SUN'S SURFACE

When Krutohlav began a new lecture on what happens on the Sun if you toss a stone or some other object into the air and about the speed with which it drops back, they, as one, pulled up their seats to be closer to him. Indeed why wouldn't his eager listeners pin back their ears and want to store up everything he told them! The more they learned, the more their curiosity grew and Krutohlav became all the more incisive in his discourse.

"Here on Earth," he began, "whenever a stone or other heavy object is thrown up into the air, or is dropped from, say, the top of a tower, the speed at which it falls to the ground is 15 Paris feet per second. If any of you is in any doubt, just try it yourself and you can't fail to be convinced that this is true. Admittedly, on my long journey I didn't reach the Moon, let alone the Sun, but I can assure you that, taking many other aspects all in all, an object falling on the Sun will go at a rate of 430 Paris feet per second. So compared with a body falling onto Earth, one falling onto the Sun will go 29 times faster."

The whole company gasped in sheer admiration of Krutohlav's erudition. Then the ever-troubled Benuš rose and said: "Yes, I believe all of that, but if objects do fall that fast on the Sun, how much does a quintal weigh there?"

They all eagerly awaited the reply.

"From what has been said you may conclude that any solid body, a stone or other object, is, on the Sun, twenty-nine times heavier than on Earth. It will also be natural that the scales on which we did any weighing would be twice as heavy. So our quintal of one hundred pounds will weigh 2,900 pounds on the Sun, so almost 30 of our quintals."[25]

"What a great earner that would be," some of them whooped. "Take whatever from here, get it weighed on the Sun and then sell it; talk about getting rich quick! That way, for one quintal of candles, a candle-maker could make as much as for thirty, a butcher for one quintal of meat could get as much as for thirty, and the price of sheep cheese, lard, bacon, butter and even the fancy stuff posh students eat would pay thirtyfold. But would it really be all that good, I wonder. It's my belief – " now it was Vratislav speaking, "that people on Earth would starve to death, because every old dear with a market stall would be bound to dash off and sell her buns for thirty times the price if the cost of everything were to go through the roof, like in this country right now."

Many of them laughed at Vratislav's joke and Krutohlav permitted himself just half a smile, under one whisker.

"Just imagine," Vratislav began again after all views that could be aired on the previous topic had been aired, "just imagine the force with which the Sun would have grabbed you and hurled you down on its own ground if you and your balloon had got anywhere near!!"

"My dear friends, you can't even begin to imagine that kind of force. Just as you were defeated over the size of the Sun, you'll hardly begin to form any clear idea of the force it exerts," Krutohlav continued gently. "Never again would I blow on my porridge if the Sun did seize me. If I had got into the Sun's orbit, it would

---

25 On past and present uses of *quintal, cent(ner), hundredweight* etc. see https://en.wikipedia.org/wiki/Quintal (accessed 03.03.2022). It follows that at different times and places it represented either 100lb (as in Reuss) or 100kg (as in today's Slovakia).

have dragged me along at such a rate that either I would have choked to death or, having actually reached it, not one whit of me would have survived. And if by some means I had actually reached the Sun, then, since I weigh a hundred and fifty-nine pounds, I would have to have weighed 4,350 pounds, so, quite naturally, I'd have been crushed by my own weight. Who on earth could carry that many pounds? Understand?"

Benuš, who was still contemplating a trip to the Sun, or any of the planets, and would have gladly lined up beside Krutohlav even at midnight, was brooding over the idea of meeting such a terrible fate. The whole company noticed and each of them was watching him with a twinkle in his eye as he so brooded.

"Meanwhile, consider this, too, my dear friends," Krutohlav chattered on. "The Sun's density isn't everywhere the same: the closer to its core, the denser it becomes, which accounts for its stupendous magnetic force. And so at the core it's all ablaze. What we can say is that – as we have seen – the Sun's density is four times lower than Earth's and might be compared to anthracite or stone pitch."

THE DISTANCE OF THE SUN FROM EARTH

"You've been telling us all this stuff about the physical properties of the Sun, and we don't even know yet how far away it is from Earth," Vratislav was keen to know. "Spell that out for us and enlighten us."

"Be bounteous and God shall not forsake thee," replied Krutohlav and began his exposition:

"The mean distance of Earth from the Sun comes out at 20,665,800 German leagues, i.e. 20,665,800 geographic leagues."

"Co-o-or!" muttered Benuš. "I'm never going to get there."

"Whether you believe me or not is all one to me," Krutohlav went on, "but it really is a long, long way away!"

"That the Sun is at such a huge distance from us is beyond comprehension," Jaroslav joined in. "Couldn't you try to put it across in some other terms?"

"By all means," Krutohlav responded. "So, if a cannon ball were fired down here and travelled at 1,500 Paris feet per second, it would take just short of ten years to reach the Sun."

"This is enough to drive you mad and make anyone's brain stop working," several of them murmured, though especially Benuš, who finally abandoned any idea of an expedition to the Sun.

THE SUN'S LIGHT

By this stage there was no getting Krutohlav to tell them anything more about the Sun. "I see you're all such sceptics that I can't be bothered wasting any more breath on you!!" he retorted testily. "If you don't believe me, stick with what you do believe, I don't have to try and convince any one of you. What would be the use? If you want to find something out, go and do your own measurements – and if you don't have faith in your findings, you should at least trust those who have put a thousand times more effort into it. Faith will be your salvation, but only if you truly believe!"

It took them a long while, but they did eventually persuade Krutohlav to continue with his truthful perceptions and findings. He was by no means keen, because the next topic upon which he was about to embark was so much more delicate, and he doubted whether his audience would be able to focus their minds on it.

That notwithstanding, despite his disinclination, he took the bull by the horns and launched into a detailed account of the Sun's luminosity:

"You enjoy sunlight every day, but maybe you've never given it a moment's thought. What would you do if it was dark the whole time? What would being without light do to your mind and body? Was it not a loving God who created you, mankind, in his own image and you have the temerity to blaspheme? Bow your head before the face of the Lord and on your knees give thanks. May you never be abandoned by your faith: give up your worldly vanity, that way alone shall you achieve your goal!"

Krutohlav would have fain gone on in the blaze of his moralising if now one, now another had not interrupted the flow of his magniloquence. So he pressed on regardless.

"Hear these wonders out," he said, picking up the thread. "Without light, as you can imagine, not only our world, but the entire planetary system would be everlasting night, an inaccessible barren wasteland, in a word, a pitch-dark grave. But light gives us power and strength, so:

"If I take this glass prism and pass a single ray of sunlight through it, I will see seven colours, to wit red, orange, yellow, green, blue, indigo and violet. If someone were to put one, any single one, of these colours to the test and break it down by means of the selfsame prism, nothing would happen, because these are light's very own true colours. But if, by means of a different piece of glass, we were to gather all these colours back together, one white ray would reappear, for the simple reason of being composed of the seven different colours.

"You may imagine how we would be if a ray of light remained white and wouldn't split up into the seven colours here on Earth.

Would not the whole of nature look white, would not any solid body have a colour like lead? Would not the dawn, or the human face look ashen? Would not our rainbow look grey? Would not the myriad of stars look grey against an ashen firmament? – Light accounts for the freshness of every green leaf, the freshness of the grass in our meadows, and without it not even your diamond would have that play of colours! Oh dear me! And wouldn't a pretty girl's blush escape the notice of her beloved?"

"How wisely has everything been ordered," Vratislav broke in, possibly the one who'd been paying closest attention to Krutohlav's words. "I've never heard from anyone such a clear account of how a ray is made up of seven colours. But does a ray of light have any other properties, or just that it can be torn apart into seven different twinkles by means of a prism?" he asked Krutohlav.

"Oh, yes. There's another bizarre thing I've observed: when a ray lands on a white slab (an absorption spectrum), you can see over 600 lines on it, some thicker, some thinner, but all black. These lines all run parallel."

"And what are they for?" asked Vratislav.

"We don't know what they're supposed to indicate, but what *is* certain is that their number and how they're arranged, and how thick they are, and their relative brightness or darkness, is always the same. But what's also true is that moonlight and the light of all the planets, even the light of our fire, all reveal the same sort of lines, but different and differently arranged. The conclusion is that every solid body has its own light."

KRUTOHLAV ENLARGES ON THE LOW DENSITY AND HIGH SPEED OF SUNLIGHT

"However, water is a denser material than air! Thanks to the density of the water struck by the wheels of a paddle steamer the boat can move against the current. Air is less dense, but much more dense than light, because birds, levering their wings against air, can fly. Light is, again, much less dense than heat because the latter can pass through walls; heat, though, can even pass through iron. Actions like these also occur in nature.

"Hitherto light has been reckoned among those materials that cannot be weighed on scales, nor has anyone yet succeeded in weighing out a certain amount of it. It may be a body, but one so thin that it defies being weighed. It comes hurtling towards us from the Sun, and it keeps coming out of the Sun without pause. In a single second it can travel 1,322,263 million leagues, so taking 8 minutes and 13.22 seconds to reach Earth. We know of no body that moves faster. What ineffable power must be within the Sun for it to keep firing off light at such a speed we can but imagine!"

ON THE TEMPERATURE OF THE SUN

All Krutohlav's listeners were still oohing and ahing at the tremendous speed of sunlight when, unbidden, he changed the subject and began:

"You also need to know about the Sun's temperature, since it goes hand in hand with light. It is our everyday experience that heat has some effect on us. The question is, should we attribute greater importance to heat or to light."

"I reckon heat," said Benuš.

"Why so?" asked Vratislav.

"Because dark people and dark animals are still alive, but without heat they'd have disappeared." And Benuš went on: "Homer and Milton were both blind, and when the surveyors Saunderson[26] and Enter[27] lost their sight, their thinking became even more profound. And Füredy[28] of Pest was totally blind when he was writing scores for Slovak folksongs."

"That is true," Krutohlav confirmed and went back to his discourse. "So temperature is the matter that gives different bodies their general physical state." Not our dry land, not our sea, our watercourses, not even our air could survive in their present form if temperature shied away from them; indeed everything would inevitably turn into a desolate, formless mass. So if you took the air's temperature away from it, what's left would fall to the ground like a compressed crust. If there were no temperature, all movement, physicality and life would be at an end. Thanks to temperature, we can change iron, copper, gold or silver into liquids. And how useful is temperature in

---

[26] Nicholas Saunderson (1682–1739), English mathematician and author of a work on algebra. He lost his sight at the age of one, owing to smallpox, later losing even his eyes. For much more on this fascinating Yorkshireman see https://mathshistory.st-andrews.ac.uk/Biographies/Saunderson/ (accessed 05.03.2022).

[27] Both printed editions of the original of this book have 'Enter' at here, but this must surely be a recurrent misprint for (or misreading of) Euler. Leonhard Euler (1707–83) was 'a Swiss mathematician who made enormous contributions to a wide range of mathematics and physics including analytic geometry, trigonometry, geometry, calculus and number theory'. He had a long history of eye problems before becoming totally blind, see https://mathshistory.st-andrews.ac.uk/Biographies/Euler/ (accessed 06.03.2022).

[28] Ladislav Füredy (1794–1850), a blind composer and teacher of music, maths and history at an institute for the blind in Pest. His main collection was published in 1837 in Vienna. His sister was also a composer.

chemistry? Temperature drives steamboats and steam wagons. There's little point in my going on and on about the utility of temperature; let's leave it at that, I know you're pretty well convinced about it."

"Yes," they all concurred and parted, well content.

KRUTOHLAV DISCUSSES
THE SOLAR SURFACE

Despite Krutohlav's insights on the subject of light and heat being more expansive than they need have been, the friends had so enjoyed the talk that some of them couldn't help themselves paying all kinds of attention to the Sun's temperature and light. But when they all met up again the following day, they persuaded Krutohlav to continue his lecture. And he did:

"You'll probably find it more interesting if we talk about the surface of the Sun as it appeared to me from aboard my balloon. Though truth to tell, I won't be able to say much more about that heavenly body than about the surface of the remotest star in the sky."

"Why so?" asked Benuš.

"Most certainly because the Sun is so very far away and because of its intense fiery light that you can't look into," Vratislav supplied the answer.

"Indeed," Krutohlav acknowledged. "The vast distance of the Sun from us makes a mockery of all our telescopes. How often did I try to explore the surface of the Sun using telescopes, yet all that ever presented itself to me was one great sea of blazing light, the whole of the Sun being a luminous inferno. The better the views I did manage to get of it, the more apparent it became that its light is monstrously mobile, as rapid in its movements as tempests here on Earth. Sometimes I saw, on that blazing sea of light, gigantic black-coloured patches four or five times the size of our Earth which completely disappeared after a few days or weeks. Next to those black spots I noticed, and quite often at that, a sort of burning blotches whose light was stronger and purer than any other solar light. And then elsewhere, all over the surface, where there were neither these brighter nor darker patches, you could see little points of paler light that kept changing the whole time."

ON WHETHER THE SUN IS NOT A FIRE

Krutohlav's ruminations fired Jaroslav in particular to the point where he came up with the idea that, if the Sun was ablaze the whole time, it could only have started from fire. His companions all agreed and they asked Krutohlav, as the most experienced of them all, what he thought.

"You're right, the Sun is burning constantly," said Krutohlav, pleased to pick up where he had left off, "but take my word for it, it doesn't burn with any terrestrial kind of fire. If it did indeed burn with a terrestrial fire, would our fire – like the Sun's – turn an African's skin black from a distance of twenty million leagues? Though it is also true that even on Earth some portion of heat is retained, as we see in the case of friction. If we rub our hands together, when savages rub sticks together and acquire fire, when our wheels get really hot if a wagon goes too fast, when things get hot during drilling, when metal strikes metal and they become heated, and so forth. True, we are not lacking in hotness, but the most telling hotness of all is that of the Sun.

"The more direct the Sun's light, the greater its power over us. In the tropics it is only as hot as it is because the Sun shines at right angles. If we concentrate the Sun's rays with a piece of glass we can light tinder with it. So great and unfathomable is the power of the rays of the Sun."

"And yet, how does it come about," Benuš began, taking over from Krutohlav, "that when I was traipsing about on Kriváň in the Tatra Mountains, the further up I went, the colder it got and the light became bluish, so the light wasn't as bright as in the valleys below. Though if one were even as little as 8,000 feet closer to the Sun, it ought to feel warmer and the light ought to shine brighter."

This really did have Krutohlav shaking and twisting his head, he began staring at the ground and seemed to be thinking really deep thoughts about this knotty problem. Eventually, as if he had had the most brilliant brainwave, he began his reply to Benuš thus:

"Precisely because we are gifted with eyes, light is, for us, something relative. It seems to me, too, that the Sun's rays may be, in themselves, cold and can burn, or reveal their power, only after they've been sundered into seven colours! Take wood, for example: wood is cold, but when it's broken down chemically it burns with a big flame. It's not impossible," Krutohlav went on, "that solar rays are cold, but are endowed with a capacity to radiate heat when they strike Earth."

"In which case, our Sun could be just as dark an entity as our Earth," Benuš yelped and rubbed his hands.

Everyone blushed at Benuš's words and from all sides had begun to reason with him when Krutohlav spoke up again:

"Let him be," he responded, "he's actually being consistent. For my own part, I'm still in two minds as to whether the Sun might not be as cold as our Earth."

"But how could that be," Jaroslav broke in, "when we constantly experience its heat?"

"We shouldn't take ourselves as the starting point," Krutohlav began his reply. "We must detach ourselves from Earth and look at both Sun *and* Earth impartially. If someone traced a ray of sunlight back on foot, they'd have the sensation of it being ever cooler and darker even if they'd gone no further than the Tatras. Ultimately, believe me, they'd be in total darkness and freeze to death if they were to float across the firmament like Icarus. The reason is quite simple and hinges on the fact that rays only emerge thanks to contact with solid bodies, so I shan't even tell you that the Sun is a dark body."

Never has anyone seen such muddled babbling as accompanied this topic. There was no end to all the brain-teasing until Krutohlav sent his companions away to cool down before they reassembled late that afternoon.

KRUTOHLAV PICKS UP WHERE HE HAD LEFT OFF

"Most people are of the belief that the Sun is an eternal fire, and their reasons cannot be dismissed lightly, being rather more compelling than the view of those who take the Sun to be a dark body. The closer the Sun's rays approach Earth, the less dense they are, and on the Sun, which they leave from a single point, the focus, they must be so condensed that their intensity over a quarter of a league is 300,000 times higher than on Earth."

"So we'd never need to buy wood for fuel there: ox or pig, anything would get roasted immediately," Benuš joked.

"Not to say crisped to a cinder and burnt away," Jaroslav rejoined with a smile.

"Stop arguing and listen," said Vratislav.

So Krutohlav carried on. "I don't want to go on for long, just long enough to tell you what most people believe. It is possible that the Sun does blaze away the whole time *despite* its blackness, but it's also possible to find not a word about its burning."

"All right, then," said Benuš, "but if it does keep blazing and burning, and goodness knows how long it has been, surely it should have got smaller."

"That's exactly what's been going round in my head. We just don't know," Krutohlav responded, "we really don't know. The renowned astronomer Newton thought that maybe comets struck the Sun now and again and so kept it stoked. But that's all wrong and I'd prefer to derive the phenomenon from electricity. And since it's true that the Sun does keep on burning, it must lose something of its bulk. But since we've only had any reasonable idea of the Sun since 1640 and since people are still wrangling over whether its diameter is around 100 German leagues, there's no way of telling whether it has shrunk a little or not. If we admit the view that over the course of two centuries the Sun has shrunk by only 2,280,000 feet, or 100 German leagues, we're no better off than we were before, i.e. we don't know if it is shrinking through burning or not."

"Great are the mysteries of God," sighed Jaroslav and Benuš in chorus. "How we humans are but dust and ashes on the ground compared to such gigantic, incomprehensible bodies; and what is the human mind compared to divine wisdom!"

KRUTOHLAV DESCRIBES SUN SPOTS

The next day, even more members assembled to witness Krutohlav's reflections.

"I've already alluded to those spots on the Sun several times. Now you need to learn rather more about them," Krutohlav resumed his philosophising. "When, aboard my balloon, I was observing the Sun's surface through my telescope – it goes without saying that I used a tinted lens, otherwise I'd have been blinded by the light – I often saw, on the surface of the Sun, dark spots, variously large and small, but always irregular and no two the same. They not only kept changing in themselves, but also shifting from place to place. I watched them at hourly intervals and saw them now bigger, now smaller, and changing their physicality. And I often saw them breaking up, or clumping together, and they often disappeared off the horizon completely. When a spot disappears, the first to shrink is the middle, its ashen fringes vanishing last. And there are spots of a different kind as well – unchanging and showing for three or four weeks at a time. Their peculiarity is that they run from east to west as narrow streaks; they're visible for thirteen days and then are invisible for the next thirteen. The closer we look towards the middle, the broader they seem, while at the poles they are, conversely, very narrow."

WHAT THE SPOTS ARE SUPPOSED TO MEAN

"What do they indicate and what might they indicate?" Benuš was curious to know.

"I was just about to explain – have a little patience, please." They all braced their minds and waited for Krutohlav's answer to this riddle.

"Since all the spots rush at the same speed from west to east, they won't be the same sort of thing as our clouds, for clouds get blown to all corners of the world, while these do keep to that one same direction. But not only their direction, but also the speed of clouds needs to be considered, because sunspots keep a steady course."

"So if they can't be clouds, what then are they?"

"And also, because they always appear bigger at the Sun's outer edges, and gain in width at the centre, they cannot be bodies in their own right, as in the case of the Moon vis-à-vis Earth. And that's why they pertain to the Sun's surface, that's where they abide. Their direction – east to west – is dependent on how the Sun turns on its axis. Other than that, my friends, there's nothing I can tell you as to what the spots actually mean. But were you to believe that they suggest some fluidity and massive movements, you would not be far from the truth."

VIEWS ON SUNSPOTS

Benuš just could not settle, having heard just how interesting the properties of sunspots were. He begged, and kept on pleading with Krutohlav to give them not only his own beliefs, but also the views of other great men on the spots.

"There are indescribable numbers of such views," Krutohlav responded, "but I can give you a rough sketch of the most important ones. So, some have been convinced that they are debris thrown up by volcanoes, others have believed them to be the Sun's own moons, spinning round it in close proximity. Galileo thought they were clouds, others the to-ing and fro-ing of light (*fluxus et refluxus lucis*) and so on. The distinguished Herschel thinks that the Sun's outermost layer consists of light, that beneath that there is a transparent layer and beneath that a third layer that moves about like clouds. If the light gets churned up like a hurricane, it can fragment and then the black patches get formed." "That idea," said Benuš, "is the most ingenious and also the most cogent conception of sunspots yet."

THE SUN'S MOTION

"The Sun turns in two ways," Krutohlav continued. "Namely:

"1. about its own axis, as is proved by the spots, which after 27 days re-appear where they had been previously. So a day and a night there take 27 days.

"2. around itself: all the planets spin round the Sun in an ellipse, but their combined mass also affects the Sun, which then follows its own tiny elliptical orbit.

"3. around a sun that is more powerful than it and of which we have no knowledge. So we, too, along with the Sun, are running round goodness knows whom, or round what star in the cosmos. In later life, Herschel observed that the Sun and its entire planetary system was getting closer to Hercules, because for a whole century the stars around it had seemed to be growing less dense, and the closer the Sun got to Hercules, the denser the appearance, to us, of the stars of Taurus.

"God works in mysterious ways. No man shall ever uncover their mystery. None shall ever discover the reach of their wisdom.

Humble thyself, oh man, before the face of the Lord! Dust thou art and unto dust shalt thou return for ever and ever, amen!"

At which they all heaved a sigh and Krutohlav closed for ever and ever the great book in which he had inscribed all these things.

PART
THREE

DESCRIBES IN DETAIL THE CONSTRUCTION OF THE DRAGON, FLYING ABOARD WHICH KRUTOHLAV EXPLORES MERCURY, VENUS, JUPITER, SATURN, MARS AND OTHER PLANETS.

Excerpted from Chlastava of Pardubice in 1855

KRUTOHLAV EMBARKS ON ANOTHER TRIP TO THE PLANETS

Once again, Krutohlav opened his book in order to re-read his past thoughts and remind himself of the things he had once written down.

"Good God, can I possibly have discovered and described all this? Can it really have been me who wrote all this down?" After he closed the book reverentially it happened to slip, flipping open at the page that recalled *Dobropán, Lada, Smrtonoš, Čistena, Žitva, Mudrena, Paroma, Hladolet* and *Nebešťan*, the splendid old names of Mercury, Venus, Mars, Vesta, Ceres, Pallas, Jupiter, Saturn and Uranus – with descriptions of them all, including pictures and important notes and speculations.

"What and why?" he wondered, holding the book up to catch the sunlight so that he could better tell one word from the next. "True – my work it is – my own records and notes." The longer he had scrutinised the planets, the more he had liked what he saw, the more he had sought to learn from it, the greater had been his curiosity... With every day that passed this curiosity troubled him more and more and gave him no peace, until, rapt in the deepest thought, his bodily frame grew quite weak. It was only after some time that Benuš, Roháč, Slavata, Vrtoš, Vlk, Hledoš, Rokyta and Krivoš, all natives of Mníšany, Štítnik, Muráň, Revúca and elsewhere, began to grieve over the chronically emaciated Krutohlav and seek the cause of his apparent disorientation. But he remained utterly uncommunicative and unresponsive. They kept on badgering him, Benuš and Roháč especially, as they tried by every means to grab his attention and discover the cause of his transformation. But Krutohlav remained obstinately silent. They guessed at all manner of possibilities and hit on the most contradictory explanations. He must, they inferred, have grand plans ahead, for his jolly disposition couldn't possibly have become transformed into melancholy. So let's wait and see where it takes him.

Then came the moment when Krutohlav summoned his companions and began to hold forth:

"You know what a restless spirit I am and that I have already discovered what there is to know about both the Moon and the Sun, but despite that, I want to take another trip into the celestial heights before I die and take a closer look at the other satellites that go round the Sun. If any of you think you're up to it, you can join me."

"Me, me too – we'll all go with you," they cried as one, which made Krutohlav very happy.

"Come on then, quick, to the balloon," the canny Roháč jumped to his feet. "Let's do whatever's needed to get us flying up into the heights as soon as possible."

"No, no, this time we're taking a flying dragon," replied Krutohlav with a grin.

"A dragon!" they yelped in unison. "How on earth...?" Benuš asked.

"Quite naturally," Krutohlav began to explain. "My travels have taught me the inconvenience and uncertainty that go with balloons, so I've had to find some better device, and that will be a dragon. It will be a quarter of a league long, 6,813 feet wide and 300 feet tall. On the inside there'll be rooms and staircases, in short everything will be so well contrived as to leave nothing missing."

"Whoa!" said Slavata, leaping for joy. "What a whopper it's going to be."

"And how's it going to move through the air?" Rokyta was curious to know.

"As a steamboat strikes the water with gigantic paddles and thrusts the vessel forward, so, in our case, the dragon will have two similar devices on its breast, like the side fins of a fish, and just one like device on its back to prevent it from floating along on the level and ensure it rises at an angle. When these gigantic paddle wheels and other mechanisms are set going, they will strike the air with the same force as a paddle steamer's paddles strike the water, and so we, too, will sail off safely into the air."

"That's some odd new invention," Roháč chimed in. "Surely we're not going to be flying through the air like birds, are we?"

"And why ever not?" Krutohlav replied. "Don't you know that, even quite recently, Napoleon would have had his timbers shivered, or ordered to be shot upstream from a cannon anyone who'd have dared tell him what we all know today, that a steamer can be propelled against a river's current? So why couldn't it be the same with air – just because air is a more rarefied fluid than water? Why do birds fly in the air? Might not we be able to soar up swifter than a swallow and higher than an eagle? All it takes is flexible thinking, amassing all the requisite knowledge and believe me, and I shall prove it, we will fly higher, and faster, than not just the swallow, but the eagle as well."

"It's quite likely, natural even, that the fluidity of air differs from that of water only in certain minor respects and that whatever applies to water, will apply to air as well," Vrtoš rationalised, and his reasoning sufficed to persuade the whole company that such a voyage into the cosmos was genuinely feasible.

The entire company was seized with indescribable joy at such a prospect and their hearts were aflame with hopes of an opportunity to take a trip, in the near future, into those faraway dominions.

Preparing the balloon had been marked by the most strenuous endeavours imaginable, but they were as nought compared to what now went into the dragon. When Babylon, Tyre, Sidon, Heliopolis and other cities were being built, not all the available workforce was enlisted and set in motion. Here, by contrast, there was a teeming of thousands and thousands of people, in such perpetual motion as if their very lives depended on breaking through at any minute either to hell or high heaven.

"I wonder what the inhabitants of Venus, the Moon and especially the Sun are thinking if they're watching us through their telescopes?" joked Roháč as he hammered the first tooth into the dragon's maw using a massive spike.

"It'll dawn on them likely enough that we mean to pay them a visit," Rokyta replied.

"Not a bit of it! They're utterly bemused and can't figure out why we're dressing this monstrosity to fly, perhaps daily, over their heads, and prefer to think we're just pulling the dragon's teeth," Hledoš jabbered as he nailed an iron scale, 24 feet by twelve, into place on the dragon's neck.

Then along trundled Vlk on a huge wagon, pulled by twelve oxen, bringing just a single claw that was to be fixed to one of the dragon's extremities. As it was being unloaded there was an unfortunate accident that cost the lives of four men and a child.

"What on earth is that?" Slavata asked as they all looked on in such perplexity that they let their tools slip from their hands.

"And just look at that round thing! It's bigger than Mercury, and the size of that wagon, then all those beasts, and all the geeing and hawing! It's staggering, just look at it, look!" Slavata went on and on.

"What is it though?" said Vrtoš as he ran across to get a better look at the monstrous sphere. "What is it, what is it?" he shouted and shrieked for all to hear.

"What else could it be but the dragon's eyeball," the oldest of the helpers replied icily.

"Eyeball, its eye?" There was no end to Vrtoš's amazement and he couldn't tear his own eyes away from it.

This eye was 72 feet high and almost as wide, and a single eyelash poking out above it measured 60 feet and was like an untrimmed billet.

Thus was the dragon made ready. People came from all over Slovakia to admire the gigantic monstrosity. The great big teeth, the massive long legs, the enormous eyes and ears, and those terrifying claws and so on, quite unlike those of any other beast, but quite proper on a dragon. No such monster had ever been seen in all the ages past, nor would one ever be seen again. If anyone wanted to see it, this was the moment to make the journey, because it was nearly finished, and they wouldn't regret it.

"To give you an idea of the dragon, Kubo, let me tell you a bit about it," said Maco to the curious Kubo having just returned home. "In all my living days I've never seen anything so freakish," he began, "it's driven some people mad, some have had epileptic fits and women have miscarried at the sight of it. It's the monster to end all monsters!!!"

Maco himself started feeling anxious as he described it, but having had a restorative gulp from his glass, he found his tongue and began, in a low tone, thus:

"You just can't imagine the thing, but I've said that already. It's lying spread-eagled right across the valley. Its snout is so huge that you could stuff our entire church tower into it. Its teeth are the size of great beams, but sharp as needles. Its eyes, which go round and round in their sockets like a ship's helm, must be able to see for miles. The surface of its tongue is covered in buildings, including the hugest ever observatory, from which the planets are to be studied. The like of its ears I've never ever seen – they rear up into the air, covered in metal plates and with ladders running all over them. And as for its tail! It sticks upwards like a whale's, with one huge paddle mounted on it and twenty-four others. Two great paddle wheels jut out from its sides and when they're set going they strike the air with such a light touch that you don't hear a sound. And there are couple of smaller ones beneath its tail. Its massive wings are a quarter of a league long and decked out with feathers, with the odd cannon disposed here and there so that if they enter hostile regions and have to do battle with someone they can meet force with force. Its whole exterior is covered in scales, each one of which takes two to four oxen to move. Inside, it is the cosiest dwelling in the world. And as for the sheer quantities of food all in one place! You could find anything there that you felt like. There's Turiec beet, Liptov potatoes, Klenová cheeses, saffron milk caps from Kohút, salted grayling and trout caught in the Zdychava and Hron, cloth from Revúca and Zips, earth nuts and peas from Zips, and even spring water from the trough at the spot they call Cross Meadows above the Revúca baths.[29] And goodness knows what else." Towards the end, Kubo had stopped taking any of this in and instead, having flung his coat across his shoulders, he had galloped off down into the valley to inspect the dragon for himself.

---

29 Revúca did indeed once have a small spa, which functioned until fairly recently; the building is still standing, but in what is described as a pitiful condition.

When all had been made ready as required, the little company of friends took their places inside the dragon. The instant the paddle wheels begun to whirr, the dragon rose up into the air at an unprecedented speed and after barely two hours it had disappeared from the watchers' sight.

Krutohlav kindled a load of charcoal, got the fire going, adjusted the oars and rowed straight for Mercury. What happened next, you can read in the following piece.

MERCURY

"Look how fast we're approaching Mercury and how much more brightly it's presenting itself. I've long wanted to have a better idea of it, but I couldn't make it out that well from Earth because it's so close to the Sun. Now we can really investigate what it is and what it's like." They all quickly followed Krutohlav into the dragon's maw and each of them, telescope in hand, kept a constant watch on it. First they began to investigate:

THE DISTANCE, ORBITAL PERIOD AND MASS OF THIS PLANET

"As we can see," Krutohlav began, leaning against one of the dragon's gigantic teeth, "Mercury is, of all the planets, the one closest to the Sun."

"Indeed so," Vlk replied as he made his own observation of Mercury. "Because it's so close to the Sun, all we can tell is that it's round. And do you see how it also shines, like the Moon?"

"Yes, Vlk's right," said Krutohlav, "not only is it small, but it must be a long way from Earth, and because it is so close to the

Sun, we can barely tell – because of the Sun's glare – what's going on on it. Its mean distance from the Sun is 8,082,000 German leagues, but as we can observe from how unevenly it orbits the Sun, being now closer, now further away, the distance can be even greater. When it's at its closest, the distance is 7,413,000 leagues, when it's furthest away it's 9,752,000 leagues. How it circles Earth is even more remarkable: calculations have shown that when it's closest to Earth, it's seven million leagues away, and at its remotest it's thirty million!"

"What have you discovered regarding Mercury's diameter?" Krutohlav asked Roháč, the latter having just come back down the ladder from the dragon's nostril, where one of the largest observatories was housed.

"It isn't as big as I thought," Roháč replied. "Its diameter is 600 geographic leagues, which is only a third of the radius of Earth."

"Do a quick calculation of its surface area," he tasked his companions, who set about it on the instant.

"Its surface area is exactly 1,073,000 square leagues," they responded as one.

"And that means that its volume will be what?"

"104 million cubic leagues."

"Just so. It has 104 million cubic leagues and so, comparatively speaking, it has only four hundredths of the body mass of Earth."

"So we could knead twenty-five Mercuries out of Earth," said Roháč.

"That's right," Krutohlav concurred.

"It's really hard to believe how fast Mercury circles the Sun," said Rokyta after a pause, as he returned from his observation post. "Just listen," he said, "it whizzes along at 6.7 geographic leagues per second, that's 578,000 a day."

"Agreed. That's what I came up with as well," Benuš piped up.

"Let's hear what Vrtoš also has to tell us," said Slavata to his fellows, "about what he's discovered regarding Mercury's mass."

"It's got only one sixth of the mass of Earth," Vrtoš replied, "I've discovered no more and no less, just that if we put Earth on one scale pan and Mercury on the other, it would need six Mercuries to balance the weight of Earth. Moreover," he went on at length, "I have established that Mercury is four times as dense as Earth. We know that the mean density of Earth is five times that of water, and so Mercury's density will be twenty times that of terrestrial water, which means that the density of Mercury equates to that of gold or platinum."

"Objects falling on Mercury," Vrtoš continued his disquisition, "do so at a rate of 14.1 feet per second."

"How did you work that out?" Rokyta asked, "and what evidence can you furnish us with, given that we're so many million miles away?"

"That's easy," the other replied, "if you know its mass and half its diameter, calculating how fast objects fall there is ever so easy. And I hadn't forgotten to work out its diameter," Vrtoš went on and the others applauded him, voicing their amazement at how clever he was. "When it's closest to Earth, objects fall in 12 seconds, when it's furthest away, it takes four. To the Sun's inhabitants, Mercury seems the same size as Earth, though we know it's much smaller. While to Mercury's inhabitants the Sun appears two and a half times larger than it does to us."

Krutohlav, having confirmed the truth of what the previous speakers had been saying, began explaining about Mercury's temperature and luminosity.

"It's very proximity to the Sun must entail a considerable change. And I have discovered that Mercury receives seven times more light than we here on Earth, and its temperature will also be sevenfold. If we had that much light, we couldn't avoid going blind and festering in seven times the heat we're used to here. And no living creature could do that. So you have to concede that any people on Mercury must be as tough as old boots! If we compare it with Uranus, where light and heat are 2,300 times weaker, and with Earth, where they are 330 times weaker, then our water would never go off the boil, while on Uranus all our fluids, including air itself, would, in that extreme cold, turn into a dense mass. So we couldn't live on either one of them."

That so put the wind up them that they hared off to slacken the dragon's paddles and propellers, fearful lest it fly them somehow to Mercury, where they risked being burned to cinders. Krutohlav himself just smiled, knowing from experience that Earth wouldn't let so much as a breadcrumb break free. "Don't delude yourselves, my friends, as humans we'll never get there, unless by the will of God," he finally muttered, after they'd begun yanking at all the ropes, folding back the paddles and reducing the steam. He could hardly hope to restore their calm.

In the end, after they had set the dragon going again, they all reassembled to hear more of Krutohlav's discourse. And so he began thus:

"As you see it there, Mercury, it's a brilliant white colour, and because it's so bright I'm sure you'll all have put tinted lenses in your telescopes. And as you're coming to realise, although we're quite close, it's almost impossible to observe it with the naked eye because, being so close to the Sun it's in a way blacked out by the greater radiance of the Sun."

"Yes, yes," Vrtoš, Roháč and Rokyta responded with their own offerings, "the light of the Sun prevents us from observing it; our best chance is using telescopes just after sunset or just before sunrise. And although Copernicus, on his deathbed, bemoaned never having seen Mercury, although Copernicus' teacher, Moestlin,[30] had it that Mercury only existed to give astronomers a bad name, and although Ricolini[31] thought it as mysterious as the alchemists had thought quicksilver, the ancient Greeks, including Ptolemy, had made a pretty good attempt at establishing its presence, its orbit and so forth. Since the invention of the telescope, it can even be found at midday, as you all know."

Following this discussion, Krutohlav gave orders for the fire to be stoked with more charcoal and the power of the dragon's paddle wheels to be bumped up, following which they shot forward at an incredible speed towards Mercury, so that they might determine certain of its other properties. Over the next two weeks they got ever closer and closer, making constant observations from the dragon's teeth, where they had installed their telescopes.

"See," said Krutohlav, "it changes just like the Moon, having a full state and quarters," and they all stared in amazement at this wonder.

---

30 Michael Moestlin or Maestlin (and yet other spellings; 1550–1631), German astronomer and mathematician. He came after Copernicus (1473–1543), so Reuss has got his facts muddled. In fact, he was the teacher of the later Johannes Kepler (1571–1630).

31 There are three or four candidates for whom Reuss might have meant here, but Urbancová (in the footnotes to the 1984 edition of *Hviezdoveda*) has settled on (and the evidence with respect to astronomy is very strong) Giovanni Batista Riccioli (1598–1671), the Italian Jesuit astronomer one of whose major works, the *Almagestum Novum* (1651) could still be described, as late as 1912, as the most important Jesuit literary work of the seventeenth century (v. https://en.wikipedia.org/wiki/Giovanni_Battista_Riccioli, accessed 13.03.2022).

"Do you see how that area that was dark just an hour ago is now shining bright, and how that shining region has since gone dark? That must be due to clouds, like ours; what else could it be? And where there are clouds there has to be air, and so we shall be of the firm belief that Mercury not only possesses clouds, but also its own supply of air. That's how it is and it cannot be otherwise," Krutohlav continued before turning to the subject of how Mercury spins.

"Whichever way I turn my telescope and no matter how hard I strain my eyes, I just cannot discern any spots of the kind the Sun has, but that could be because of the glare. But that it turns on its axis is obviously true, because the coign at its pole reappears at the same time, which is evidence enough that it is spinning. And its rotation is like time on Earth. So Mercury's rotation is the same with regard to the Sun. If there were the teeny-weeniest difference in the rotation of Earth and Mercury, all the greater would be the difference in Mercury's weather. You'd never believe how quickly that can change: its seasons last three weeks, actually just 22 days, while with us they take no less than 91 days. So one of our seasons lasts more than four times longer.

"Such abrupt changes in the weather leaves the impression of everlasting spring. But since the Sun does such a stalwart job of scorching it during the day, the night isn't long enough for it to cool down. Then when we consider the great changes effected by light even on Earth, here it must be quite different: there will be greater differences among the colours and it will penetrate the ground more keenly. So how could Mercury's flora and fauna not be quite different from ours?" Krutohlav ended his deliberation and the others stopped making their tireless notes on all those important matters in their books.

As they sailed on through the air, they kept a constant watch on Mercury. Then Roháč let out a yelp – he'd spotted some mountains on Mercury. So they all extended their telescopes in readiness and likewise saw great mountains stretching for 40–60 geographic leagues. They quickly set about measuring the height of each one, finding some to be as high as 58,000 feet, so twice as high as any on Earth. There appeared to be more mountains on the southern half, as they had already noted on other planets. "It could be," Krutohlav concluded, "that the height of its mountains goes a long way towards tempering the blazing heat."

Thus ended their scrutiny of Mercury. It was a long time before the dragon could transport them to a different orbit, this part of the journey being at an end and the intention being for it to fly them elsewhere – to the next nearest body, Venus. So the boilers on board the dragon were fired up again, the new direction set, and they rowed away, determined to reach Venus in the shortest possible time.

The wheels span at a monstrous rate and the dragon was tossed hither and yon like a ball. Its swishing through the air was like a marmot's whistle as it flew way above the clouds, ever higher and higher until they had a clearer view of Venus in all her beauty.

VENUS

"We're approaching Venus, for us the most important of the planets, which is unequalled in terms of its attributes," Krutohlav began and each of them focussed hard on it, now quite close, and they were loath to take their eyes off it. "As I said, it's the brightest of them all and gives out the most beautiful light. It's the closest to Earth and its brisk rotation, as we see it, is the fastest. And we should be grateful to it for enabling us to determine the Earth's distance from the Sun. While the dragon was being constructed back on Earth, we could recognise it with the naked eye by its bright, white light, twinkling there even in daylight. We also discovered that, apart from the Moon, it's the only light in the sky that can be seen with the naked eye at the same time as the Sun. Despite being, like Mercury, so close to the Sun, and spinning in the latter's rays, it's best observed at dusk or dawn: at such opportune times – with the Sun rising or setting – its light shines so bright that you can even make out its shadow. That is probably what makes it so hard to observe from Earth even with a decent telescope and why we never see its light clearly defined. Another possible cause, besides its lusty light, is its vast, but unsteady atmosphere."

"And where did the planets get their names from?" Slavata was eager to know.

"Their Slavonic names come from Slavonic mythology, just as the Greek and Latin names come from their pagan religion," Krutohlav replied. "The Sun (*sol*) is called *Chasoň* in Slavonic and its sign is figure 1. *Dobropán* (*Mercurius*), also known as *Zeloň*, was associated with quicksilver and in both astrology and metallography it was given the sign in figure 2. The cross-shaped stick represents the stick with which Mercury accompanied the souls of the dead to Hell. *Lada*, *Krasopani*, *Zízlila* or *Venuša* (*Venus*) is usually given the symbol in figure 3. The circle represents a mirror with its handle as evidence of the attribute of beauty. In metallography the symbol means copper and it is possible that the first mirrors among the ancients were indeed made of copper. *Smrtonoš* (*Mars*) (fig. 4) is the god of war and his symbol represents a shield and an arrow; in metallography it signifies iron.

Kráľomoc or *Perún* (*Jupiter*) (fig. 5): its sign is the first Greek letter in the name of Zeus. *Hladolet* (*Saturn*) has the sign in fig. 6, showing a sickle or scythe, as if this god were to cut everything down with the passage of time. The sign also means lead, though the star itself has very little resemblance to it in terms of its light. Earth (*Terra*) (fig. 7) represents an orb and cross, which relates to salvation. *Nebešťan* (*Uranus*) (fig. 8) doesn't mean a thing. *Žitva* (*Ceres*) (fig. 9) denotes harvest. *Mudrena* (*Pallas*) (fig. 10) represents the pike of the militant Pallas.[32] *Jovina* (*Juno*) (fig. 11). *Čistena* (*Vesta*) (fig. 12) signifies an altar with a constantly burning flame. We ought also to mention *Kvetena* (*Flora*), *Dužena* (*Iris*), *Česena* (*Hebe*), *Vehlasa* (*Mesis*), *Hviezdena* (*Astraea*) and others, and apart from all these I have observed many other satellites which, if I live long enough, I'll give names to, and give them their proper specifications. However, let's pause there and start to take a proper look at Venus," Krutohlav concluded.

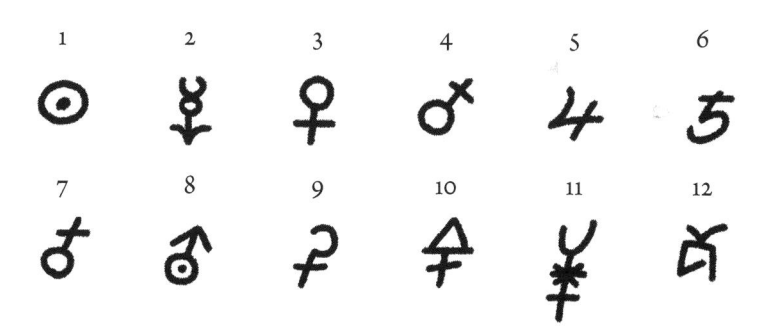

1	2	3	4	5	6
☉	☿	♀	♂	♃	♄
7	8	9	10	11	12
♂	♁	⚳	⚴	⚵	⚶

---

[32] Reuss has this Pallas as male, and there were several such in ancient mythology, hence, too, the symbol of a lance or spear, but the reference is thought properly to be to Pallas Athene, also symbolised by a lance.

KRUTOHLAV'S COMPANIONS LOOK FOR THE DISTANCE AND ORBIT OF VENUS

As soon as his allies had recovered, each hastened to his assigned post from which to make an adequate study of Venus' physical attributes. Krutoslav himself went off with his Herschel telescope to the far end of the dragon's tongue, where there was a huge observatory. Slavata scrambled up onto its eyebrow to be that much closer to Venus and give his all to the observing of it. For his immediate task Roháč chose a 30–foot projection erected on the dragon's forehead, while Vrtoš sat on the white of one of the dragon's eyes, and not a word could be heard, just the rattle and clank of the turning paddle wheels.

After quite some time they all started to make their way to the tongue, to join Krutohlav in the main observatory, where he was watching Venus unceasingly and with the greatest diligence.

"So how far is Venus from the Sun?" Krutohlav asked Slavata, who was still perched on the eyebrow.

"I have established that Venus has 0.723 of the radius of Earth," he replied, "and so it's 15 million geographic leagues from the Sun."

"That's exactly right," the others chorused, "our calculations have brought us all to the selfsame figure."

"I've also observed that it always orbits the Sun at the same distance, with only the slightest deviations, whereas in Mercury's case we found the difference when it is furthest from the Sun to be two million geographic leagues."

"But in relation to Earth it's quite different," said Vrtoš as he scrambled back down his ladder. "When Venus comes closest to Earth, it's five million leagues away, while at its most remote the distance is 35 million leagues. That's quite a difference, eh? So won't that explain why it looks different in size at different times? When it's close to Earth we see it as bigger than Jupiter, bigger even than the ring of Saturn, while when it's furthest away it hardly matches Mercury for size."

Having come down off his projection, Roháč explained that the diameter of Venus came to just 1,680 geographic leagues, making it actually slightly smaller than Earth. It has a surface area of 8,376,000 square leagues, so almost as great as Earth's. Its volume, at 2,230 cubic leagues, also almost matches Earth's. It orbits the Sun at 4.9 leagues per second. Its mass is slightly higher than that of Earth, and a solid body falling drops on Venus at a rate of 15.87 feet in the first second, or 0.7 of a foot more than on Earth.

Now that he had listened to all the observations made by his comrades and compared them with his own findings and calculations, Krutohlav confirmed the truth of their assertions: "So then, when we put all this together we shall find that Venus comes closest to Earth in every regard. But what differences have we found? Hardly any, but our next observations will show what we will find actually on Venus and what we should look for." And with that he brought the day's observations of Venus to a close.

THE LUMINOSITY AND MAXIMUM VISIBILITY OF VENUS

Next morning they all rose and, armed each with his own telescope, scurried off to their respective posts. From his eyebrow position Slavata observed that the gleam from Venus was similar to that from Mercury, with the difference that Venus being closer, its gleam seemed stronger.

"Since we've heard that Venus's orbit is never far from the Sun," Vrtoš began to shout down from the eye-white, "it is always exposed to the glare of the Sun, but when we, I mean our Earth approaches it, we're bound to see it as now smaller, now bigger. Even at its closest to us its light is 3,000 times weaker than the Moon's, which is why it really does twinkle like a star. I've read in *Svetozor* that it shines like a lighted candle 230 feet away. When on 21 July 1716 it was shining precisely that bright, the people of London thought it was a portent announcing some imminent disaster, and in 1750 crowds of people in Paris had to be broken up by the police because its brightness had stirred them to revolt."

"Exactly so," Krutohlav concurred, "that's where the greatest human folly and stupidity breaks out, whereas we know that once every eight years Venus is going to be just as luminous as in 1716 or 1750."

At that moment the welkin turned dark, which put an end to the day's observations. So they all clambered down and tucked into pork washed down with both beer and wine.

KRUTOHLAV'S ASSOCIATES ARGUE ABOUT SPOTS ON VENUS AND ABOUT ITS ATMOSPHERE

"To your stations, my brethren! Observe Venus now: now that that dark cloud cover has been riven apart, it appears to us as a flash of sunlight," said Krutohlav and they all dispersed up flights of stairs and ladders onto the dragon's eyebrows, tongue, ears and tail etc. to marshal their telescopes with a view to exploring the spots on Venus as they grew ever larger, and so to studying the matter of the planet's air.

Several weeks passed before Venus yielded her all to them.

"But we have her now," said Vrtoš with a shake of his head. "I'd never have imagined how much work and trouble she'd put us to."

"It's because she's well-known for her virginity, she won't let anyone near her," Roháč responded, sitting up there on his projection.

"Not only that, though," Slavata called down from his eyebrow. "She has the spirit and wit to outdo a dashing young man, yet we oldies have had the audacity to try cajoling her, so it's no surprise that she's treated us the way she has."

"Amen to all that," Krutohlav wound up that exchange. "Let us see whatever we can and pass on to our earthly descendants what we have discovered and what there is to be said about her."

They gathered round a table and began discussing the matter at hand in earnest.

"From my position on the dragon's eyebrow I observed spots very like those on the Sun, same form, constancy and velocity," Slavata ruminated aloud.

"He's right, I spotted the same thing," Vrtoš concurred, "actual sunspots."

"It isn't possible," Roháč carped, "for any spots on Venus to move as fast as on the Sun. It's an altogether different kind of body from the Sun, which makes any such notion ridiculous. Admittedly, I saw something similar myself, but they looked flimsy, opaque and greyish in colour, very like clouds on Earth. They're not dark spots."

"That's true, Roháč is right about what he saw," Rokyta agreed.

Krutohlav himself acknowledged the truth of Roháč's assumptions. The latter, overjoyed at having got to the bottom of such a knotty problem, which required experience and pertinent observational skills, continued: "This planet also has air, which is of the same density and reaches almost the same altitude as the air round Earth."

"So let's hear why," Krutohlav responded, his head resting on the tabletop, and so they all listened to Roháč, their mouths agape.

"Listen up, then," said Roháč in turn. "If our Earth had no air, we would see neither dusk, nor dawn, and the Sun's radiance would turn at once into the deepest dark. But I have seen that the mountains on Venus are still shining bright, while its valleys have long been overtaken by darkness, just as on Earth. From this we may conclude that dusk will be darker and longer-lasting in proportion to the density of the air and how high it reaches. Or not? In the Moon's case we can see with even the smallest telescope that the dark (reverse) part is sharply separated from the part that shines (its disk), one kind of light transitioning abruptly, not at all gradually, into another, that's to say into darkness. This tells us that either the Moon has no air, or that it is so thin that our eyes cannot detect it. If you are still not convinced, let me say this, too: as the Moon rotates on our horizon, other more remote suns (fixed stars) disappear – with no gradual loss of light – reappearing just as suddenly when the opposite applies."

"But with Venus it's all quite different," Roháč[33] went on, getting quite carried away. "Despite how brightly it shines, if we look closely through our telescopes towards its edge, its duskiness changes and doesn't extend far beyond it. The same applies to fixed stars. The only conclusion we can draw from that is that

---

33   Reuss has here, presumably as an oversight, not Roháč, but Vrtoš, but that does not make sense, given a) the verb *went on*, and b) the first sentence in the following paragraph, referring to Roháč as the last speaker. Both Slovak editions retain, despite this contradiction, Vrtoš.

Venus is enveloped in an atmosphere that is almost identical to our terrestrial atmosphere, as least as regards its height and density. Any talk of spots is misplaced. If dark areas show that look like clouds, they're actually more like thinner mists and fogs. The people of Venus, if there are any, enjoy clean air and live in a drier environment, because they have no large lakes or seas to vaporise into vapours, which is precisely why it must be so very arid!"

Roháč having had his say, they all voiced their admiration for his acuity and how far he had progressed in astronomy, and more than once they turned cautiously to look at Krutohlav to see if he wasn't shaking his head at these reflections. But Krutohlav did not shake his head, not even once, so that was that.

THE COMPANY DETERMINE VENUS'S ROTATION ABOUT ITS OWN AXIS

In his quarters, Roháč was just munching an apple when there was a knock on his door. "Come in, come in, I've just been eating a most excellent black pudding and need to refresh my stomach."

"That's why I'm here. These papers from Krutohlav's office say you killed a sick pig. All such accidents are to be avoided aboard the dragon in transit," said the visitor, grinning into his whiskers.

"The pig was a bit bloated, that's all, but it hadn't gone off," came the reply.

"All the same." The visitor fished pointlessly for the paper, smiling.

Then Roháč's mama said: "Do come into the other room, the kids are making so much noise in here." And so he did and, extracting a florin from his pocket, asked for some roasted black pudding and a sausage, because he'd gone off beef and had no pork of his own.

"Of course, you're very welcome, why not? Let me do that for you," whereupon Roháč took his keys, went ahead and showed him their stock of sausages and other meats.

Then his grandmother stoked the dragon's fire and roasted two gigantic black puddings. My, they were good!

"Where are you headed?" asked Roháč.

"I have to take a smaller balloon and drop down to Red Rock to get some shingles. I'm under strict orders." And drop down he did, the dragon having moved on.

At that point Slavata tapped on the door: "On your feet, come up and watch Venus rotating. You've had plenty of time by now for your black pudding to wallow about inside your belly."

As for me, I grabbed my cape, scrambled up to my original post, i.e. on the dragon's ear, and watched Venus with extraordinary diligence, the black pudding still giving me that nice warming sensation.

"Have you seen that rotation before?" Krutohlav asked me, sitting there on the ear.

"Yes."

"Talk to me."

So I began to elaborate:

"Before we found the mountains, it was almost impossible to verify Venus's rotation, since all it affords are trifling little spots that look like clouds. But I did find that it rotates on its axis once every 23.3 Earth hours."

"Wrong," retorted Vrtoš, "I made it 24.1 hours."

"You're also wrong, Vrtoš," Krutohlav settled the matter. "One spin takes exactly 23 hours and 21 minutes."

SLAVATA DISCUSSES THE DAYS AND WEATHER ON VENUS

"Let's hear what Slavata has to tell us."

And he duly began:

"Dear old Krutohlav has given a firm decision as to the time Venus needs to turn on its axis. This rotation is almost identical to Earth's and so its day and night will also be the same. But the matter of Venus's weather will be quite different if it holds that the axis round which it spins is tilted at 72°. Any such tilt, or declination, determines what the weather is like. And the same applies in the case of Venus. Thus each half of Venus ought to have a very hot zone where the Sun rises and sets. This ought to be around its poles, and on both sides; here the Sun could never shine straight down on the heads of Venus's inhabitants. The temperate zone would be such that for a time the Sun would never appear – the way it does on Earth – and then it would fire straight down on the crowns of people's heads once again. This shows that the temperate zone on Venus is made up of wintery cold and great heat."

Here Krutohlav took over and, having confirmed what had been said, began explaining the whole matter thus:

"Away from the poles, the Sun will sometimes shine down on the inhabitants at an angle. In the gap between the cold belts, the sun will beat down on their heads almost vertically, as the Spaniards and Greeks get it with us. For inhabitants of the poles, the Sun is still shining, during the longest days, at midnight, just as in St Petersburg at midday. Those who live around its equator are lucky not to get burned alive during one period, and during the other, just as long, they'll get very cold as the night drags on and on. We see from all this that Venusians have to cope with quite contrary weather and they're lucky in that Venus orbits the Sun in half the time it takes our Earth, which is what governs and accounts for the abrupt changes in the weather." Thus did Krutohlav bring the discussion to a close.

ROHÁČ HAS THE BRIGHT IDEA OF GETTING TO VENUS IN ORDER TO DISCOVER WHAT EARTH MIGHT LOOK LIKE FROM THERE

All those aboard the dragon noticed the way it was being violently tossed and jogged about. For a time they ignored it, but finally it got so bad that the entire dragon seemed about to smash up with a bang. "What is it? What's happening?" They all came out running and examined the injured dragon.

"Nothing, it's nothing," Roháč replied, having turned quite pale. "I wanted to hurry it on towards Venus so as to have a view of Earth from there."

Krutohlav just shook his head sadly and wagged a menacing finger at him, until, having talked sense into him, he gave orders for the dragon to be set back on its steady course and began:

"We don't need to get to Venus, which we'll never reach anyway, in order to have a good view of Earth. The human mind is a greater gift from God than anything else in the world, and so all it needs is for the mind to be bent to a task for an end to be achieved. So listen while I try to satisfy Roháč's desire: if we did get to Venus, we might survive and

1. obtain a stupendous view of every corner of Venus from its six-league high mountains. If we were looking similarly out from Vienna, we could, with the aid of a telescope, take in Hamburg, Paris, Naples and other places within a hundred leagues;

2. for a long time ahead the Sun would still shine on the mountain tops, while the valleys would have long been overtaken by darkness;

3. we would be refreshed by the purity of the air, which is rarely subject to any kind of transformation;

4. the stars would shine for us with a consistently bright light;

5. we should the see the Sun four times as large as we see it from Earth and its light would be twice as powerful, like bright midday sunlight in our world;

6. the Earth itself, at its closest to Venus, appears nine times larger than Venus appears to us, and its light is nine times brighter than Venus's is to us.

"Would you really want that, Roháč? To embark on a trip to Venus where no human creature from Earth can ever alight? All you did was place us in mortal peril, for which you deserve a fat fine! But since your aspiration was driven by curiosity, you are forgiven."

Roháč blushed and made himself scarce.

JOINTLY THEY SCOUR THE SKY FOR VENUS'S MOON

"Seek and observe Venus's moon," Krutohlav began, aiming his own monstrous telescope at the region around Venus. "Fontana back in 1645, Cassini in 1672 and 1686, Schort in 1740 and others saw it, so we ought to be able to locate it." Krutohlav and his band spent three months on the look-out.

"Have you found it, Vrtoš?"

"No!" came the reply.

"And you two, Slavata, Roháč?" he asked them and then the others.

"No," they replied.

"I may well have seen it," said Rokyta, "but it could just have been my eyes playing up, because as I twisted my telescope, the moon twisted as well."

"That's a sign of how the Moon's great luminosity deceives our eyes," said Krutohlav.

"I also saw something similar, but eventually decided they were sunspots."

"So there's an end of it – Venus doesn't have a moon of her own," said Krutohlav irritably as he closed the huge book in which he kept all his notes.

MARS

"Right now Mars is getting close, so let's be done with Venus and find out about Mars instead," Krutohlav began, "and let's have a look at its particular attributes."

The two previous planets, Mercury and Venus, are otherwise referred to as the innermost planets because their orbits fall within that of Earth, that is, Earth travels round them. But Mars is a real planet because on its journey around the Sun it travels round our Earth and not the other way round. Thus it is first among the outer planets.

MARS'S DISTANCE AND ORBIT

"The average distance of Mars from the Sun is 32 million geographic leagues. But on the one hand it gets as close as 29 million leagues and on the other it moves as far away as 35 million. But the relation of Mars to the Sun differs in other ways, too. It comes closest to Earth at seven million[34] leagues and is farthest from it at 54 million leagues. That's a huge difference. It is a thousand leagues in diameter, so just slightly over half the diameter of Earth. Its surface area is nine million square leagues, only three-tenths that of Earth. Its volume is 467 million cubic leagues or two-fifths of the corporality of Earth. When it's closest to Earth it is as big as Jupiter, but at its most distant it's as big as Uranus. Its circuit of the Sun takes 686.9 days, so its velocity around the Sun is less than 3 and two-thirds leagues per second. It is hard to determine its mass, for it doesn't possess a moon. It appears that the speed of an object falling on it is 6.3 feet in the first second."

Krutohlav had so hit his stride that he might have gone on goodness how much longer throwing light on Mars except that his companions advised him to stop since it was an ideal time for breakfast and a rest: they'd been out and about for a fortnight so now was the time for some much needed refreshment and relaxation!

KRUTOHLAV'S COMPANIONS ARGUE ABOUT SPOTS AND THE ROTATION OF MARS

"How does it strike you?" Vrtohlav asked Roháč, who was squatting up above on his coign.

"It's dark-red in colour, like the colour of molten iron," came the reply.

"Do you see any spots on it?"

"Why yes," Roháč replied. "They're like the red of iron ore or red sand, and it could be dry land; elsewhere it gleams green like

---

34 Both editions of the original text say only seven leagues here, clearly calling for a minor edit.

our mountain lakes or seas, and they could be actual seas and lakes."

"And have you worked out how Mars turns on its axis, Slavata?" Rokyta asked him.

"I've reckoned one axial rotation at 24 hours and 40 minutes," Slavata replied.

"That's not true," came the response from Vrtoš. "It takes 24 hours, 39 minutes and 21 seconds."

Then there was a spate of calculation and disputation over who was right. In the end they asked Krutohlav and he settled matters:

"I've been observing Mars and its rotation for a long time now, and have established beyond doubt that only Vrtoš's reckoning is correct."

"True, that's true, it's what we found as well," others replied.

"Well, hear something new now, my friends, something you haven't suspected in your wildest dreams, a property peculiar to Mars and other planets close to it."

"Go on," said the others, gathering round.

So Krutohlav began: "What's remarkable is that the four planets revolving closest round the Sun and being closest to it are almost identical as regards the length of their days. And another thing: the further they are from the Sun, the faster their rotation." They were all pleased to learn of such a grand commonality among these bodies.

Krutohlav went on: "You've all been deliberating about those spots, but so far you haven't established what they actually mean. Let me explain. Since these spots always present themselves as unchanging with regard to their location and habitus, they cannot be compared to clouds, which are prone to change, and it is apparent that they are a permanent fixture on Mars. There's also no disguising the fact that – as I have observed on more than one occasion – the spots are of two kinds as to their essence. One we've already had explained, the other resides in the very opposite: spots that manifest themselves as extremely variable and moving very fast, at twice the speed of our most terrible tempests. And so Mars evinces both fixed spots and marks that are cloudlike and mobile. This is why we should gain from further enquiry."

MARS'S ATMOSPHERE

We readers shall be taught what to think on that score by the intimations arising from Krutohlav's companions' enquiries:

"The atmosphere on Mars is very dense. I know this because, as it rotated, I noticed a large star which, on its approach to the edge of Mars, grew dimmer and dimmer until it disappeared, and I saw the same thing on the opposite side," Rokyta reported.

"Using a better telescope, I saw quite different things and can attest that Mars's atmosphere consists of only very thin matter," Roháč contested. Krutohlav then found that it was Roháč who was right.

"We have now examined and revealed practically all there is about Mars that lends itself to human enquiry. So we have no alternative but to turn the dragon towards another planet." Whereupon they tightened all the screws and sails, stoked the fire and promptly rowed off in a new direction. "But before we abandon it completely, I should just remind you that Mars appears oblate, flattened at the poles. Besides that, we can find white specks on them, glinting like snow. These, having been warmed by the Sun over a period, disappear, and when a wintery cold returns, they sparkle beautifully.

This permits us to conclude that these are vast areas covered in snow. Finally, and to be brief, for another planet is already looming, I would recall that, to date, Mars has not been recorded as having any moon. Mars itself does not shine brightly, so if it does have any moons, they are not visible in the gloom." So ended Krutohlav, the others having heard him out, mouths agape. Finally, closing his book, he gave the order to make for another region and row ever onward so that he and his companions might develop their image of the cosmos further. The dragon whizzed along and after a long journey they drew ever closer to Jupiter.

JUPITER

The closer they got to Jupiter, the more they wondered at its size, luminosity and the horizontal bands that they discerned on it. Never yet had Roháč clung so firmly to his projection, not because he was afraid of falling off, but because Jupiter proved to be so very, very interesting and he didn't want the hand with which he was holding his telescope to move one jot. The same went for Vrtoš, Rokyta, Slavata and the rest, all so intent on observing Jupiter that their eyes remained glued to it. Only Krutohlav remained on the dragon's tongue, where he twisted and turned his Herschel telescope on such sudden impulses that some of its little wheels came adrift and fell off, leaving huge depressions in the hills near Kameňany[35] in Gemer county, and on the Bükk Mountains.[36] Anyone inclined to go digging there would easily unearth one of the fallen telescope wheels.

---

35 A village about 20 km SSE of Revúca as the crow flies.
36 A range of limestone mountains in northern Hungary, between Eger and Miskolc, famous for its caves, ski slopes and its status as a national park. It is *c.* 80 km S of Kameňany.

"Listen up, my fellow scions of Revúca," said Krutohlav as he commenced his memorable discourse, made at their request. "Jupiter, whom we Slavs have long known as *Perun*, has also been known as *Královoc* [≈ 'Theocrat'] for the great power that he wields over others. It is the largest of the planets known to us at present. It shines with a strong, yellowish light, so big that it's easy to see if you've got good eyesight, as are its four moons, which keep circling round it, distinguishable even to the naked eye... Observe! Its average distance from the sun is 108 and a half million leagues, so it's five and one-fifth times as far from the Sun as our Earth."

"And is the line of its orbit the same as with the previous four planets?" Vrtoš was curious to know.

"Not quite! It's almost constant: to be precise, its greatest distance from the Sun is 133 and four-fifths of a million leagues, and at its closest it is 103 and two-thirds of a million," Krutohlav enlightened him. "So, as you see, the difference is slight. But all the greater is the difference when compared to Earth, which comes roughly to 79–130 million leagues."

"And its diameter?"

"That is 19,980 geographic leagues, so 11 times greater than Earth's. And its surface area will be 121 times greater than Earth's and its volume 1,333 times greater. So if someone wanted to make Earth-size spherules out of Jupiter, he could make 1,333 of them. Or again, out of the Sun he could make 905 Jupiters or 13 million Earths."

"Oh, my God," Rokyta sighed, "such numbers are too huge to get one's head round, not to mention the size of the heavenly bodies themselves."

"Its mean rate of movement round the Sun is a mere 1.7 leagues per second, so it rotates around the Sun two and four-fifths more slowly than Earth, and four times slower than Mercury.

"Jupiter's mass is 340 times that of Earth, which is why its density comes to only a quarter of that of Earth, which makes it rather similar to our amber. Yet despite its low density, the rate at which solid bodies fall on it comes to 38 and four-fifths feet in the first second. From this it is obvious what a huge body we are dealing with, why it is plainly second only after the Sun and why its mass is three times that of all the other planets taken together."

JUPITER'S ATMOSPHERE

"On the surface of Jupiter, as you are discovering, we can see horizontal lines running round it, rather like our equator. In addition to these long lines we can also see smaller, dark, cloudlike spots. Some of them, the widest and darkest, are static and lie around its equator. Others are constantly mutating. The latter appear and disappear in a matter of a few hours, but they are always parallel to the large spots. When these smaller spots break up, they seem to reveal some darker space, which could be the actual surface of Jupiter."

WHAT THE LINES AND SPOTS OBSERVED ON JUPITER MEAN

"Oh, please, Krutohlav, do try and be a bit more precise and explain these things to us, what they mean, or ought to mean," some of them implored him.

"It is unlikely that the lines and spots observed on Jupiter belong to its ground. This is because the motion of the lines and the spots keeps almost constantly to a west-to-east direction and their velocity does not match the body's rotation – they're always two or three hours behind. Some of the spots closer to the planet's equator have been observed to travel at 300–400 feet per second, which is eight times as fast as the greatest hurricanes on Earth. Many have asserted that their velocity can be as high as 10,000 feet per second. In their motion there is considerable similarity to the way in which our trade winds move. If these spots had anything to do with the weather on Jupiter – take good heed, my friends! – such enormous body movements and the tossing and turning would make the surface of Jupiter uninhabitable, because it would be ever in motion like the terrestrial ocean before it withdrew into its proper confines. If all the movements are happening in the air above Jupiter, then it is quite different from ours and much denser. I myself have observed areas measuring 10–20,000 square leagues suddenly, in the space of a few hours, turn bright from having been totally dark. Especially at the poles. In a nutshell, Jupiter is racked by colossal hurricanes, changing by the hour and thus resembling primordial Chaos." So spake Krutohlav, then he began again:

ON JUPITER'S ROTATION

"On Jupiter," he went on, "there are only a few static spots. From them we can determine that a day and a night there last 9.93 of our hours. From that you can appreciate that Jupiter, in all its great size, must spin very fast indeed. This great sphere's velocity being indeed so high, its rate has been calculated at 1.7 leagues, or 39,070 French feet per second. The rate at which it circles the Sun amounts to 1.3 leagues per second. And so both speeds – its rotation about its own axis and its orbiting the Sun – are very close, almost equal. And this points to the peculiar attributes of Jupiter and its close relations. In this respect, there is little difference between Jupiter and Saturn, and none between Jupiter and Uranus. A consequence of its velocity is that it is considerably squashed at the poles, to the extent that while such flattening on Earth comes to two leagues, in Jupiter's case it amounts to 800 leagues."

THE SEASONS ON JUPITER

"In view of its position, the weather on Jupiter is always the same, so winter and summer will be alike. The same applies to days, except at each pole, where the Sun is below the horizon for longer and shines longer. Over most of Jupiter, days and nights are equal, with a duration of five of our hours.

"As for the climate," Krutohlav pursued his narrative further, "the difference is greater, depending on how close to or far from the equator. Around its equator, there is permanent spring or summer, with the Sun floating constantly right over the inhabitants' heads. Things are different at the poles, where the Sun shines at an angle (3°), which is why it is permanently winter, with mountains and plains of ice that never melt, because the Sun is so very far away. The actual distance is 10 million leagues, and the Sun appears 27 times smaller than it does to us Earthlings. There is a clear boundary in the weather between either pole and the equator, because one year of theirs takes twelve of ours, and so the consequences of the climate are longer-lasting."

JUPITER'S MASS AND OTHER CONSIDERATIONS

"It has not yet been established accurately how long Jupiter's orbit takes, or exactly how flattened it is at the poles, and the same applies to its mass. To be brief: it is around 1/1073 the size of the Sun, and if we did ever reach Jupiter – the Sun's largest satellite – the entire cosmos would certainly appear different from how we see it from Earth. Its air is so dense that we might compare it to wood, and despite that density it has massive bursts of rapid change. It could be that it has vast oceans and rivers that release vapours and create woody clouds. One season up there lasts a whole three years, that is, spring, summer, autumn and winter at three years apiece, twelve years in all. Below its equator the Sun blazes down at right angles, and its distance from the zenith is a mere 3°. At the poles there's daylight for six years, then it's dark for six years, and when day does break after six years, the Sun is rotating so low above the ground that come lunchtime it's still only 3° up.

"The great contrast is that against the many years' perdurability of the weather, the days and nights are very short – a night and a day barely take ten hours of ours. A day lasts for five and a night likewise. This rapid turnover must affect the inhabitants' pace, and who's to say that they don't get our twelve-hour shift done in five? People who enjoy a lie-in wouldn't be happy here, but gluttons would rejoice that it's time to eat again."

HOW THE WORLD LOOKS FROM JUPITER

"From Jupiter, the Sun appears 27 times smaller than it does to us, and its luminosity is also 27 times weaker, and 180 times weaker than that of Mercury. Because it's so dark, all the stars in the sky shine bright on Jupiter, by day and night. The whole lot rotates in ten hours, as it takes 24 hours with us. It is quite beautiful when Jupiter is eclipsed by its own four moons. And I could explain much more to you, my friends, but right now its four moons have come floating along."

A DESCRIPTION OF THE FOUR MOONS OF JUPITER

Krutohlav's companions came and stood around him inside the observatory that had been set up on the dragon's tongue. He kept his enquiring eye clamped to his Herschel telescope, just now and again letting the others take a peek. And he began to explain:

"See the four moons that circle constantly around Jupiter, just as our Moon circles the Earth. From Earth a mountain shepherd with good eyesight can make them out, but ordinary eyes need an ordinary telescope for the purpose. They often disappear quite suddenly, then reappear a few hours later – having been eclipsed by Jupiter in the meantime. Of the four, the smallest is the second one, the largest the third. But even the first and fourth are twice the size of our own Moon. The third has five times the diameter of Earth's Moon, and the second is more like ours."

Having been advised on all that was to be discovered about Jupiter, they went back inside the dragon in order to concentrate on redirecting it, so that it might convey them all to another planet. They piled on the coal, got the fire blazing, set the paddles turning, slid out the oars and prepared everything for the dragon to sail at an unimaginable speed from this heavenly body to the next until, after a considerable time, they found themselves in the proximity of a – to them – previously unknown satellite of the Sun, which they were to assess and identify.

SATURN

After a very long journey, Krutohlav and his companions had finally reached Saturn and they could scarcely take in its stunning, extraordinary physiognomy, with that ring round it. It sparkled there before their eyes like a gigantic star girt with a hoop. Spontaneously, they gathered round Krutohlav to learn all about this satellite, which has no equal throughout the entire universe. Krutohlav directed his telescope towards Saturn and calculated:

ITS DISTANCE FROM THE SUN AND ITS ORBIT AROUND IT

"The distance of Saturn from the Sun is nine times greater than Earth's, and it travels round the Sun once in 29.5 years. So its year lasts twenty-nine and a half Earth years.

"As you can see, it shines with a pale, almost white light without rays. Once someone has found it in the vault of heaven, they'll easily seek it out again, because it moves only slowly and takes two and half years to transition from one sign of the zodiac to the next.

"It travels at 1.3 leagues per second, so it goes round the Sun five times slower than Mercury and three and a half times slower than Earth. To Saturn's inhabitants the Sun appears 90 times smaller than it does to us. And its luminosity is also 90 times lower, so on their loveliest days it's like dusk is to us."

KRUTOHLAV OBSERVES SATURN'S MAGNITUDE AND MASS

"Its diameter measures 17,690 leagues, slightly less than Jupiter's, but almost ten times that of Earth. Its surface area is 95 times and its volume 928 times greater than Earth's, meaning that if you rolled it out, you could make 928 balls the size of Earth from it. Its mass is but a three thousand five hundred and twelfth part of that of the Sun, so 95 times greater than Earth's mass. It is easy to deduce from that that Saturn's density is trifling, only a tenth of the density of Earth. What's more, it is the softest of them all, having twice the softness of our cork oak (*Quercus ruber*). A body falling onto it almost matches the rate on Earth – 14.5 feet per second. The effect its flimsy mass has on the flora, fauna, not to mention the inhabitants of Saturn, is easily imagined.

KRUTOHLAV DISCUSSES THE LINES ON SATURN AND ITS ATMOSPHERE

"Like Jupiter, Saturn also has lines like an equator. These will doubtless also have something to do with its atmosphere, though that must be quite, quite different from ours. The lines can be seen to undergo great changes, and although we're seeing it from such a huge distance, they indicate and confirm that it gets very stormy there.

"The pole of Saturn that faces away from the Sun is whiter and brighter, possibly because of the uninterrupted reign of winter and snow. And why not indeed? With the Sun shining on it 90 times less brightly and their winter lasting seven and a quarter years? The fact that Saturn and its moons are swathed in an atmosphere is proved by the stars that, as it moves along its orbit, vanish from sight only slowly."

SATURN'S RING

Having thus learned plenty about this heavenly body itself, Krutohlav's comrades now kept badgering the expert to have him explain Saturn's luminous ring and unravel its meaning for them.

"Before I could begin to throw some light on this wonder, this unprecedented miracle, take up your stations and observe it; I shall do likewise." And so they dispersed.

About four days later, Roháč climbed down from his perch and reported what he had established:

"In form, Saturn is quite different from all the comets we've come to know so far – it's egg-shaped. Despite my best efforts and despite not being able to delve deep inside it, it's my view that Saturn consists of three bodies clamped together (*Saturnus triformis*)[37] as if consisting of three moons."

"Wrong," declared Rokyta. "They're not moons that rotate separately, but are part of the body of Saturn itself."

"Wrong again," said Vrtoš, "it's just that it's elongated and has two dark patches on its sides."

---

37 As discovered by Galileo in 1610.

"You're all wrong," Krutohlav launched into his explanation: "Like the astronomers who came before us, you, too, have got it wrong. Listen: around the actual body of Saturn, around its sphere, that's not a solid, wide, freely suspended ring running round it."

"So where's it from then?" some of them asked.

"What do you think, Vrtoš?"

"I think it was caused by vapours and is being kept supplied," Vrtoš replied.

"But it seems more likely to be Saturn's air," Roháč interrupted. Rokyta was coming to the view that it was some residue of the sphere, squashed flat round its equator.

"Keep it up, lads, try telling me how a certain astronomer explained that the ring had snapped off the tail of a comet, got caught in a loop round Saturn and was left hanging there," Krutohlav brought his comrades' insights to a head, laughing. Then he started orating again:

"The ring we see floating before us is double, an inner and an outer ring. The latter is wider and darker, with a black line separating it from the inner ring, with which it lies at the same latitude and is on a common plane. Here and there, the inner ring reveals itself to be made up of many finer rings. To understand all this better, we must resort to

MEASURING SATURN'S RING

"It averages 8,545 leagues across, the outer ring 2,283 leagues, the inner 3,708 leagues; the width of the gap between them is 387 leagues, and the distance of the inner ring from Saturn itself is 4,122 leagues. From this we can ascertain the actual size of the ring encircling the planet: its total diameter is 38,090 leagues, or 22 times the diameter of Earth. Its volume is 13,980 million cubic leagues or almost five times that of Earth. Some would have it that its volume is 27 times greater.

"Like Saturn itself, the ring consists of dark solid bodies that get their light from the Sun, which explains why, by turns, the ring casts a shadow on the sphere of Saturn and the sphere on the ring. The colour of the ring is also different from that of the sphere: the sphere is yellow, the ring white.

"That there could be empty space between the ring and the sphere has only been attested once so far, by a star's being spotted through the gap."

After this conversation they all retired to Krutohlav's quarters to be informed about the way the ring often disappears from view according to the direction in which it lies. So twice a year (i.e. twice in 25.5 years) it gets completely lost. In addition, he told them about its huge variability.

KRUTOHLAV OBSERVES MOUNTAINS AND DESCRIBES SATURN'S ATMOSPHERE

Krutohlav's determination to investigate the surface of Saturn was driven by the fact that the planet does have an atmosphere. As for the ring, it has many little points of brightness, which have been considered to be mountains. Their height has been put at around 200 geographic leagues. Meanwhile, hear something about the ring's rotation: some would deny it altogether, but most people think that it turns on its axis once every nine and a half terrestrial hours. That will all be clarified once a telescope has been put together that improves on Herschel's. For now we have no alternative but to make do with what we have found so far. So let us examine instead:

WHAT THE RING OF SATURN LOOKS LIKE

As you know, even when shining its brightest, the Sun gives only the appearance of twilight on Saturn, so everything sits benumbed in the dark. Added to that there are those sudden changes between day and night, huge seasonal variations in the weather, one of which lasts seven and a half years, that is, three times longer than on earth, while winter at the poles can endure for a full fourteen years. Then it will dawn on us that for our own flora and fauna such a state of affairs could only have injurious and unprecedented consequences.

Since the ring is set at an angle to the sphere, any inhabitants dwelling below the equator will always see it as a dark band overhead. Dark because the Sun can never illuminate it there. Therefore it will also prevent them from examining other stars. And even the seven moons that rotate beyond the ring are quite invisible to them. Those who inhabit the poles have to put up with a night that lasts fifteen years and a fifteen-year day, and they never see the ring, because it's too close and beneath their horizon. Being as broad as it is, it can only be seen by those who live below 45°. From that point on, the closer to the equator, the narrower it grows until it stands at a right angle. So the people see it shining like a band of brightness, like a rainbow in the sky, but illuminated only piecemeal, one belt at a time.

URANUS

The dragon headed at speed straight for Uranus, and its occupants made notes as they gazed upon it:

The distance of Uranus from the Sun is almost twice that of Saturn. Its mean distance from the Sun is 400 million leagues. To afford ourselves a better idea of such a distance, we should note that if someone took up position in a fast rowing boat that might do four leagues in an hour, then they would cover the distance in 11,400 years. A sound travelling at 164 leagues an hour would take 280 years to reach Uranus from the Sun, while light would make the same trip in two hours and 39 minutes. It is 424 million leagues distant from Earth and 348 million geographic leagues at its closest. In the latter circumstance it can be detected as a sixth-magnitude star even without the use of a telescope.

We owe the discovery of Uranus and some other satellites to Herschel. He spotted it at Bath,[38] near London, on 13 March 1781 with a telescope having a seven-foot focus. Since Uranus moves across the sky only very slowly, and takes a mere 30,687 days, i.e. almost 84 years, to make one revolution of the Sun, he would have to have waited a very long time to assess everything about it. But his predecessors had discovered certain signs and opened the way to his further researches.

---

[38] Frederick William (originally Friedrich Wilhelm) Herschel (1738-1822) did indeed discover Uranus from Bath (his house there is now the Herschel Museum of Astronomy), though when he immigrated from Hannover he settled in Slough, which *is* near London; he spent most of his life there. In both Slough and Bath he made endless telescopes and numerous astronomical discoveries. His musical alter ego as a composer of note saw him become organist at the Octagon Chapel in Bath. For much more on this fascinating figure and his sister Caroline (1750-1848), a productive astronomer and musician in her own right, for whom William also made telescopes to aid her comet-searching habit, see the respective, highly informative pages on Wikipedia.

URANUS' SIZE AND MASS

From its transformations, the surface of Uranus may be calculated to be 18 times greater than Earth's and its volume 76 times greater. Its mass is 17 times greater, its density reaching only one fifth of the density of Earth, so it is like our water. A solid body falls at 14.5 feet per second – half a foot less than on Earth. The speed at which it rotates round the Sun is almost one German league per second, so four times lower than the rate of Earth's rotation. They see the Sun the same size as Venus, or 19 times smaller than we see it, and its luminosity will be 360 times weaker. It follows that the brightest day on Uranus will barely compare with a starry night on Earth.

Because it is so exceedingly remote, we know very little about its surface. It is a small, round sphere, uniformly illuminated throughout. No spots and lines can be discerned, so there's no means of telling the ways it rotates. That it spins round its axis at a precipitous rate may be inferred from how it is flattened at the poles.

KRUTOHLAV LOOKS FOR A MOON AND DETERMINES THE DAYS AND WEATHER ON URANUS

Krutohlav opened up his gigantic, Herschel-like telescope and, lo and behold! – he immediately spotted six moons. Though thereafter they only ever saw two. Because they are so remote, they are very weakly illuminated, though they seem quite large. At that distance not even our own Moon could be detected.

"The true fact that any variation in the weather is completely lost on Uranus will be due to its ecliptic (angled at 90°), so twice a year the Sun will shine straight down on the heads even of those who inhabit its poles. The tops of the heads of those living below the equator will get scorched in early spring and autumn, while below the poles they'll only see it on the horizon. So everywhere on Uranus night and day are also alike, but then the poles will get a night that lasts 42 of our years with a day of the same duration to follow."

With those words Krutohlav ended his discourse. Then he withdrew to his quarters and said not a word for forty days, almost forgetting even to eat and drink and languishing like some dry old stick. His companions took fright at his lamentable condition, though they were in no doubt that he was pondering some new topic, previously untouched.

KRUTOHLAV DISCUSSES AT LENGTH THE POSSIBLE INHABITANTS OF THE PLANETS

Record by Zlatoklas based on Krutohlav's own book in 1855

Almost six months had passed when Krutohlav, twisting his head this way and that, invited all his companions to dinner the following day so that he, too, might have a proper meal at last. They were all delighted because not for nothing were they looking forward to, and cherishing their hopes of, a detailed lecture from him on whatever fascinating subject he'd been puzzling over for so long. Then, after dinner and for the first time in ages, having filled his pipe and lit it, he commenced in all gravity:

"As we have flown across the firmament on our sprightly dragon, all of us here have been tossed around and subjected to untold hardships and tribulations. But despite having made so many discoveries, what we have learned and discovered amounts to less than a single grain of all the oceans' sand, or than a single starlet among the billions of stars in the sky. What is the handful of planets that we have come to know but superficially in comparison with the innumerable quantities of gigantic heavenly bodies? We hanker after more, yet what do we know about our very own Earth? About the interior of Africa and Australia, about our very own poles?"

Upon hearing these words, they all sank into an even deeper silence and huddled close together. Once their mental animation was restored, Krutohlav went on with his philosophising:

"I wouldn't want you to think that I'm suggesting that we clip the wings of our flying dragon and seek out those places which I have mentioned. No, we can leave them to people, for their benefit, let them have that pleasure. Our task now is to throw light on a much more glorious subject, following our survey and partial, if uncertain, description of the planets, namely, whether they can be or are inhabited."

At this unexampled turn in Krutohlav's disquisition, some of them went red in the face, while others rejoiced – the latter desirous of flying even higher, the former keen to drop back to Earth. In the end, this new topic – so important and interesting – over which they had all often racked their brains, did draw them all in, and the desire to learn of Krutohlav's view of the matter fired them all. And so, after a brief pause, he launched into this fascinating account as to:

WHETHER THE PLANETS ARE INHABITED, OR NOT

"Listen up, my friends! You will surely share my honest belief that we must not judge the inhabitants of other planets – if there are any – by our own sense of such things as love, concord, wellbeing and other needs that they may have, and even less should we see them embedded in the bleakest circumstances imaginable, just because that's how it strikes us. If we wish to speak about them, we have to have seen them with our own eyes and only then measure them by our own yardstick. So let's not beat our brains out over their lot, but be resigned to investigating how we would be affected by their circumstances if we were different by nature. We shall not tarry too long here over the sagacity and philosophising of other astronomers who, taking the essence of the planets into account, have portrayed their inhabitants according to what the planets' fundamental nature carries with it. But before I describe their suppositions and the images they formed, hear this, my modest preamble."

And all his fellows, pensive now, prepared earnestly to hear him out. Then Krutohlav, following a short pause, began again:

"In all likelihood, the planets will be full to bursting with sundry creatures and, there too, communities beyond number will be glad to be alive. Since we on Earth see that even the tiniest grain of sand, the least droplet of water is endowed with life, how could we conceive of such mighty spheres being mere lifeless, barren wastes with no inhabitants and other living creatures? Since we on Earth encounter an endless array of different animals and even humans who differ from one another – the African from the Finn – how could the creatures that dwell on Mercury and Uranus not differ from one another, and grow ever further apart the greater the distance between them?"

Whereat each of his fellows nodded wisely.

"But let us proceed further and hear some of the funny things others have thought."

HUYGHENS' ASSUMPTIONS ABOUT THE INHABITANTS OF THE PLANETS

"In his day, Huyghens[39] was one of the foremost astronomers and even corresponded with the distinguished Kempelen.[40] His view resided above all in the fact that despite how the planets differ from Earth, each of them had to have water, chiefly because without water neither plants nor animals could survive. True, such water has to be qualitatively different, because on Saturn it would always be ice and on Mercury it would be constantly on the boil. So where any such water exists, any plant will grow like ours, sucking its fluidity through its roots and air through its leaves. And wherever there are plants there will also be animals that live on them and they will multiply just like our animals! And so forth: where there is enough water, we must also run into

---

39 Christiaan Huyg(h)ens (1629–95) – "Dutch mathematician, physicist, astronomer and inventor, ... regarded as one of the greatest scientists of all time and a major figure in the scientific revolution. In physics, Huyghens made groundbreaking contributions in optics and mechanics, while as an astronomer he is chiefly known for his studies of the rings of Saturn and the discovery of its moon Titan. As an inventor, he improved the design of telescopes and invented the pendulum clock, ... the most accurate timekeeper for almost 300 years. An exceptionally talented mathematician and physicist, Huyghens was the first to idealize a physical problem by a set of parameters then analyse it mathematically, and the first to fully mathematize a mechanistic explanation of an unobservable physical phenomenon. ... [H]e has been called the first theoretical physicist and one of the founders of modern mathematical physics." (https://en.wikipedia.org/wiki/Christiaan_Huygens).

40 Johann Wolfgang Ritter von Kempelen de Pázmánd (1734–1804) – Hungarian author and inventor, known for his chess-playing 'automaton' *The Turk* (a present for empress Maria-Theresa in 1769) and for his speaking machine (see https://en.wikipedia.org/wiki/Wolfgang_von_Kempelen). The Slovak Reuss would surely approve of von Kempelen as a native of Pressburg, today's Bratislava, though, given the latter's dates, Huyghens could scarcely have been in correspondence with him.

air, otherwise all the water would quickly evaporate and seas and rivers would dry up. Huyghens had it that the air on different planets was different, being as dense on Jupiter as our water, so that we could swim in it; and this allegedly was what gave rise to the lines and the constant spots and clouds.

"Dissatisfied with all this, he populated the planetary realms with rational beings, there to proclaim the might of God and to marvel at nature. For why should man of all beings have been created for tiny Earth while other gigantic bodies remained empty, and why might Earth alone have all these benefits? So these creatures, too, Huyghens goes on, have minds exactly like ours, and among them, too, we find but one truth, justice, goodness, and they are endowed with the same senses as we are. For if, for example, they didn't have eyes with which to seek their nutriment, how would they be able to tell friend from foe and why should the Sun stand guard over them if they didn't have a material interest in its light? Elsewhere he mentions that one and the same planet could be home to more than one species of rational beings, though it soon dawned on him that that would be at variance with divine wisdom, since such different kinds of beings would just decimate, devastate and destroy one another. Earth people are of one kind and see how they carry on! So instead he populates the planets variously with sages and scholars, especially astronomers. He also maintains that the only reason why people are born naked is for distress and affliction to open up to them the gateway to such mental prowess and progress that they can even take care of their raiment, which animals don't need. That's what brought him to the idea of scholars living on the planets. And he says there are also craftsmen there, and a social life, and they haggle and drive hard bargains, and, just like us, they shorten their lifespan through pain and vitriol, kill each other in conflict and so on. He is undecided as to whether these rational beings eat the flesh of the irrational ones, though he inclines to the view that that particular bane is peculiar to man on Earth.

"As to what those scholars actually look like, there he is somewhat hesitant. His forerunners had determined that people on Jupiter and Saturn must be ten to fifteen times larger than elephants, so at least whale-size. He thought that inconceivable, the planets being of different sizes. Others had concluded that their inhabitants must be the size of mice. He obviously didn't like that idea for the compelling reason that such tiny people wouldn't have the knowledge or dexterity with which to operate or repair any larger pieces of astronomical equipment."

Krutohlav might well have gone on about Huyghens's assumptions if some of the others, Slavata and Vrtoš in particular, hadn't burst out laughing and scoffed at such foolish, fantastical notions.

"But why didn't he invest the people of the planets with at least one additional sense?" Vrtoš jested. "That way he would have given us something important to go on."

"Because he didn't know, any more than we do," Slavata responded. "We'd not be people any more, and the whole of nature would take on a different aspect if we were one sense short or if, say, we had more holes bored into our bodies, like eyes or ears, and so had some senses extra! Well! And what might be the sense of that? We could only know that if we did have the extra. Our Earth has been so shaped by Nature that we can take in everything that it affords to man and beast with the five senses that we do have. But a different planet with a different natural environment predetermines different senses, so we're in no position to attest that whatever we find on Earth must also be proper to the planets."

Slavata having thus convinced Vrtoš and enlightened the others, Krutohlav picked up the thread and continued talking about Huyghens:

"On Mercury, where the Sun beats down seven times hotter, it is so hot that all our plants would be scorched and we, too, would be roasted in no time. So there the plants and animals will have been so fashioned as to be able to cope with the heat. We would just perish there. The inhabitants of Mercury must surely believe that because of the cold we froze to death long ago, just as we believe the same about the people of Uranus. But since the life of the body is governed by temperature, and intellectual prowess depends on that, Huyghens is of the belief that Mercurians surpass Earthlings by far. I wonder! So why don't the peoples living in Africa, where it's mostly hot, share the minds and aptitudes of Europeans? Also, if Mercury is peopled by none but geniuses, Jupiter and Saturn must be full of asses and oafs. Huyghens duly abandoned that train of thought, the more readily for being unable to concede that the inhabitants of Saturn and Jupiter would be incapable of investigating the sheer beauty of the moons that shone out above them or of appreciating the beauty of the entire firmament, and all for the simple reason of being stupid! And so *eo ipso*," Krutohlav concluded, "I shall refrain from trying to explain things of which I know nothing, and leave the matter there – to take care of itself."

KIRCHNER'S SUPPOSITION ABOUT THE INHABITANTS OF THE PLANETS

"Kirchner, a Jesuit, tells of the journey he made from planet to planet on the arm of Genius and reports at length on his discoveries.[41] On his journey he was not so circumspect as Huyghens and his imagination is not so well organised, his account lacking the support of an adequate breadth of knowledge," Krutohlav commenced his assessment of Kirchner. "But hear me out, my brothers! So that you may also judge him from another angle. He had always been hostile to Copernicus and here he claims that all the planets are empty wastelands quite devoid of inhabitants of any kind. That there are no plants or animals on them. On Venus he found everything beautiful and pleasant, such as if Venus herself dwelt there. Dawns gleamed pink and spread pleasant aromas all over it, gentle breezes blew into its babbling brooks, and everything glinted with gold and pearls. On Jupiter he found healthy, clean air, beautifully pure water and ground that shone like silver. Everything was ruled, he said, by all the powers at Jupiter's command. He said he felt well enough at ease

---

[41] Reuss is presumably referring to the German Jesuit polymath Athanasius Kircher (1598/1602–80), whose countless interests did include astronomy, as revealed by certain websites, though not Wikipedia. See, for one, https://www.encyclopedia.com/people/science-and-technology/mathematics-biographies/athanasius-kircher. The work referred to is presumably his 1656 imaginative fiction *Itinerarium exstaticum quo mundi opificium*, where the narrator is guided through the planets by the angel Cosmiel (see https://en.wikipedia.org/wiki/Itinerarium_exstaticum). The two birth dates above reflect the contrary data to be found on the internet. That there are general uncertainties about this figure is perhaps reflected by the absence of any footnote on him in the 1984 Tatran edition of the book, whereas, for example, the previously mentioned Kempelen is footnoted, as are most other historical figures.

on Mercury, but here everything drifted about exquisitely and was reminiscent of quicksilver.

"Everything he saw on Mars – the god of war – he described as frightful: its watercourses flickered and flared as with burning pitch, overflowing and veiling all there was in dense smoke. And that Saturn was desolate and dark, looking like nothing so much as a grave from which no good could possibly be expected, hence he had tried to get away from it as fast as possible."

At this account the entire company laughed even more raucously and pitied such stargazers for indulging in such follies. Whereat Krutohlav gave up on Mars and switched to:

FONTENELLI'S HYPOTHESIS

"Fontenelli[42] assumed that that it was so hot on Mercury that if its inhabitants migrated to even the very hottest parts of Africa, their teeth would still chatter with cold and they'd eventually freeze to death. Gold and silver as we know them would have to be, because of the heat, in liquid form like our quicksilver. And precisely because metals are their water, it will never occur to them that for Earthlings they'd be the solidest matter and be carried around in pouches in the shape of coins. Its days, he says, are very

---

42 The reference is undoubtedly to the French (not Italian, as Reuss's form of the name might suggest) Bernard Le Bovier de Fontenelle (1657–1757), a strawberry-loving nephew of Pierre Corneille and, from 1697, permanent secretary of the French Academy of Scinces. Reuss's 'analysis' of his ideas is clearly drawn from his *Entretiens sur la pluralité des mondes* (1686). He wrote in a novelistic style to give his work wider accessibility, making him something of a forerunner of Reuss. He also has a lunar crater named after him. See https://en.wikipedia.org/wiki/Bernard_Le_Bovier_de_Fontenelle and https://en.wikipedia.org/wiki/Conversations_on_the_Plurality_of_Worlds (accessed 19.07.2023).

short – though we know that they are almost as long as ours – and so it must spin very fast, otherwise the inhabitants would be roasted to death. It is unsurprising that, as a consequence of the heat, their scorched brains drive them crazy, making them dance tirelessly and unceasingly, revel in hare-brained frivolities and be as carefree as human children and madmen, and that they can barely wait for nightfall and some time to get their breath back.

"The inhabitants of Venus," he says, "are all Celadons and Sylphs, champions afire and ablaze with perpetual love. All they ever talk about is love, spinning time out endlessly, like our poets. There's never a word about philosophy, mathematics etc. They don't read any newspapers, never so much as look at a book, living only for love, which they fret about the whole time. Even the tiniest children learn about love in school and have entire books on the subject off by heart. This love-struck race is otherwise the worst in the world, almost burnt to a cinder by the Sun, but always gleeful and frolicsome. You've never counted so many poets, so many musicians, seen so much dancing as on Venus. There is simply no end to all these pleasures and since all they live on is air, they have all the more time to give over to fun and games.

"Fontenelli has little to say about Mars beyond that it is exquisite, so we'll let it go at that as well.

"He'd prefer not to say anything about Jupiter either, because, being so huge, he hardly takes any notice of us. To him we appear 144 times smaller than he does to us and we appear to him only as Mercury appears to us, by sunlight. And when he does spot us and puts something in whatever kind of news-sheet, what good does that do us? Jupiterians know even less about Venus and Mercury because they're always paddling about in the rays of the Sun. They won't know much about Saturn either, its rings and moons, unless some Galileo were to pop up there. Because it's so cold they're hardly likely to bother about the stars, and if we relocated them to Lapland they'd burn up instantly. Their watercourses are like polished stone and alcohol will look like a diamond. While that other crowd do all that dancing, these folk are phlegmatic and in all likelihood never stop whinging."

Krutohlav lapsed into silence and the others all took a deep breath. Finally Krutohlav finished what he'd wanted to say:

"Let's bother our heads no more and set aside things of which we know nothing for certain and perhaps never will. Instead, let us give thanks to God for granting us habitation in the very centre of inapprehensible space, where we are neither roasted like Mercury nor frozen stiff like Uranus. Let us praise God like that philosopher who was glad not to have been born an animal, but a man, and that he had been born a Greek and not a Barbarian. Let us rejoice that our abode is more hospitable, that we are in Earth's middle zone, that the Sun doesn't burn us like in Senegal and that we don't have to suffer the cold that reigns at the poles."

Whereupon Krutohlav closed his book.

PART

FOUR

**CONTAINS AN ACCOUNT OF THOSE
BODIES WITH TAILS CALLED COMETS, OF
HOW KRUTOHLAV AND HIS COMPANIONS
WERE DRAWN INTO GREAT PERIL AND HOW
THEY SAFELY ESCAPED THE DANGER.**

*Excerpted from old texts by
Černoboj from Ranostaj in 1855*

MIGHT KRUTOHLAV ALSO KNOW SOMETHING ABOUT COMETS?

I wonder! Let's hear it, my friends.

Well, well, it was Christmas, it was *We Believe* time! When, together, Slavata and Roháč climbed down from the dragon's horn and, as they descended, also knocked Vrtoš off his perch on the dragon's eyebrow.

"Help, we've had it!" the others screamed. "We're done for!"

"What's the matter?" yelped Hnevoš, jumping down to join them.

"Our last hour has struck," Rokyta snuffled, barely able to stand upright as the dragon pitched and tossed.

"Oh, hell," Vrtoš yelped, "this is the end!"

"On your feet, lads, grab the oars or it's all over!" a voice rang out.

"I doubt even God can help us now," came from the dragon's belly. "Everything's breaking up, we're out of steam, we're going to suffocate and die the death, the dragon's already lost its eyebrows, ears and teeth, it's all over. Help! God have mercy!"

"Aargh, the light's getting to me!" "I can't stand the noise!" "The light's making me giddy!" "I've got pins and needles in my arms and legs! We've had it!" Such screaming and shouting echoed the length and breadth of the dragon. No one knew what was happening and why they were all suffering so. The dragon really was pitching so crazily up and down that none of them could stay on their feet. One started to light a fire, another to put it out, one loosened the bolts on the wheels, another screwed them back tight, one rowed to starboard, another steered to port; confusion followed confusion and there was no end to the general derangement.

At all this hullabaloo Krutohlav woke up and could scarcely recover his wits to realise he was no longer asleep, but had come to. So he took up his snuffbox, took a few good pinches, and having sneezed roundly three times, he bellowed so loud that even the dragon itself became briefly motionless:

"What's all this?"

"It's bad, boss, bad," several voices responded, "we've had it, help!"

"It'll have been that – *We Believe!*" Krutohlav grumbled and rushed off to investigate the cause of the disaster.

He had barely crossed the threshold of his quarters when he saw all round him spikes pointing downwards, pulley wheels upside down, a candlestick with the candle flame at the bottom, and his own very pen writing backwards – in a word, everything was so topsy-turvy and back to front that he could scarcely find himself. The greater haste he made to ascertain the cause of their predicament, the more he observed that he could move forward with only one half of his body at a time. This circumstance was the most compelling evidence that he and his companions, along with the dragon, had fallen into the hands of villains. What to do about it? He hurried on and lo! – there at his feet Vrtoš was writhing and gesturing, beneath the boiler Roháč was rolling about struggling with something, further on Slavata was slaving away trying to tie some knots, while Rokyta was rocking on his heels in a daze – and goodness knows what else there was; in a word it was such a shambles that I can't believe things could have been any worse at the building of the Tower of Babel, let alone at the Creation.

"Golly, never have I seen the like in all my living days!"

Just then, he was hurled with such violence against the dragon's tongue that he smashed right into his largest telescope, the one modelled on Herschel's, and the tongue itself split two-thirds along its length.

"Whoa now, think," the terror-stricken Krutohlav cried and in his terror-stricken state he – whether from gumption or fright – was about to hide behind the gigantic lens that he himself had made.

"God, great God," were the last words Krutohlav uttered before being laid flat out, his limbs being pulled towards all corners of the universe. And when, half an hour later, Vrtoš tried to pull him back together, Krutohlav came round and asked him what he wanted.

Once properly awake, he first took a pinch of snuff.

"Save us, boss, or we're all going to perish," Vrtoš replied.

"Yes, yes, all right, all right, sure," and he promptly set his spectacles back on his nose and also began staring through the telescope at all the ends of the universe to try to discover the cause of this monstrous catastrophe.

"Harrumph! Nothing happens without due cause. One word leads to another, any cause has its own roots, any matter its reason, valour is followed by self-neglect, gloom by light, frozen limbs by infuriation, anger by joy, – oh, balderdash, that's all rubbish and delusions of the senses and our feelings. Of course we are where we are, no two ways about it – no action is without a cause, and, lo and behold! – by the look of Vrtoš here, we are in some sort of great peril."

"What kind?" the only half-alive Vrtoš asked him.

Then, adopting a tone of gravity, Krutohlav replied.

"We're in the grip of a comet."

Just then, the dragon received such a massive jolt that Krutohlav himself, though he had now found his feet, could barely even shake his head. Poor Vrtoš just wriggled and writhed in pain.

"A comet, aha, a comet, eh! That'll give us what for!" the almost lifeless Vrtoš grumbled and, rising to his feet, he could now make barely a single twist or turn.[43]

"Yes, yes, a comet," Krutohlav replied. "Because Roháč's endless curiosity made him make the dragon fly ever faster, we've entered its gravitational field and it's now got our lives to work away at. But never mind, if we can just break clear of its gravitational pull, we'll…" But at that moment the dragon jerked so violently that all its teeth fell out and it started whizzing about like a butterfly tossed in the wind. Krutohlav himself bashed his head so hard against a twisted pillar that, once again, shaking his head was more than he could manage.

"We've had it," yelped Vrtoš, bent double, "we're done for," he said with a fivefold wriggle.

The pensive Krutohlav, having come to again, fished out his snuffbox and took a good pinch. Then he bent his mind to their liberation. Lost in thought, he selected his best telescopes, lay them out on the tip of the dragon's tongue and wound a solid belt around himself to keep him from falling.

As he looked through his telescope, he observed that the comet's tail was brushing them and that it was a serious, huge, bright and glittery comet. He was dumbstruck, but believing he could help his companions, he was fired with the spirit of endurance.

---

43 Vrtoš's name is suggestive of twisting, turning or fidgeting.

Then he was blown over again – and without a word picked himself up off the floor.

"What the hell's going on?" he growled, increasingly irate. "Next thing they'll be singing a requiem for us!" Anyway, he redirected his gigantic telescope and – would you believe it! – discovered that they were being tossed about by a comet dating back to the 1600s, but he also calculated that it was retreating at speed and that they would soon be out of danger.

To expedite the process he ordered those whose minds were still boggled to be brought round, chided others into making a fire, which he himself blew into life. He adjusted their sturdy oars, unfurled the sails, tightened the ropes, tensed all the bindings and oiled the axle of the paddle wheels; he re-aligned and loaded the cannon, set up the lusty mortars and distributed, dispensed and delivered all the necessary orders to get every conceivable thing ready for them to be able to break out of the comet's stranglehold.

It was only with great difficulty that Vrtoš, Roháč, Slavata, Rokyta and others – indeed all of them – endeavoured to drag themselves out of their doldrums into dayspring, and despite the fact that Krutohlav himself tested the solidity of the mast with his head several times more, he it was who proclaimed: "Who dares place such hurdles in our way, when we are but seekers after truth and have God on our side? Pah! You blackguard! It's all your fault! You dastard of 1832![44] We know what you're about, so, my lads, onwards and upwards," he roared, "and we'll soon be free."

---

44 A most peculiar imprecation, possibly alluding to the conference of 1832 that had sought liberation from serfdom, as our heroes now sought liberation from the clutches of the comet. The tone doesn't seem quite right for it to be alluding to Biela's Comet, 'recovered' by Herschel in September of that year.

Words fail me to describe the sheer determination of his subordinates. His own unfailing word was *faith* – the faith underpinning their hopes, their faith in themselves – the ultimate consequence, throughout the entire world, of all being and doing. How their work proceeded and how everything was ordered shall be seen in the sequel.

The dragon reared up and gave the comet's tail such a resounding thwack that it struck 10,000 sparks off it at once, then it soared on past it and headed off to ever more remote parts.

"Amen, my brothers. I say to you, God is taking care of us!" Krutohlav brought the matter to an end, though for a long, a very long time, he never stopped shaking his head in wonderment. "Amen, we did it – thanks be to God! Amen!" And the dragon shot off so fast that even Krutohlav, having got back on his feet, could hardly get his nose back in the right place. But so what... They had all now escaped from danger, but, that notwithstanding, the enraged dragon drove itself so hard and so fast that no other satellite or comet had a hope of catching up with it.

Following their terrible plight, the companions congregated on the dragon's head. Each one, in his own behalf, rendered thanks unto God for his deliverance, and Krutohlav himself even knelt down to pray! Meanwhile, the dragon soared ahead at an inconceivable speed.

Then Vrtoš, Roháč and others, having had a bite to eat, begged Krutohlav to tell them, in detail and at length, something about these godless entities, in all the more timely fashion for their having just been saved from one. And Krutohlav, with a customary shake of his head, began:

COMETS

"Apart from the satellites mentioned previously, whose numbers grow from year to year, there are yet other bodies that orbit the Sun and are part of the solar system. Even at first sight, they differ clearly in form from all the satellites proper. Since time immemorial, as we all know, people have been particularly fascinated by them. Whole nations have held them to be omens of some impending disaster and of the wrath of God. Only now, at least among the more enlightened, have prejudices been set aside and we are able to examine them more closely and assess them more clearly from calculations of their course. Our deepest regret is that we know so little about their nature, and their purpose – the very reason for their being – remains a total mystery.

"Hitherto, as historians have recorded, some 500 or so comets are spoken of as having made themselves visible to Earth. But this is a trifling number. Without telescopes, people registered only the ones that caught their eye, and of those only the more remarkable ones. But some are so tiny and invisible that without a telescope they cannot catch the eye. Just consider this: in the thirty-seven years from 1769 to 1807, thirty-six were spotted and duly described, though the common man saw not one of them spinning with its tail through space. Since the days of Messier[45] and Pons,[46] two, even three, new comets have been discovered every year. If, over 6,000 years, as the Jews count them, our forebears had discovered and described just two comets a year, we'd

---

45 Charles Messier (1730–1817), French astronomer who discovered 14 new comets and compiled a catalogue of nebulae and star clusters, the bodies today known as Messier objects.

46 Jean-Louis Pons (1761–1831), French astronomer who discovered 37 new comets, more than anyone in the history of astronomy.

have 12,000 to be talking about today. And if we allow also for the fact that some are visible only from the southern hemisphere, where the Australians keep no kind of records, and that some comets are only visible by day and may run their course and slip away when the skies are overcast, the true number of comets must of course be much higher than we have indicated.

"The motion of comets: As I said earlier, the planets are little involved in eclipsis and they all move from west to east. Neither one nor the other can be said of comets. They travel round the Sun quite haphazardly and at an angle that varies between zero and 170 degrees. Because of their elongated orbital track they can only be properly assessed when they are closer to the Sun and so have also come nearer to Earth."

THE NUMBER OF COMETS BETWEEN THE VARIOUS PLANETS

"Within the orbital track of Mercury there are presently twenty comets, and between the Sun and Venus almost seventy. Taking this into account, we might calculate that there should be at least 51,880 comets between the Sun and Uranus. But even that number will be too low when we appreciate that we have taken as base only the seventy planets that are known and have not added in all the ones we do not know. What a great host of heavenly bodies that is compared to the handful of planets! Neither we nor our planets constitute a state, but in comets we have the peasantry. Our planets are the chosen ones who encircle the Sun's throne and get grilled by the Sun. By contrast, the comets have always come by, as it were, to pay their respects before moving off into the vastness of space.

THE FORM
OF COMETS

"Who among you hasn't seen a comet? On closer inspection of one we'll find, however: its core, or nucleus, the surround, or coma, and its tail.

"The nucleus is usually tiny, round and brighter, but not with the kind of light we see in planets. Some don't actually have a nucleus and seem to be just a gaseous cloud. They are invariably poorly illuminated, so their size is hard to determine. Let's just take a look at the measurements of comets:

"The coma appears to be of the essence, because comets have been seen that had neither nucleus, nor tail, but never one without a coma. The coma surrounds the nucleus, the circle being slightly extended on the side where the tail is, as if it were the start of the tail. Otherwise it is so fluffy and sparse that it is reminiscent of our mists and fogs, and other stars can be seen through it. We don't believe it to be wrapped tight around the nucleus, but, on the contrary, to surround it at some distance, so that there is a dark line between it and the nucleus. In some cases, more than one such ring has been detected. That way it looks as if a comet's nucleus consists of many concentric lines and bright clouds. Herschel supposes these rings to be the comet's gases for they have been seen to undergo frequent transformations. So, for example, the comet seen between 1799 and 1807 shrank by a quarter in the course of a day, then got bigger again.

"The tail, as we have said, is thought to be an extension of the coma, and its size varies. Some comets have two or three tails, even more, and all keep one direction. The 1823 comet had two tails opposite each other: one pointed towards the Sun, the other turned completely away from it. The 1744 comet had six tails, that's to say its tail was split into six.

"More worthy of attention is the rapid breakup of the tail's light. Thus of the comet that appeared in 1811 Chladni[47] noticed that its luminosity – one million leagues per second – kept dropping, then rising, and was also in excess of the speed of light as we know it.

"What makes a comet's tail? The cause has to be sought in the Sun, for as a comet approaches the Sun, its tail grows longer, and the further it moves away, the more the tail shrinks. It is possible that the great heat of the Sun converts the nucleus into steam which cold then draws back in, thus it regresses as its distance from the Sun rises.

"Large comet tails are darker in the middle and marked by a broad streak, which is why they look double. Some hold that this line is the shadow of the nucleus; others see such a tail as a hollow cone, simple brighter on the outside and darker in the middle."

KRUTOHLAV EXPLAINS HOW COMETS ORIGINATE AND EVOLVE

Krutohlav's companions, having learned about certain peculiarities of comets, their size and other attributes, wouldn't let up and kept badgering him to continue and tell them yet more. So Krutohlav, having got his breath back, went on:

---

[47] Ernst Florens Friedrich Chladni (1756–1827), German physicist and musician of Slovak provenance (Reuss gives him the original family surname of Chladný), often called the father of acoustics and known also for his pioneering work in the study of meteorites.

"It is possible that the darker ring between the nucleus and the coma is nothing but a separate transparent, elastic material in its own right. And the very daintiness of comets may be another reason why it gets so blown up by extreme heat. In the same way, the atmosphere of our Earth, if it were a hollow void internally, might equally easily turn into a tail – considering how it orbits the Sun.

"The matter that makes up the coma and the tail is very thin, very flimsy, given that other stars can be seen through it, and it is possible that our water, if it were exposed to the same great heat, would change in a similar way. Some bodies have no nucleus at all, being nothing but steam, and if they come close to another, larger body, they crumble away completely, disappear and fall as dew onto the planets or rain onto the Sun.

"Why comets have such an odd way of going round the Sun is very hard to work out. We know that each body has its weight, which may be negative or positive. So it could be that comets are not drawn towards the Sun, but hurled away from it, explaining why they form such vast ellipses. In this context, much is often said about the ether, but I'll say nothing about that because it strikes me as no more than a product of human fantasising.

LIGHT CHANGES
IN COMETS

"Only yesterday, Vrtoš asked me whether comets are dark bodies like the planets and whether they get their light from the Sun or not. I can tell you this much: that could be easily investigated and ascertained if only we could look into the changes in their light the way we can in the case of Venus, Mercury or the Moon. While there is no such chance, the matter must remain obscure. It is said that Cassiori[48] investigated certain light changes on a comet in 1744, but he refers only to irregularities in the core. Others know nothing about this either, so I, too, deem the matter uncertain and would rather we moved onto

THE MASS
OF COMETS

"I have already told you, brothers of mine, that comet matter is so sparse that it cannot really be compared to our clouds and fogs. So, despite their size, it is not unnatural that the rays of the Sun can break through them and drive them back. It may also be that the core is concentrated steam and that the core proper consists of little more than dust of the meteorites that so often hit Earth. Even at first sight it is obvious that they bear no similarity to other solid bodies, such as the planets, for even the best telescope reveals them to be no more than clouds of steam. We sometimes can't see more than ten to twenty paces through our fogs, but through these – and they can have a diameter of many thousands of leagues – we can clearly see other stars beyond. And the same goes for their tails, but even more so. From this it follows that the matter that makes up comets must be extraordinarily thin, like air, and if we were in it, we would see nothing and hear nothing. There may even be some truth to the assertion that many comets have already threaded their way right through Earth without us even knowing."

---

48 Cassiori, unidentified. This could be a misremembering or miscopying, or indeed a more recent misprint, of Cassini (Giovanni Domenico, or Jean-Dominique, 1625–1712), variously described as Italian or French, or his unequivocally French grandson Jean-Dominique, Comte de Cassini (1748–1845), both astronomers of note.

This fascinating account so fired his audience's minds that they couldn't prevent themselves from again trying to persuade the wilting Krutohlav to take such an interesting topic further.

HALLEY'S COMET

"This curious comet is distinguished by certain peculiar attributes that we find nowhere else. It is the only one we really know, even despite the long duration of its orbit, because it has been back so often. We can trace it with certainty as far back as the middle of the fifteenth century, and with reasonable certainty back to the earliest years after the birth of Christ. That apart, it is one of the largest and most likely to catch the eye. It is the one that people have been able to foretell and luckily always get it right. It is the one that has provided so much from which we've been able to learn about comets generally. And because it has so much to its credit, we'll look into it in greater detail."

THE TIME IT TAKES TO ORBIT, ITS AXIS, SPEED AND DISTANCE FROM US

"It orbits the Sun once every 75 or 76 years. The major axis of its orbit is almost eight times that of Earth, so its orbital track measures 744 million leagues. The minor axis comes to 380 million leagues. At its closest to the Sun it's only half as far from it as Earth; then when it's farthest from the Sun it's twice as far away as Uranus is from the Sun. It moves along its orbit track in the opposite direction from the planets, that is, from east to west.

"As for speed, that varies and is dependent on the Sun. At its closest to the Sun, it travels 59,500 leagues in an hour, and it revolves four times faster than Earth; when it's farthest from the Sun, it covers a mere 980 geographic leagues and revolves fifteen times slower than Earth.

"What's really good about it is the fact that its orbital track means that it can never come too close to Earth; even at the best of times it will still be many million leagues away, while the orbit of Biela's Comet once brought it as close as 3,000 leagues.[49] That was in 1832. This matter brings with it the reassurance that in the future we needn't be afraid of Halley's Comet either, so the apprehension of some that it might be a threat to Earth is unwarranted.

"If we count blocks of 75 or 76 years since 1456, when Halley's Comet was identified, then we can easily trace, from the records left by historians, when exactly it has appeared."

THE EARLIEST GUARANTEED SIGHTINGS OF HALLEY'S COMET

"*First appearance.* This was in 1456, when it was equidistant from Sun and Earth and shining most pleasingly. Its tail was 60° long and the end looked like a peacock's. At first, it was visible only early in the morning, then, later, having completely vanished in the meantime, only in the evening, leading many to believe that there were two different comets. Investigators were of the view that the only reason for its invisibility was sunlight.

---

[49] The comet is named after Baron Wilhelm von Biela (1782–1856), a Bohemian-German officer in the Austro-Hungarian army and an amateur astronomer, and became only the third comet known to be periodic. The reference to its orbits in the plural relates to the fact that between its various apparitions it was seen to have split in two.

"*Second appearance.* This was in 1531. This time it wasn't nearly so beautiful and Europe didn't even get so worked up about it, and the best observations of it were made by Peter Bienevitz[50] at Ingolstadt; he it was who first stated that comets' tails point away from the Sun. It was still only appearing early in the morning and in the evening.

"*The third time it appeared* was in 1607, when it looked very much as it did in 1835.

"*The fourth time* was in 1682. And it was Halley, a contemporary of Newton, who pronounced that the several previous appearances were of one and the same comet.

"*The fifth appearance* was in 1759. We saw it last in 1835.

"It is the latest comet of which we know things. Biela was an Austrian officer who had observed the comet that carries his name on 28 February 1826 at Josephstadt[51] in Bohemia and duly identified it. He set its revolution of the Sun at six years and 270 days. Its greatest distance from the Sun is 6.26 and its shortest 0.94 times that of Earth's.

"Biela's Comet was first observed in 1772 and again in 1805,[52] but not properly identified. It still appears as a small, round, glimmering mist, tailless and with a bright spot in the centre of it. The diameter of the mist is 9.460 geographic leagues, or five and a half times the diameter of Earth; by contrast its nucleus has barely 20 leagues. The last time it put in an appearance was in 1832 and again in 1838."

---

50 Better known as Peter Apianus (1495–1552), Saxon Humanist mathematician, astronomer, cartographer and printer. His *Cosmography* was translated into French, Dutch and Spanish.

51 Today's Josefov, a former military fortress and now protected monument, built in the 1780s at Jaroměř in Eastern Bohemia.

52 By Jacques Montaigne and Jean-Marie Pons respectively.

ON THE DANGEROUS POSITION OF THE ORBIT OF THIS COMET

"But look now, brothers, what may befall Earth one day. Hear this:

"The orbits of, say, Jupiter and Earth have been so well calculated and are so regular that they can never go wrong, unless they happen to be thrown off course by some other, unknown bodies. The same applies to the paths of most comets, whether in relation to one another, or to the planets. Until even a few years ago it wasn't known if the route of this or that comet or planet might not cut straight across another's, that's to say whether it might not actually touch it. This does apply to Encke's Comet, which frequently crosses the path of Mercury, so it will come as no surprise if they smash into each other one day. Many are they who'd love to see that catastrophe come to pass and as soon as possible. As for Biela's Comet, the same goes for its relationship to Earth, in the sense that it could come very close to us some day and our pathways could almost overlap. So if it does happen that their pathways come close, they're bound to meet and the consequences of such a conflict will definitely be unkind to us. But the upset caused needn't affect just the Earth, but the Biela and Enke comets as well. To get a better idea of all this, let me tell you about

OLBER'S COMET

"Up until 1815, it had been possible to predict the return of Halley's comet only. But on March 6 that year, Olber discovered a new, if small, comet that was conspicuous for having an orbital period of 75 years despite its small size, so it was to be visible again in 1887. Its greatest distance from the Sun is 33.98 times half the diameter of the Earth's and at its closest 1.22 times. It runs a course from west to east. Its orbit is so positioned vis-à-vis Earth that it can never come close to us or do us any harm.

ENCKE'S COMET

"This one was discovered by Pons in 1818, but Encke was the first to compute its orbit at three years and 115 days. It had been observed, but not identified, in 1786, 1795 and 1805. Its greatest distance from the Sun is 4.07 and its shortest 0.33 times half the diameter of Earth's. It rotates like a planet, is tiny, with an icy sheen, almost round, and has hardly any tail. It sometimes comes closer to Earth, but cannot crash into it, so will never place us in jeopardy.

"I can tell you no more than that, my friends, only that Encke investigated it and found that its orbit round the Sun was constantly shrinking, and that he believed that one day it would collapse into the Sun. But more of that anon. So enough of this one; I shall move on to Biela's Comet.

A DESCRIPTION OF BIELA'S COMET

"We must hope that neither we, nor indeed those who come after us, will be reduced to cinders because of Biela's Comet," said Krutohlav, now shaking his head in dismay more violently than his companions had seen in a long time. They all gathered round, heads thrust forward in one direction, and listened closely, hearts pounding, to what Krutohlav had to say about Biela's Comet, which seemed to threaten Earth with fire and brimstone. Then Krutohlav began his sonorous account in these memorable terms:

EARTH'S CLOSE ENCOUNTER WITH BIELA'S COMET IN 1832

"There's no point in us trying to rationalise whether Earth ought not perhaps to be afraid on its account. Because it's not impossible that Biela will one day give Earth a solid poke in the ribs, so it's in our interest to take a closer look at it.

"In 1826, this ominous comet had already come so close to Earth's orbital path that it swished past only about twice as far away as the Moon from Earth. But on 29 October 1832 it was thirteen times closer to the orbital path of Earth or the Moon, or maybe even closer, for its elements haven't yet been fully established. From the orbital path of Earth – but not from Earth itself – it was fortunately over thirteen million leagues distant, and long before Earth might have caught up with it it had gone on its way. The clash – and this applies to the future as well – can only come in late November. That at the time we needn't have been so terror-stricken as we were, we were taught by the future.

"For the comet to crash into Earth, and do remember this, it has to be late December, when it's closest to the Sun. That can't happen in this century, but only in future centuries, in 1933 and 2115, on December 26. And there remains the question of whether it might not change course, also whether it might not indeed crash into the Earth where their paths cross, or whether it will be as in 1832, with the comet simply overtaking Earth.

"If it did come to a crash of one into the other, well, the comet's elements are just like our steam and clouds, its nucleus is tiny and we don't even have to worry about its tail, because it doesn't have one."

"But we shan't live to see the day," said Roháč.

"Let alone 1933," Slavata added.

"What's it to us anyway," said Vrtoš selfishly, "why should we care about the deaths of those living at the time?"

"Hm," said Krutohlav with another shake of his head. "And your children, in whom you will live till eternity, doesn't it matter to you if they die such a wretched death? What a mean and miserable lot you are!"

KRUTOHLAV TURNS TO THE VITALLY IMPORTANT SUBJECT OF WHAT IF ANYTHING EARTH SHOULD FEAR FROM COMETS

"Even if we've nothing to fear from Biela's, the question still arises as to what we should and might expect from other comets. Their numbers are huge – as we saw above – and they come trotting past Earth in every direction. Is it not possible that one might brush against Earth, lay waste to us and fly off with us to all ends of the cosmos? In the event, which we must allow for, that its nucleus were as hard as Earth's and as big, and if it struck at an angle, a terrible fate would surely await us."

At which they were all gripped by anxiety. But Krutohlav went on thus: "So hear now what Laplace, the greatest geometrician of modern times, said of any crash between Earth and a comet:

"As in olden times, even more recently the appearance of a comet has been seen as ominous. In our own day people are hugely fearful of what might become of us if any one of the countless comets revolving round Earth bumped into it. The truth is that if Earth's axis changed because of it, the consequences can be easily surmised. First, the length of the days would change; all waters, lakes and seas would abandon their banks and shores and adapt quickly to the new equator; most people and animals would drown in the flood or would die from the gash inflicted on Earth, entire genera of animals would die out and so forth. In a word, all signs of life as people know it would suddenly vanish.

"There's no doubt that this is a bleak picture, but it's also true," Krutohlav went on with his narrative. "Who among us hasn't observed that when we're haring along at speed in a carriage and the horses suddenly stop, we get jerked forward. The more violently, the faster we'd been going. Our experience would be the same if we were hit by a comet. On our planet we really are almost like a coach-load of people, travelling round the Sun at such a speed that we are covering 17,000 leagues in an hour, in other words 120 times faster than a ball shot from a cannon. If our Earth and a comet crashed, our houses, gardens, hills, storehouses, everything and everybody would be hurled in the direction of the crash site. So, too, the ocean, rising up and over its shores, would rapidly cover our highest mountains in its waves and we would all drown. Can you, my friends, even imagine such a catastrophe?" They were all thunderstruck, lost in wonder at the nature of the jeopardy in which they found themselves.

THE CASE AGAINST SUCH CONCERNS AND FEARS

"Now you're all scared stiff and white as sheets, but remember also that – as I mentioned earlier – comets and their nuclei are much like our steam and clouds," Krutohlav continued. "So if you imagine one hitting solid ground, the effect would have to be fairly gentle. To which I would add that all comets move very fast and if one did come close to Earth it would only tarry in our proximity for a few hours and the duration of any gravitational pull would also be short-lived."

KRUTOHLAV LOOKS INTO ANCIENT VIEWS ON COMETS

"The very fact that the ancients didn't know what comets are means that their views on them will vary. I'll set out some of them for your benefit, but only the main ones.

"Pliny considered that there were twelve families of comets, from which each derived its particular characteristics. So, those that were equipped with a mane were meant to fly very fast; conical ones always had a pale appearance; those that resembled hair appeared at the greatest distance, and so on.

"Aristotle divided them into bearded or tailed.

"Plutarch didn't acknowledge them as solid bodies, but thought them mere reflections of the Sun's rays.

"In the early seventeenth century, after sunspots had been observed, they thought that comets were fumes exhaled by the Sun. Similarly Johannes Hevelius[53] in Danzig pronounced them to be fumes exhaled by the planets. Kepler[54] saw them as monsters,

---

53 Hevelius (1611—1687) was a Polish astronomer of Bohemian German-speaking Lutheran origin who mapped the Moon ('the founder of lunar topography') and drew up a list of fixed stars. (He and all others mentioned are well catered for by Wikipedia.)
54 Johannes Kepler (1571–1630), German astronomer and astrologer, mathematician and music theorist. Known also for his collaboration with Tycho de Brahe in Prague.

peculiar whale-like things flying about the celestial spheres. Others said that they were infectious vapours. Most thought they were harbingers of misfortune. That was also believed by Cicero, Seneca, Pliny, Riccioli and many others.

"That comets might have any influence on temperature, climate and the purity of the atmosphere is worthless drivel. On how matters stand with epidemics I shall be quite brief:

"In 542 AD an epidemic broke out and lasted for fifty years, but no comet was sighted throughout that time.

"In 717 AD there was a plague in the east, and in Constantinople alone 300,000 people perished. But neither hide nor hair of a comet.

"In 990 AD St Anthony's fire,[55] which terminates quickly in blood poisoning, raged for the first time in Europe. Around then, only two comets were observed, but actually later.

"In 1092 people began dying for a whole five years. Some countries lost half their population, others died out completely. Antiochia was one where almost everyone died including 200,000 of the soldiers stationed there. But comets of any size were only seen in 1071 and 1097.

"From 1310 on, the plague raged for seven years. 13,000 people died in Strasbourg, 14,000 in Basle, 16,000 in Mainz and 13,000 in Cologne; a largish comet had only been seen in 1305.

"In 1347 the black death was raging. 22,000 people a month died in Gaza, while Baghdad and Damascus were totally wiped out. In London 80,000 died, in Lübeck 1,600 in a single night, while for three months people in Vienna were dying at a daily rate of 700–800, one time reaching 1,400. Even royals died back

---

[55] Ergotism, known throughout medieval Europe as 'holy fire', from Lat. *ignis sacer*, or 'St Anthony's fire'.

then: the Byzantine Andronikos III, Alfonso XI in Spain, Joan in Portugal,[56] Simeon Ivanovich the Proud of Moscow and his brother and seven children. The plague lasted five years. Comets appeared in 1347 and 1351.

"In 1356 the black death broke out again, also lasting five years and with even greater vehemence. For every 1000 Italians only 100 survived. 20,000 people died in Cologne, 17,000 in Avignon, including five cardinals and 100 bishops while they were all there in council, and not one remained unburied or just left by the roadside; but at this time there is no mention of any comet.

"In 1367 the black death broke out yet again and raged until 1374 in the form of a dancing mania after which the victim's belly burst open.[57] People sought refuge in convents and monasteries, until a special order went out banning the practice. It was beginning to look as if the whole of humanity would die. No comets appeared at this time.

"The same goes for cholera, which has begun to plague us in a big way – as in this very year of 1855 – but we've heard nary a word about any comet."

---

[56] The reference is to Princess Joan of England, who died in 1348 on the way to her wedding with Prince Peter, son of King Alfonso XI of Castile and Queen Maria of Portugal.

[57] This refers to the first major outbreak of dancing plague or choreomania, which started in Aachen and spread across Europe over the next several years; also called tarantism in the Italian context. Some believe it was another manifestation of ergotism.

KRUTOHLAV COMPLETES HIS DISCOURSE ON COMETS WITH A LAST MENTION OF THEIR INHABITANTS

"We firmly believe that everything is inhabited by living creatures, so should comets, given their sheer size and numbers, be left empty of them? Particles of their elements already indicate that such creatures will differ from those to be found on the planets. What they might be like we do not know. We should certainly not survive on them because they must be dominated by extreme heat and extreme cold. Thus the heat of the 1680 comet as it approached the Sun was 260,000 times greater than the heat of the Sun as felt on Earth and 2,000 times hotter than white-hot cast iron. As it moves away from the Sun, the cold is so extreme that it would be like Earth turning into ice. So what must those creatures be like if they have to be suddenly reduced to ashes? And how can they look out into the darkest night, once it has moved far away from the Sun?"

With these words, Krutohlav closed his huge tome and the others gave a deep sigh of relief.

PART

FIVE

**CONCERNING FIXED STARS,
DOUBLE STARS AND, FINALLY,
THE BIRTH AND ULTIMATE LIFESPAN
OF EARTH, ALSO ON KRUTOHLAV'S
STRANGE TALES.**

As written up by Hromovín of Libušice in 1856

FIXED
STARS

"What exactly are fixed stars? Do they shine the way our Sun does?" Benuš asked.

"Indeed they do," Krutohlav replied. "As far as their blazing fire is concerned, they are bodies just like the Sun, shining with light of their own. But don't go thinking that they're identical to the Sun in terms of their size. They are simply immense and keep in check goodness knows how many million systems around them. In all probability, our own Sun isn't standing still, but has to revolve round some other fixed star, unknown to us.

"Even as we first glance up into the heavens we can tell not only that there are far too many stars even to begin counting them, but also that they vary in size. Some gleam very bright and start to twinkle the moment the Sun sets, others are duller, smaller and only appear in the deep of a dark night. Yet others can only be made out with the aid of a telescope. How wrong we would be to assert that the stars that seem bigger really are bigger. No, no, that's all to do with distance.

"We astronomers know nothing, or next to nothing, about just how remote and how large they really are. So since we are going to talk about fixed stars, we shall only refer to their apparent size. In that sense, we shall say that the largest ones are of the first magnitude, progressively smaller ones of the second down to the sixth magnitude, those being all the ones visible to the naked eye.

"This classification is by no means exact. We have to take into account their relative distance, size, luminosity etc.; their rotation varies, and we sometimes see the same one as now larger, now smaller, so their light will be different. So for example, to the ancient Greeks Sirius still shone red, now it's quite pale; Castor was once larger than Pollux, now it's the other way round. One star in the Snake, or Serpens constellation, used to be of the first magnitude, while today it barely passes for the second. Even the seven stars that make up Ursa Major keep changing size, the fourth one being of the fourth magnitude, while in the days of Tycho de Brahe it was still a second-magnitude star.

"So far we've only mentioned ones that are visible to the naked eye. Stars visible only through a telescope are divided into ten groups and so together make up the six.

THE NUMBER OF FIXED STARS IN THE FIRST SIX GROUPS

"The present number of first-magnitude stars is fourteen, with 70 of the second magnitude and 300 of the third. Those of the fourth magnitude are too numerous to count, but are reckoned to be around 5,000. Those of the seventh magnitude cannot be counted at all, so many of them are there. Bode puts them at 17,240, Lalande at around 50,000 – but even that is only from the northern hemisphere, so there should be as many again from the southern. Littrow assumes there are about 70,000.

"But if we consider that a better telescope might raise the numbers tenfold, the total must be reckoned at 2,726,000. But through his telescope Herschel saw not a hundred, but a thousand all at once, so the total must come to at least 273 million."

THE AREAS OF THE SKY
RICH IN STARS

Krutohlav's audience had barely got their heads round this much when he began talking about areas of the sky that were rich in stars.

"Herschel says that there were over 50,000 stars that he could clearly distinguish at one point in Orion's club. Huyghens put the number of stars in Orion at 2,000, Herschel counted 258,000 in the Milky Way. From such counts as these we may infer that the total number of stars comes to at least 534,600 million.

THE MILKY WAY

"Despite the above number of stars being so huge, it still seems on the low side. The truth is that within infinity we can only see the closest stars, and of any others beyond them we know absolutely nothing.

"If we go outside on a clear evening and scan the sky, we shall see as many stars as there are grains of sand in the sea, distributed here more densely, there more sparsely. An especially large, infinite, number are concentrated in that pale band known as the Milky Way. It stretches right across the heavens. With his giant telescope Herschel managed to disembroil this fog so it, too, broke down into individual stars. All the stars that make up the Milky Way certainly belong to a system all its own. We know little of the size of any of the stars, about which there has been more guesswork than certainty. For example, the large star called Vega, which has been observed by many, but especially Herschel, is so huge that its radius is 34 times that of the Sun. Others are as remote as 2,000 million times the width of Earth.

So we can imagine what gigantic bodies they must be! What is the Sun compared to them? No more than a flea compared to Earth! How lamentably tiny is our solar system when compared to those other systems! It's a mere droplet on the end of a needle in comparison to the infinite ocean of the heavens!!!"

Thus did Krutohlav bring this important subject to a close.

The following day they all met up again and kept pestering Krutohlav to tell them yet more new things of which they knew nothing. In the end he couldn't counter their importuning and began again thus:

DOUBLE STARS

"You have all been so very keen to know what those heavenly bodies are that are called double stars," he began his next lecture.

"In some languages they are called twins, meaning they are two, but very close, or paired, situated close together and rotating round each other. There are many such, to date we know of over 6,000. Many people hold to the view that they are optical illusions, but that's not at all how it is: they really are two, close together, belonging to each other and constituting their own system.

"Because of the sheer numbers, they have had to be divided into classes: the first includes those that are less than four seconds apart, of which there are around 1,316. The second is for those that are 4–8 seconds apart and they number 1,318. The third class are 8–18 seconds apart and of those there are almost as many again. The fourth class are 16–32 seconds apart, and in it there are 1,450 stars.

"In relation to single stars, the ratio is two double stars to ten singles. However, I don't fancy going into that, so let's go on to another matter that is of greater concern to us all.

"Usually one of the twins is smaller, much smaller than in the case of, say, polar stars: one may be of second magnitude, the other of eleventh. But sometimes they are equal in size.

"As for the way they rotate, each one moves in its own way, though why this is so remains unknown. So, for example, a double star that was already double in the time of Jesus is still double despite the billions of leagues it has travelled.

"The distribution of double stars across the firmament is uneven. There are parts that have very few, but the closer we get to the Milky way, the more their numbers grow. There can even be 2–4 of them quite close together.

"It is apparent that all these double stars move within the infinity of the cosmos, always spinning around together, in a brotherly fashion. The most momentous double star is within Cygnus; there the distance between the twins is 15 seconds. In a hundred years they travel 607 seconds, so since the birth of Christ they have passed through three degrees or six times the diameter of the Moon, but they have never drifted apart. Besides that, it is clear that the weaker twin rotates around the stronger one elliptically, just like the Moon around Earth."

THE BIRTH OF THE SOLAR WORLD, OR SOLAR SYSTEM

"It is a fact that the Earth on which we dwell, indeed the entire solar system was not always in the condition in which we know them today. Just as there is a progression in the life of man, of fauna and flora – in the sense that they are engendered, brought forth, mature and die – it is conceivable that the same proceeding also applies to the entire solar system. Is such a thing possible?"

"Of course it is," the company chorused.

"Precisely because the world as we know it is awash with so many blessings, perhaps no one thing has attracted so many conjectures as the debate around the beginnings of Earth and the cosmos. True, the gigantic teeth found in Ohio were declared to be an angel's, but that notion has now fallen quite out of favour, and yet... today's hypotheses about the beginning of the world don't sound any better. Listen up, my brothers: the windbag Burnett, happily a Quaker,[58] was followed by the ingenious Woodword,[59] a bold fellow and unyielding, who in discussing the ancient permutations of Earth was not ashamed to assert that some of the laws of God at the Creation must have lapsed. And it is possible that at the moment when he arrived at this determination his deranged mind promptly turned to ice. And do you know that even in our own day there are many who have affirmed that Earth is an animal that endures, possesses entrails, gives evidence of being sensate, digests and excretes, breathes and breeds without pause. But let's

---

58 Reuss must mean the Yorkshireman Thomas Burnet (1635–1715). The serious account of his life and work at https://www.famousscientists.org/thomas-burnet/ speaks specifically of his defence of the authority of the Church of England, making Reuss's description of him as a Quaker distinctly odd, but his contribution to science includes such works as *Telluris Theoria Sacra* (*Sacred Theory of the Earth, parts 1 & 2*, 1681), which contained a theory of the structure of the Earth and an explanation of how the earth was formed; it attracted much attention and was duly translated into English. The third and fourth parts were published in 1689 and a *Review of the Theory of the Earth*, published in 1690, completed the large work. I do not doubt that this is the man whom Reuss had in mind, despite the misspelt surname.

59 Another doubtless misspelling, for John Woodward (1665–1728), who was "perhaps the greatest exponent of the Flood as the creator of fossils. In the words of an admirer, Woodward's book, *An Essay toward a Natural History of the Earth*, 'Vindicates, supports and maintains the Mosaick Account of things, as exactly agreeable to the Phaenomena of Nature.' Woodward held that the Flood had dissolved every rock and picked up every living thing into 'one common confused Mass.'" (https://ucmp.berkeley.edu/history/medieval.html. See also https://en.wikipedia.org/wiki/John_Woodward_%28naturalist%29. Neither Woodward nor Burnet are treated to a footnote in the critical Tatran edition of Reuss's book.

abandon the ideas of those bright sparks: better is it to envy their genius than argue with them. So I shall step aside from all such and give you instead the view of our foremost observers."

"Oh, please do, please," they all cried.

LEIBNITZ'S VIEW OF THE ORIGIN OF THE WORLD

So Krutohlav began a brief account of the ideas of the celebrated Leibnitz, who is incidentally a Slav by origin.

"All planets, as well as comets, not excluding Earth – says Leibnitz – were, in their youth, suns. But then they aged, leaving their youth behind them and with it their own luminosity. Where these suns came from, however, and why the surviving Sun didn't lose its light, of that Leibnitz says absolutely nothing. It appears that he just tossed out this product of his mind for us to chew over, lest we get bored."

WHISTON'S IDEA

"This man[60] mused with such tireless dedication upon the origin of the world that some other topic might have better merited the attention. He had fallen hopelessly in love with comets and

---

60 William Whiston of Leicestershire (1667–1752), in his day a well-regarded natural philosopher, mathematician, historian and a Cambridge professor. During an impressive career he, amongst much else, gave talks on astronomy at a London coffee house and produced a book, *A New Theory of the Earth* (1696), "in which he presented a description of the divine creation of the Earth and a posited global flood". As Reuss says, he "postulated that the earth originated from the atmosphere of a comet and that all major changes in earth's history could be attributed to the action of comets" (cometary catastrophism). It was well received by such persons as Isaac Newton and John Locke. (See https://en.wikipedia.org/wiki/William_Whiston and https://en.wikipedia.org/wiki/A_New_Theory_of_the_Earth, accessed 14.05.2022.)

deduced everything else from them. He held that Earth was originally a comet without an axis, without inhabitants, a lifeless dimwit, though one that did revolve around the Sun. After many millions of years it eventually crashed into another comet and then acquired an axis to spin round. With that came the alternation of days and nights that gave rise to plants and animals. This was the onset of a millennial paradise. Then everything went wrong: another comet struck Earth and the naughty populace all got drowned. Eventually yet another one will show up and destroy everything by fire. Never has anything so ridiculous been read so avidly as these particular views."

THE VIEWS OF BUFFON

"Nor did Buffon[61] lose any time before turning his attention to such an important matter. He believed that the origins of everything were rooted in a radiant Sun and the infinite number of comets spinning round it in every direction. Now and then, a comet might have happened to make contact with the Sun in one of two ways: either a hurtling comet hurled itself into the Sun, thereby adding to its mass, or a comet glanced lightly off it at an angle, grabbed a portion of its mass and made it its own. The comet then dragged the chunk snatched from the Sun behind it like water, split it into more than one smaller streams and into

---

61 Georges-Louis Leclerc, Comte de Buffon (1707–88), French naturalist, mathematician and cosmologist, and author of *Histoire naturelle, générale et particulière* (1749–1788) in 36 volumes. Accorded various academic honours, national and international. His speculation that the solar system was created following a comet's collision with the Sun is in his *Les époques de la nature* (1778). (See https://en.wikipedia.org/wiki/Georges-Louis_Leclerc,_Comte_de_Buffon, accessed 14.05.2022.)

spheres which, depending on how far they were from the Sun, had to spin in different ways. This was also what gave rise to planets and moons. Buffon imbued his views with such grace and beauty and his presentation of them to the reader was so matter-of-fact that it was as if he himself had been present at the birth of the universe. So, for example, of the piece torn from the Sun that became our Earth he asserted that it burned with a constant fire for 3,000 years after which it became a fluid mass for the next 34,000 years. The ocean was pure steam until 25,000 years later water finally fell out of the air and covered Earth to a height of 12,000 feet. Over the next 20,000 years the water accumulated around the Equator, and so he went on and on."

FRANKLIN'S VIEWS

"When air is compressed, it becomes as dense as the weights by which the compression is achieved; thus under twice or three times the pressure, air will become twice or three times as dense. It can become so compressed that even gold will float on it. The deeper into Earth, the denser the air: at seven and a half leagues beneath Earth's crust water will float on it first, at ten and a half leagues tin, at eleven silver and at eleven and a half gold. And if gold were to be somehow pushed below eleven and a half leagues, it would bob up to the surface of the air like a cork. Earth is said to be liquid inside, but the liquid is denser than solid bodies that we know on Earth, and so they would all float on it. So it is not impossible that even Earth originally sprang from gases that became dense. Bodies of different weight occupy the layer appointed to them and somehow float on the air. Our rocks, mountains etc. have been – as the lightest – cast up onto the surface of the Earth that we inhabit, and above that floats an even lighter air.

"The original matter from which Earth arose was not a gas, because gas is only an end-product, and it is possible that as water arises from steam, so Earth, its rocks, mountains, water and air also came from that original matter."

Krutohlav had long done with this and gone over to another topic, but his companions took a long time to get over their amazement at the profundity of these ideas.

"Listen, my brothers, I still have to tell you about Laplace's idea about the origin of the world, which is probably closest to the truth."

"We're all ears," they chorused.

LAPLACE'S VIEW
OF THE ORIGIN OF THE WORLD

"Before I go into this at length, there are still some things you need to know about asteroids and comets.

"1. We observe, not without some surprise, that all the planets keep to one and the same direction: from west to east. The same goes for moons. So a total of 34 known bodies all take the same path, and as new asteroids are discovered, that number will only grow. Do you suppose that is merely by chance? Surely not, this universal direction of their motion will at bottom have the same cause.

"2. With all asteroids we observe their orbiting of the Sun to be more or less circular, without forming any distant ellipses. The greatest wanderers are Pallas and Juno, but even there it is very slight

SELECTED TITLES PUBLISHED BY JANTAR

Barcode is one of many collections of short stories published by Jantar in English. In 2022, we published **DEAD** and **Mothers and Truckers** by Balla and Ivana Dobrakovová respectively. Another, very popular, collection of short stories was published in 2018 called **And My Head Exploded**. Featuring 10 short stories, the book features works and authors from the Bohemian fin-de-siècle era never previously translated into English.

In 2017, we published **Fox Season** by Agnieszka Dale, a collection of dazzling stories set in a London bracing itself for Brexit. It is now making its first appearance on university literature courses. The stories were described by Zoë Apostolides in the *Financial Times* as 'fascinating and refreshingly honest stares at life in a foreign place, whatever that definition might be'.

City of Torment by Daniela Hodrová, published in 2021 attracted very positive reviews in *The Los Angeles Review of Books*, *The Irish Times* and *New European Review*. The book begins, 'Alice Davidovič would have never thought the window of her childhood room hung so low above the Olšany cemetery that a body could travel the distance in less than two seconds.'

Birds of Verhovina by Ádám Bodor contains a cast of weirdos and miscreants left to make their own way in the Carpathian Mountains. It was described by Diána Vonnák in *The Times Literary Supplement* as 'one of those places you might visit but might never leave; it is reality on its way to becoming allegory'.

Carbide by Andriy Lyubka was published at the end of 2020 when we all thought the worst that could happen was to be locked-down by a global pandemic. Set in what now appears to be the very quaint Ukraine prior to its attempted evisceration by Russia, Lyubka describes another Carpathian periphery world populated by criminals, corrupt local officials and a delusional history teacher. *Carbide* was described by Kate Tsurkan in *The Los Angeles Review of Books* as 'a fast-paced tragicomedy which establishes the young author as Ukraine's modern-day Voltaire'.

These titles and all our other titles can be purchased postage-free world-wide from our website:
www.JantarPublishing.com

FORTHCOMING TITLES

Jantar is an independent publisher based in London that has been praised widely for its choice of texts, artwork, editorial rigour and use of very rare and sometimes unique fonts in all its books. Jantar's guiding principle is to select, publish and make accessible previously inaccessible works of Central European literary fiction through translations into English… texts 'trapped in amber'.

Since its foundation in 2011, Jantar's list has been made up, mostly, of works of literary fiction. In 2023, we begin to broaden our mission to include works of science fiction from Central Europe, a region rich in authors and stories in this genre.

Being Jantar, we begin our new SF list with the first recognised works in the genre written in Czech and Slovak. **Newton's Brain** by Jakub Arbes and published in a new translation by David Short, was first published in 1877, 18 years before *The Time Machine* by H.G. Wells. It first appeared in English translation in 1892. Arbes was much admired by Émile Zola.

Our second SF title was written in an uncodified version of 'Old Slovak' and published in 1856. ***The Science of the Stars*** by Gustáv Reuss is arguably the first title to feature a balloon travelling to the moon. It is certainly the first to appear in any version of the Slovak language.

Also forthcoming in 2024, is a new novella by Balla, **Among the Ruins**, and our first novels translated from German. In May, we shall publish **Winterberg's Last Journey** by Jaroslav Rudiš. Later in the year, we launch the much-anticipated new translation of ***The Grandmother*** by Božena Němcová. Together with Erben's *Kytice* (Jantar 2014) and Mácha's *May* (Jantar 2025), *The Grandmother* is one of the three founding works of modern Czech Literature. This new and complete translation will show, for the first time to English-language readers, the subversive, feminist, anti-theological and anti-Habsburg elements in this classic text. It will be published in a regular prose version and another illustrated by Míla Fürstová.

These titles and all our other titles can be purchased postage-free world-wide from our website:
www.JantarPublishing.com

in comparison to comets. Asteroids differ from comets in that not one travels from east to west, nor do they form any major ellipses.

"They also differ in the angle of their orbits to the ecliptic. In comets this is huge, with planets and asteroids only slight.

"Taking a cool look at all three of these considerations, we will infer that their force must surely relate to the entire systems that were operative at the start of time. The cause has to be sought in the gaseous fluidum that kept the asteroids far apart from one another. If this fluidum gave the asteroids their circular orbit, it really must have been wrapped round the Sun as atmosphere. Previously, the Sun may have been even hotter, its heat reaching far beyond Uranus, until it cooled down and shrank to its present condition.

"So the Sun may be supposed to have looked like a gigantic luminous core, wreathed in vapours. The actual core of the Sun might even have been missing originally, being instead just a massive blazing, scorching haze.

"But now concentrate really hard: we're going to take a closer look at this hypothesis, which does seem closest to the truth," Krutohlav continued.

"We're listening, we're listening," they chorused.

"So keep it up. If that shining core, the embryo of the future Sun, happened, through some force of which we can know nothing, to revolve around itself, then the atmosphere that enfolded it must have revolved along with it. And if the originally refulgent Sun released heat from its innermost layers, that brought about an imbalance, though the parts released didn't stop circling round the core. As a denser mass formed around the various layers, this drew thinner vapours towards it, rolled them into balls and so gave rise to asteroids."

At these words, they all whooped with delight.

"And we may conclude from this," Krutohlav went on, "that their direction was also the same as the Sun's and that they had to have travelled from west to east. And since these bodies rotated the faster the more distant they were from the Sun, it makes it easy to assess their rotation about their own axis and their direction. Until they cooled down, they took up more space, but having cooled down, their density is as we know it today.

"As for comets, they originated in the same way and they seem to concentrate into spheres only slowly.

"The only other thing that can be said here is that the Sun and the planets were probably liquid at the outset. Without conceding that, we should not be able to explain either the rotation of Earth or that of the Moon and other planets. How the planets lost their light is hard to determine; nor does this hypothesis help us determine why some planets are denser than others. Uranus is denser than Saturn, Saturn is less dense than Jupiter, and Mercury is the densest of all. The Sun ought to be the densest, yet its mass is 15 times more rarefied than Mercury's."

THE DURATION OF THE WORLD

Benuš was curious to know how much longer the world, or, rather, the solar system, was going to last, or what we and our descendants might be in for, at which Krutohlav frowned so intensely and shook his head so fiercely that some of them began thinking that he'd gone out of his mind. But then he stood up four-square and required that the question be repeated, before remaining totally engrossed as he pondered where and how to begin, or whether he shouldn't scrap the whole idea and give no thought whatsoever to the world's duration. He was well aware that this was no time for levity, indeed the gravity of the issue was as great as that of the subject itself. After their repeated entreaties he finally unburdened himself of the view that on this unfortunate point nothing at all could be said with certainty. Then canny Roháč took him by the arm and continued to badger him: it might not be possible to state everything with certainty, but he might at least address some of the possible outcomes. So in the end, after such a barrage of supplication, he finally yielded and began again.

THINGS THAT CAN GO WRONG

"Since I was able to speak at some length about the origin of the world, especially of the solar system, it is indeed proper that I should offer a glimpse of the world's future, or what we may hope for, or expect, or what we might reasonably fear.

"In our previous discussion, we arrived at the properties of the solar system, and with all the certainty that we can muster at present. It is right and proper that we should explore the future and consider whether any new findings about the solar system might not tell us more about how long the world will last. Since even we shall pass and fall victim to immutable nature and our own destiny, the bosoms of each of us will father the transcendent question of whether the Sun, Moon and other celestial bodies will keep on turning forever and aye, in a word, whether they will retain their attributes and how.

"I shall not go into the things that could go wrong merely at random, for it does remain possible that some hitherto unknown comets might burn up and destroy us, or that some other unknown body might burn up and destroy the entire solar system, the way one fixed star in Cassiopeia came a cropper, of which I shall say no more. But where such unforeseeable catastrophes are concerned, we should, given our ignorance, say nothing. The death of one man struck by lightning tells us nothing about the fate of the whole of mankind. But the aging of the human frame, how it shrinks and grows threadbare across the generations does lead us to conclude that nature itself, in its parts or as a whole, may survive. So we shall speak only of individual bodies within the solar system, where two things can go wrong:

1. Periodic, or localised, as relating to the planets' orbits,

2. Everlasting (sempiternal), which might bring about a permanent change in the planets' orbits.

"Clearly matters of the first order may destroy an entity, but what of the second, the eternal? Maybe they'll never happen."

THREE ELEMENTS IN THE ORBITING OF PLANETS

"I shall, then, lay before you this hugely interesting subject, which is of interest to us all and from which we can then move on to others.

"Any orbit, whether of a planet or comet, consists of six definable parts, or elements. And these are: 1. the major axis, or the time of an orbit; 2. its deviation, or eccentricity; 3. its tilt or inclination; 4. the length of its perihelion (distance from the Sun); 5. the longitude of the ascending node; 6. the epoch of a planet in orbit at a certain time.

"The last three will have no impact on the perduration of the world, but with the first three it is a different matter.

"A major axis must not change, not even periodically, for it would keep on growing, inevitably, and that would cause things to go wrong. The other two might conceivably change, but only to a limited degree, otherwise they could damage the entire system at some future date. For example, if the eccentricity of Earth's orbit kept rising, becoming more elongated, or if, in consequence of that, the Moon came ever closer, then in the former case the Earth's climate would change completely, while in the second the Moon would have to crash into Earth with a bang. And other planets would be affected likewise: some would come closer to us, others would move further away, and our years would be now shorter, now longer, and ultimately Earth would be constantly awash with the plague, and it could happen that one or other planet would also crash into it."

CONSEQUENCES OF THE FOREGOING

"I don't want to carry on now with something so straightforward, or launch into any complicated mathematics, but believe me, as Littrow and Poisson believe it, that the present condition of the solar system is no different from what I shall now present to you."

"Let's hear it then, come on!" they all cried.

So Krutohlav proceeded further:

"From all the calculations that I have worked on, and with me likewise Newton, Littrow and Copernicus, it is quite apparent that precisely because the solar system is an integral whole, it will stand its ground forever; and precisely for that same reason all the orbits of the major axes will be and shall remain unchangeable.

Eccentricity and inclination do change, admittedly, but so slightly, and within a certain finite range, that they can never let us down. Added to that, their rotating only in one direction gives them the seal of permanence for all time. Hence neither we, nor those who come after us need – on this score at least – have anything, absolutely anything to fear."

"Gosh, what a relief!" said Benuš, "That both we and our descendants will endure forever."

"I'd actually have preferred to see something of the Great Flood: I'd have scrambled up Mount Ararat or Kriváň[62] and looked down on the world in its frenzy, like when from up on Avas I watched the fighting going on around Miskolc.[63]

Thus did they all twitter and jest until Krutohlav uttered these words: "But then you'd all perish anyway. Just wait a moment while I tell you how things look for us and stop being silly."

---

62 Kriváň, second highest peak in the Tatra Mountains.
63 Avas Hill, once volcanic, is the highest point of the north-Hungarian city of Miskolc, at 234 m. above sea level and a 104 metres above the city. There is a reproduction of an old view from Avas over the city on the Miskolc Wikipedia page (https://en.wikipedia.org/wiki/Miskolc). The 'fighting' probably refers to 23 June 1849, when, towards the end of the 1848–49 Hungarian revolution, "the Hungarian units had retreated all the way to Miskolc", meanwhile "General Rüdiger had entered Prešov and Field Marshal Pashkevich was having lunch in the palace of the Bishop of Košice" (v. https://noveslovo.sk/c/Ludovit_Stur_jeho_zivotny_pribeh_14; I am grateful to Karin Kilíková of Revúca, whose persistence resulted in tracing this lone reference to the Miskolc dimension for me. During the Hungarian Revolution of 1848, the Baltic German General Friedrich Alexander von Rüdiger took part in the Russian intervention that helped defeat the rebellion, and he was the Russian signatory of the Instrument of Surrender at Világos [v. https://en.wikipedia.org/wiki/Friedrich_von_R%C3%BCdiger, accessed 21.06.2022], while Field Marshal Count Ivan Fyodorovich Paskevich-Erevansky, Serene Prince of Warsaw, commanded the Russian troops sent to assist Austria against the rebellious Hungarians and finally compelled the Hungarians' surrender at Világos [v. https://en.wikipedia.org/wiki/Ivan_Paskevich, accessed 21.06.2022]).

OTHER REASONS
WHY THE SYSTEM WILL LAST

"The entire system and all of its parts have been so well and properly organised that there can be no thought of any harm coming to it. This order is autocratic, or absolutist. At the centre shines the Sun and the planets run around it. The Sun's mass is 700 times greater than all of them, so it is well placed to dictate to them autocratically. The same relationship applies to others as well, especially moons. So Earth's mass is seventy times greater than the Moon's, and Jupiter's is 6,000 times that of all its moons taken together. Since the Sun has dominion over its moons – and no mean dominion at that – it is naturally impossible for any disorder to break out. So should someone suddenly take Jupiter away, one of its moons would immediately go whirling in an ellipse around the Sun and another would do its orbiting in a hyperbola.

"The eternal order that we see in the entire system must also apply to Earth. So the ends of the Earth, its poles, have been the same, unaltered, since time immemorial. Likewise the oceans have kept to their beds for thousands and thousands of years. Such had been God's desire, and his watchword from the very beginning was 'Halt!', to stop his work of such delight from ever changing!"

THE MOTION
OF BODIES IN MATTER

"The light of the Sun as we know it today niftily shows how all the planets move within it. But there could be other, rarer matters that would cause the planets' motion to stop. We don't have to bother about that, no matter how delicate they might be. Suffice it to say that given the solid matter of our planets, nothing in particular has yet been observed, though with the translucent fluidity of comets things are different."

"Go on, we're listening," they urged.

"A comet – as I've told you already – can sense that it is moving within matter, and so with almost every passing year its course shortens by one day. Many calculations have taught us how a comet's course keeps growing shorter and shorter until, in a word, and unless something changes, it is bound to crash into the Sun. An observation made ten years ago showed one comet to be travelling one thousandth faster. So in 16,000 years' time, it will be only half its present distance from the Sun. If Jupiter shifted its course by one millionth in a million years, then in seventy million years its speed would rise by one thousandth and its orbit would halve in a mere 700 million years, by which time it would be revolving round the Sun at twice its present velocity. Although this time scale seems like an eternity, it would eventually come to pass that Jupiter would hit the Sun."

THE MATTER BROUGHT TO A CLOSE

"So even given that we can be sure of the solar system for many millions of years to come, we do know that it won't last forever: much as all things on Earth last only a certain time, not staying in one and the same form, but reshaping themselves into other bodies. Every year winter upsets everything, entire species of animals have died out and whole nations have proved ephemeral. Everything is trapped in time and, as predetermined, comes to naught. So are Earth and other cosmic bodies to be spared subjection to that same general law? By what right may we require that exception? Have not some stars passed away, never to twinkle again? To us, such catastrophes are incomprehensible, but that is due to our own pettiness! Out there things are measured differently, and the Milky Way is but a far distant trace of a world that is infinite!

"So since this Earth of ours will grow old and become as nothing, are we to start whimpering against a law that is eternal, or try to oppose it? All things that have their beginnings on Earth must also die on Earth; there may be progress, but it will culminate and come to an end. Anything that has form will die away. And so all things will pass, but one alone, to us unknown, will remain – our eternal God!"

At these words, all Krutohlav's listeners heaved a deep sigh and he himself, having praised the Lord, closed his book.

KRUTOHLAV'S LAST STORIES ABOUT LIFE

Having said all there was to say on the subject of the world's duration, Krutohlav gave orders for the dragon to fly a few miles above Earth at eagle-speed.

"Look, you see the country we're flying over," he said, "that was once full of aurochs and marshlands, and now it's inhabited by lots of people. The leftovers of previous peoples are forever rampaging over this and that: some dream of a kingdom, others an empire and yet others a republic. These people are doughty, honest, impassioned, learned. Such a pity that their watchword is: *fashion!*"

At which point, Benuš looked down and saw a young woman entering a church with a pretty prayer-book. What's that then? – Fashion, precisely – and, indeed, the entire populace was getting cluttered up with books.

"Amen to that! Let me tell you, this morally debilitated nation will soon be laid even lower, and if it wants to survive it needs to be reborn. So what shall I tell you about the country lying down there beneath us?" Krutohlav picked up on the questions they'd been asking him. "Not three centuries have passed since it was Europe's bugbear. Now its glory is hidden in the shadows," he began. "It's a beautiful country, once a match for Italy or ancient Greece. And rich in metals."

"And what do those monstrous great buildings mean? All I see in them is affectation with a rope round its waist," Svatovit interrupted him.

"Be quiet," Krutohlav said, "that's this nation's lot."

"And what are those redcaps doing in those narrows?"

"Quiet, I tell you, that's a sign of the nation's weakness."

"We seem to have been flying for ages now over an endless plain, with not a hill in sight!" Roháč suddenly gave vent to what he'd been mulling over. "What sort of country is this?"

"Stop complaining, you'll get plenty of hills and mountains and upland meadows in due course. This people above whom we are dawdling right now keeps a look-out over other peoples. Meaning? Think about it! The question is: What am *I*, what *am* I, did the world come into being out of half zero or whole zero?"

"But what's that? I can see long, wide mantles – and hats full of holes," Benuš shouted Krutohlav down.

"Leave it, this people's concern is that 'I am' thing! Once it was a quite amazing and memorable nation, but now a great gloom hangs over it. The truth is that all women, even girls, go about hooded. And for why? Because of the want of enlightenment hereabouts!"

"And this here, what's this? Nothing but boats. Utter squalor and such opulence! Nothing but redcaps. Joy beside woe, industriousness beside sloth, profit and utility. Surely that means they're all merchants."

"Forget them," Krutohlav replied to Slavín, "they'll also only last a certain time; in the east as in the west dark clouds are gathering. Time will tell, time will decide, the hour has already struck!"

"This is a land where the sun will never set," Krutohlav lapsed back into his musings, "a vast land, huge. Its intellectual prowess grows ever mightier and in the very near future its mental and physical prowess will give Europe a good shake. This country is… is…"

At that very moment it was as if a thunderbolt had hit the dragon: it shuddered mightily and threatened to crash into the Tatras, into Kriváň. They were all scared out of their wits, especially Krutohlav, who'd even anticipated the peril that loomed ahead.

"Oars aloft, be smart about it, fill the drums and pipes with smoke, or we're done for!" he bellowed with all the urgency at his command.

Everything was working, but twenty-four hours passed and nothing had helped.

"Amen, I say, keep at it in every way each of you can."

The entire company was in a trance. Amen! A dense mass of clouds had hidden the tossing and turning dragon from sight, and it was all over.

Note. Many friends have been asking itinerant pedlars of herbs, spices and precious oils, as well as astronomers and others, if they haven't perhaps heard something about Krutohlav's terrible demise. None of them has been able to say anything for certain, but astronomers from Stuttgart and Munich have reported that they had indeed observed some orbiting monstrosity though they had no idea what became of it. So nor can we say anything about what became of Krutohlav, his dragon and his companions. He may have been swept up by the latest new planet, in which case he is almost certainly leading a happier life there than on wretched Earth.

PART

SIX

THE EARTH.

EARTH

Never since the world began was there ever such a confusion of the senses as that time when Krutohlav shook his head in order to quell the impulses of his fellows. But his effort had been in vain, for there was no man, woman, child or whoever who would not have brought ladders, planks, spikes and so forth and hauled them up to Gerlachov.[64]

"Goodness gracious! What do you make of it? Is this the Day of Judgement or what? So much banging, shouting and screaming – such a hullaballoo can't have been heard even during the Flood. What on earth's got into you all?"

"Quiet, woman!" Hnevoš[65] had responded, "Whatever our great master Krutohlav may have to say about it, we have to reach the summit of Gerlach to get a good view of the world from there."

"But Hubby dearest, take pity on yourself and on me, there isn't a living soul can make it to the top."

Thereupon Hnevoš grabbed a ladder and galloped off to set it up at a point beneath the corrie half way up the mountain. His wife began chiding him again, growing quite angry: "For goodness sake, what on earth are you after?"

For a while Hnevoš was silent, then he said:

"I want to learn from our master. You can stay down here with the children, but I'm going to climb up there, using the ladder to get to the spot where Krutohlav means to tell us about the world."

---

64 The context suggests that he is referring to Gerlach(ov) Peak, rather than the eponymous village that lies on the plain directly south of the mountain (next to Poprad-Tatry Airport). The mountain is the highest in the High Tatras and the highest point in all of Slovakia, first climbed in 1855, i.e. in Reuss's own day.

65 All the new names in this section are telling; this one literally connotes *hnev* – 'anger' or perhaps ill-temper.

His wife was all flushed and knew she couldn't douse the flame that was gaining an ever stronger hold in her husband's bosom. She yielded to her fate and aided Hnevoš by taking the other end of the huge ladder and then helping him set it up safely. Then Hnevoš launched himself onto it and kept climbing till he reached the corrie, where all his pals treated him to a loud and gleeful welcome, for they'd spotted that he wasn't going to get away from his pretty Libuška that easily.

Now Krutohlav shook his head, leaned against a boulder that not a living soul had ever touched before him, picked himself a little bunch of alpine gypsophila and bellflowers, stuck them in his hat and, sunk deep in thought as he gazed out over the vast expanses of Slovakia and Galicia, began as follows:

"Everything's so futile," and at those opening words even his audience's breathing became inaudible, such was their devotion as they listened. "What are we, mere Earthlings, what is this summit of Gerlach compared to Dhaulagiri? What is Grape Hill[66] compared to us up here? Our little world doesn't know what it's missing!"

ON WHETHER THE EARTH IS FLAT AND PROPPED UP ON SOMETHING

"I'd bet two to one that Earth is an endless plain, and so it must lie on top of something. The more I think about it, the more I believe that is so," Hniloš[67] responded.

---

66 Vinný vrch, a small hill, the highest point in the village of Španie pole, some way due south of Revúca. The village's claim to fame is, beside its Lutheran church, as a site where a type of prehistoric urn of a specifically Slovak type has been found.

67 His name suggests 'rot'.

Such philosophising sparked huge arguments among many of them and these would doubtless have come to a ludicrous end if Krutohlav hadn't begun to explain matters.

"Whether or not the Earth is flat and lying on top of something you can appreciate if you take the following images into consideration." Silence descended and all ears were pricked. "If Earth is an endless plain whose end will never be found, and if it is propped up on or lying on top of something, tell me, are the Sun or the Moon, which we see rise and set, the same bodies we keep seeing or not?"

"Of course the Moon and the Sun are the same ones as we saw in the sky any day before," they chorused, Pochyba[68] alone voicing his doubts, though the reasoning behind them was soon dispelled.

"Since you believe this is the case – and there is no other possibility – another question arises. If you think Earth is a flat expanse lying on top of something, why does the Sun rise day after day from the edge of it and then set beyond the edge? If it were lying on top of something, the Sun's passage would be blocked by whatever that support is and could neither rise nor set. Answer me that, Sprostoš, Hlupoš and Tarandák!"[69] Krutohlav addressed the men by name.

"Perhaps," Hlupoš began, "some special holes have been left in the support for the Sun and Moon to pass through during the night."

"So what then is Earth's underpinning or holdfast itself resting on? You see my point, just what is holding Earth up?" Krutohlav persisted.

---

68 His name means 'doubt'.

69 These men's names all suggest stupidity in one way or another.

"Surely it must be held in place with crossbeams and pegs," Chytroš[70] chipped in.

"No, no, it's all held together with chains," was Radoš's ingenious retort.[71]

"That's all well and good," said Mudroš,[72] "but what are the crossbeams attached to, what's holding the chains in place? Tell me that!"

"Hm, you're right, I suppose. For all the Silly-billys and Twaddlemongers that there are, one would have to hit on the idea that Earth is held fast to the legs of the Ineffable One."

"Don't you be taking the name of the holy Ineffable One in vain," Krutohlav muttered sharply. The deniers, lacking all evidence about Earth, were shamed into silence.

KRUTOHLAV PURSUES THE MATTER FURTHER

"The only thing that follows from all this," Krutohlav began again, "is that if the Sun, Moon and billions of stars rotate about our Earth, that's to say they keep passing from sight and coming back again, this Earth of ours cannot be some endless plain, but has to be – no matter how great its magnitude and extent – somehow limited in size. You must believe that."

"Of course," they chorused.

"If, then, we cannot contemplate some endless flat expanse, but have to admit that Earth's size is limited, it naturally follows that it is freely suspended in space. So try telling me again, what's

---
70   Ironic, 'Brightspark'.
71   This speaker's name implies 'counsel'.
72   'Wiseman'.

it supported by, what's it kneeling on? And ultimately, what's the end-support that holds in place all the other supports that hold the Earth up? And the billions of stars: do they pass through the Earth's support or trip their way through holes in it? I don't mean to mince words: willy-nilly, you have to accept the truth that the Earth is delimited all round, that it has nothing to prop it up, and that it stands suspended within the infinity of cosmic space. The why and how it can be there unsupported and not fall away somewhere I'll deal with in due course."

Most of them were accustomed to seeing Earth as terra firma; if Krutohlav were to be right, that wouldn't make any sense. And yet, musing on the arguments that had gone before, they still found things likely to be both true – and untrue.

For all the company's temporary stupefaction and the disagreements they had had, most became convinced that the truth was none other than as given them by Krutohlav.

ON WHETHER EARTH IS SPHERICAL OR CUBIC

"Since Earth is finite, that is, not endless, meaning it is limited as to its mass, the question then arises of the shape it has or must have: whether it's like a squashed lentil, round like a ball or pyramidal. In short, what shape is it? Because any finite, limited mass must have some shape or other!"

"Indeed so," some of them concurred.

"So look all around from here on Gerlach and see where the Earth's skyline ends."

They all stared hard and took a long, long look.

"Everywhere I look I see my own skyline shrinking, and the more I strain my eyes, the more everything drops lower," said Pozorovateľ.[73]

"And I, when I was sailing across the flat of the sea to Kamchatka, I kept seeing the ends of the firmament dropping lower than they should be. We used to say the horizon was setting," said Mudroš.

"What causes it?" Krutohlav mumbled.

"I think that if the skyline really does seem lower, then it really must be lower," Mudroš replied.

Some of them had their doubts, and Krutohlav merely affirmed that this had even been substantiated instrumentally.

But hear now another reason.

"If we take up a position such as we're standing in now, we can observe, from here on Gerlach, that the horizon is circular, and so Earth cannot be four-sided, but spherical, since only a sphere can afford the same spectacle from all points."

This was followed by a tremendous hubbub, much yelling and endless argument; however, in the end they did all arrive at the conviction that only a sphere could afford such a view as they were having from Gerlach.

---

73 'Observer'.

KRUTOHLAV LOOKS ABOUT FOR MORE EVIDENCE THAT THE EARTH IS ROUND

Some of Krutohlav's companions had come round to accepting that the Earth was definitely spherical, but without being totally convinced. Hence they kept pleading, nay, badgering him to unravel the problem as quickly as possible and simply prove that the Earth really is spherical. First he immersed himself in thought, then eventually explained matters thus:

"Have any of you ever trudged across the barren great plain of northern Hungary?" was the first question he put to them

"I've done a fair bit of that," "Me, too," many of them replied.

"Did you ever notice, as you drew closer to some village or other, but especially to some tallish church tower, how it changed?"

"True, that really is a remarkable thing," Zvedoš[74] interrupted, "something me and my fellow-journeymen could never understand, and we had endless arguments over it. Let me tell you," he went on, "the further we travelled across the completely flat land away from this or that village, first we lost sight of its walls, then the roofs, and gradually the main body of the tower disappeared until all that remained was the cross on top, and before long even that vanished. Believe me, my friends, what I'm telling you is the honest truth."

"You're not the only one," Mudroš took over from Zvedoš. "When I was heading across that barren landscape towards the village of X, I ran into this Magyar and asked him roughly which way it lay. And he said: 'Can't you see the cross on top of the church tower?' I strained my eyes and, my, was I surprised to see

---

74 The name suggests inquisitiveness.

it there, at ground level! I was seeing Földi[75] growing right out of the ground. 'And how far away is it?' 'One German league and a bit.' And the closer I got, the more the tower rose up out of the ground. Then first one lantern, then the second, and the third,[76] then the tower wall and some treetops until eventually the roofs and walls of the houses became ever more clearly visible. The more clearly, the closer I got to the village."

"And at sea it's just the same with ships," Tvrdoš[77] took over. "When a ship leaves harbour, first its bottom half and any dinghies disappear, then the whole ship, leaving only the masts and pennants visible, and finally just the tip of the main mast. And the same in reverse when a ship is coming towards you."

All this while Krutohlav was sniggering away as he observed his audience's faces. In the end, Tvrdoš having had his say, he began again:

"What you've been telling us is absolutely true. But what follows from it, or how are we to explain this extraordinary natural phenomenon?" No one dared utter a word and he went on with his explanation. "Since, hitherto, this extraordinary natural phenomenon has manifested itself throughout the world, the only thing that can follow from it is that Earth must be spherical. If that were not the case, then, for example, that church tower would not disappear piecemeal, all the way up to the cross on top, or, conversely appear from the cross downwards, but would have to stay as one whole, from top to bottom, though growing ever

---

[75] This may well refer to the actual village of Földes in Hajdú-Bihar County on the border with Romania.

[76] The church spire at Földes is indeed crowned by three lanterns, one above the other, see the photo at https://en.wikipedia.org/wiki/F%C3%B6ldes (accessed 25.06.2022).

[77] This name suggests hardness or assertiveness.

smaller and smaller. If it was far, far away, it would be all there for the eye to see, but teeny-weeny as a poppy-seed, until it was too far away to be seen at all. And the same goes for those ships, and so our Earth is not flat, but a spherical body."

The assembled company could not begin to conceal their amazement at the way Krutohlav had expounded this phenomenon so emphatically, and stated its cause so aptly.

"And now here's another reason why we must believe that Earth is not flat, but a sphere. Do you know the constellation called the Big Dipper, otherwise known as the Great Bear – those seven gloriously radiant stars?"

"We do," came the response from all round.

"Looking from here along the line of the Dipper's two end stars, you will see an extremely beautiful star, called the Pole Star. It is suspended directly above our North Pole, never moving from our perspective, and with all other stars revolving round it. If you look up at it from the south, it appears to be almost on the horizon, but the further north you go, the brighter it appears until, at the Pole, it's directly overhead. As many leagues as you progress from south to north, so many will be the degrees of the Pole Star's elevation, that is, it will have climbed that many leagues. How could this happen if the Earth were not round?" Some of them understood this elucidation, others not at all, and Pochyba was particularly sceptical.

"All right, then, Pochyba, I'll give you a third proof that the Earth is round, so listen closely and think about it," Krutohlav said. And he, straining his ears, listened:

"What do you think: you've got on a boat anywhere in the world, say, Gibraltar, and you've travelled steadily, without stopping, from west to east, where would you arrive?"

"Gibraltar's in Spain, isn't it?"

"Yes, so where would you arrive at?"

"I've no idea, but I'm dead sure that with the Earth being flat, I'd never see Gibraltar again but would just get further and further away from it, the Earth going on and on forever."

"Indeed you would get further and further away," Krutohlav assured him, "but listen up and I will convince you that if you kept sailing eastwards you'd be surprised to find yourself back in Gibraltar three years later. Oh yes, and that's with only ever having rowed eastwards."

"That's not possible," Pochyba objected.

"No, it's entirely possible, and natural," Krutohlav went on, all fired up. "If you don't want to believe me, then get this: if one boat will row east from Gibraltar and another westwards, ever westwards, both will be back in Gibraltar in two to three years' time."

"I don't believe it," said Pochyba, shaking his head.

"If I can prove it to you, will you then believe the Earth is round and not flat?"

"If you do, I will, otherwise not!"

"All right. If we set off by boat from Gibraltar and keep going in an easterly direction, what sea will we have entered?"

"The Mediterranean," many of them replied.

"Good. So we'll pass by Sicily and Malta and end up in Alexandria. From there we'll take it overland, by Suez, into..."

"... the Red Sea," replied Záboj.[78]

"Right. And from there we'll pass Java, Sumatra and reach..."

"... the Pacific Ocean."

---

78 Not a punning name, but one associated with a hero of Old Czech literature.

"Going down from there, we'll take the route taken by Magellan into the Atlantic Ocean and so back to Gibraltar from where we'd set out. And had we not been going constantly eastwards?"

"Yes!" they cried in unison.

"So now do you believe the Earth is spherical?"

And, surprisingly, they all cried: "Yes, we do."

"That apart," Krutohlav began in pursuit his fourth proof, "since the invention of the telescope, all heavenly bodies have presented themselves as spherical – I mean we see the Moon, the Sun and the billions of stars as round – so why should our Earth be a cube or flat? The fact that Earth is a sphere is also proved by lunar eclipses: when Earth casts a shadow on the Moon, that shadow is circular, so Earth itself must be round."

Krutohlav's audience, having been convinced by all this solid evidence, no longer doubted the roundness of this gigantic body, Earth. But just like those wiseacres in our own day who fail to grasp that Earth can hang about in space unsupported by anything, some of his listeners were still deeply troubled.

"But how *do* the Sun, Moon and those myriad of stars just stand there? None of them being tied down, and yet they glitter? It is the power of God that, at the beginning of the world, created these huge bodies, endowing them at once with great might and mutual attraction. In due course, you shall see, for I shall prove it to you, that the Sun attracts to it not only our Earth, but other, much larger bodies, keeping them at a fixed distance, just as Earth itself has, from the beginning of time, managed and taken care of the Moon that is attracted to *it*."

With that Krutohlav brought his discourse to a close.

THE DAILY ROTATION
OF EARTH

When the companions had rested awhile, there in that huge corrie on Gerlach, Krutohlav clambered once more up the ladders that had been got ready, up to the mountain's very summit. Scrambling up through various gullies, the entire company followed him. Once they had spread out across the site, Krutohlav, having climbed to the topmost spot, began holding forth on how Earth could revolve about its own axis.

a) on the basis of its velocity

"Up there the firmament is spinning round our Earth, yet we abide at rest; but let's leave that, let's leave the firmament be and let's have Earth at the Equator travel at 225 leagues an hour. Certainly, that might appear somewhat flattering at first sight, given that none of us has detected that speed and we ourselves are not moving, but sitting here peacefully. But just let me get up a head of steam and I'll explain what can be adjudged about Earth from where we are right now."

Whereupon Krutohlav blew his nose and then went on:

"Such speed on Earth's part is very hard to grasp, and it's like sound, which travels at 2,724 leagues a minute. We shall familiarise ourselves in due course with the much higher velocities of some other bodies. Furthermore – and please don't interrupt me – it bowls along fastest at the Equator, and the further we move away from there towards the poles, the slower the speed, so the poles as Earth's axial points barely move at all. So the summit of Gerlach, where we are standing now, is moving faster than St Petersburg, but slower than Rome or Constantinople."

"Where's this leading us?" Netrpoš[79] butted in. "You're changing the subject."

"Just keep listening and you'll see what follows from the velocity of other bodies if Earth is standing still, that is, how fast other bodies must be revolving around a motionless Earth."

At this point some of them detected what Krutohlav's words were leading up to, but they let him continue.

"Our Moon is, as you'll believe in due course, almost 52,000 leagues from Earth, and around a motionless Earth its orbit, of a length of 326,730 leagues in every 24 hours, must come to 227 leagues a minute, which would be six times faster than the velocity of Earth. The Sun, which is 21 million leagues from us, would have to cover 90,000 leagues a minute and travel 24,000 times faster. With the velocity of these bodies we haven't reached the end of it, because even the distance of the Sun from Earth is a mere dot compared to the distance of other heavenly bodies. At what speed would they have to be moving round Earth and with what force would they have to have been hurled – and why? Just so that we could be left in peace? How ridiculous is that! That billions of stars should have been created just for our peace and freedom?!"

Such a din as broke out after Krutohlav had finished hadn't been heard for quite some time. Some had failed to fathom his perspicacity and thought processes, others were just amazed. Some mocked and jibed, especially Hniloš and Vadoš,[80] while blushing at being so slow on the uptake. Pochyba, his head propped on his elbows and cupped in his hands, was lost in the deepest cogitation.

---

79 The name implies impatience.

80 Names suggestive of rot and flaw, respectively.

Then they all, sunk in thought, hauled themselves back down into the corrie and waited upon the coming day, when Krutohlav had promised to present yet more arguments in favour of the Earth's rotation.

Which, next day, he duly did.

b) on the basis of the size of other heavenly bodies.

"Do you not think it an injustice to declare Earth to be a motionless body merely in order that, at our behest, other monstrous masses should go whirling around us? Is it not folly, for example, to allow even just the Sun to revolve around the Earth when you could make a million and a half Earth-size globules out of it and expect its huge mass to move 2,400 times faster around the million and a half times smaller Earth? And how many billions of stars, whose magnitude and remoteness are beyond our ken, such that the Sun's distance is but an invisible dash by comparison, do we expect to go circling round the speck of dust that is Earth, which, in comparison to others, will vanish one day and perish like a grain of sand in the ocean? And why? I ask you: for us to dwell in peace and quiet, is that why? Just because it's where we live??"

"That's rubbish," exclaimed Mudroš. "That's not possible. How on earth could the entire heavens circle around a speck that's so tiny in comparison with the Sun! Or do you think that a smallish entity should govern the monstrously huge?"

"You do have a point there. And the more I think about it, the more likely it seems to me that Krutohlav is using this argument to bring us round to thinking as much," the ever troubled Pochyba added.

"Me too, me too, I'm coming round to the same idea," came from various quarters.

"Well, just wait," said Krutohlav, "there's also the fact that

c) the uniformity of the motion of the stars permits us to conclude how Earth is revolving."

"How so?" asked Smeloš,[81] "That's not possible."

"I'd also very much like to know how that is," came the response from Vrtoš.[82]

"So just listen to what our master has to say," several other voices responded.

"All the stars in the sky, whether large or small, whether close to us or extremely remote, swing past once every twenty-four hours."

"I get that, I do," exclaimed Umoš.[83]

"No matter with what ineffable power our Earth might be endowed, it ought, by the laws of mechanics, to react differently to something that is far away from how it reacts to something close by. And what actually happens? It reacts to them all in exactly the same way, be that the nearby Moon, or the Sun or the billions of distant fixed stars. And this sameness of response relates precisely to a twenty-four hour period."

"Ho-ho! Ha-ha-ha," some began to chuckle at the notion that Earth was left in state of shame and disgrace, whizzing willy-nilly through the cosmos like a piffling little poppy-seed. Only Vrtoš, Hnevoš and Vadoš bit their lips and, outraged by the shame inflicted upon Earth, turned their backs on those who mocked them as a defence against any jokes at their expense and to secure the peace and quiet due to them, and to our Earth.

---

81   This name implies boldness.

82   The nit-picking one.

83   The brainy one.

Presently, Krutohlav, having taken a breather, raised the question whether how the Earth revolves

d) depended on its want of a central point.

"If the Earth is supposed to be static, then it must have a central point around which all the stars turn. But where are we to seek this central point – surely in the middle of the Earth, or not?"

"Indeed so," some responded.

"Right then. But we can see that the stars and their orbits do revolve, but not around the centre of the Earth. Indeed, we can also see that they turn outwards, not only from any central point of the Earth, but away from Earth itself. So, for example, the Big Dipper revolves around the Pole Star. So how are we to track down that point on Earth that would attract them so that they revolved round it?"

"It really is silly to harbour any further doubts about how Earth rotates."

"It's pure madness to keep thinking Earth is static."

"Oafish to cling to that delusion."

"Crazy to lay claim to more than actually exists."

Those who'd run out of patience inveighed thus against the non-believers, especially Pochyba, who stubbornly continued to doubt this greatest of all truths. He really was so adrift that when with all the pushing and shoving, a rock came loose and he nearly went flying over the edge.

At which Krutohlav wagged a finger and silence reigned once more.

e) the way bodies fall from a height is also evidence of Earth's rotation.

"If Earth rotates, then solid, small bodies dropped from a height must shift if not yards, then at least inches away from their starting point and so not land where they ought to, but a little further off."

All minds were already spellbound by these words, but Krutohlav pressed on:

"All bodies dropped from a height fall straight down. But if one has been dropped from a greater height, Earth will have, during its fall, run on a bit and so the thing cannot land where it really should have. If I can prove this to you, you will have acquired further evidence that Earth does rotate."

"So we shall," Benuš concurred.

"Tomorrow, or any other time you like, you can check this for yourselves, especially from Kriváň, at the spot where the source of the White Vaag is. Hard by it, there's a 7,000-foot sheer cliff face from which it will be easy to throw balls down. That's all I'll say for the present – right now I can't be bothered to go into it any deeper – but at another time I'll elaborate on how a falling body shifts as Earth rotates not only eastwards, but also slightly to the south, and that happens everywhere except at the Equator. Take good note of that. Let me give you a few examples to make this whole thing more interesting.

"In 1802, Benzenberg[84] wanted to check this, so he climbed the tower of St Michael's church in Hamburg and found that a ball dropped from a height of two hundred and thirty-five feet retreated eastwards by four Paris lines.[85] From a different tower, measuring two hundred and sixty feet, the ball shifted by five lines. If someone were to drop a ball from the top of Mt Etna,

---

84 Johann Friedrich Benzenberg (1747–1846) German physicist, astronomer and geologist, who wrote widely on the laws of gravity (1804) and the rotation of the Earth (1807). His ball-dropping experiments were inspired by an idea of Isaac Newton's.

85 How the French line differed from the English one I have not ascertained, but it is roughly 1/12 of an inch.

which rears up to a height of 10,000 feet, the shift would be seven feet, five inches and eight lines.

"Tomorrow, by Jove, I'll do my own test from the summit of Kriváň and I bet we'll see a shift of seven feet or more. That should make Pochyba, Hnevoš and Vadoš happy!" said Mudroš with a sting in his tone.

"You needn't bother. But all this does furnish incontrovertible evidence that our Earth really is spinning round, and if you do do an experiment, whenever that might be, you're bound to find this is all true."

The were now all dancing with glee at the inexhaustible profusion of evidence that Earth rotates and no one entertained any further doubts. But Krutohlav, with yet another shake of his head, was not yet giving up on convincing his friends and also mentioned that

f) Earth's rotation can also be inferred from its centrifugal force.

"Consider, too," he began again, "if we might not – from the rotation of the Earth, which at the Equator is whizzing round at one German league in sixteen seconds – track down evidence on the ground that would provide further confirmation of that rotation. Before we look into the various causes and issues, I need to explain to you what centrifugal force means. If you take a catapult with a stone in it and just swing it round, the stone won't go flying. If you tie some string round a ball, you can swing it round and round. The longer you swing it, the sooner the string will snap. If you fill a bucket with water, the water will settle level, but if we had the strength to spin the bucket in the air around its axis, the water would press outwards and climb up the sides, leaving a depression in the middle. If you could spin the bucket at an unconscionable speed, it would eventually become dry.

"If you sprinkle some sand on a board, tie a string to it and start swinging it round, the sand won't go flying, but collect round the rims until it grinds itself to nothing.

"If you attach a ring of elastic to a stick and spin it very fast, it won't stay circular, but become elongated.

"If you take some soft clay and place it on a potter's wheel which you then set turning, the clay will flatten at the edges and bulge at the centre."

"We get it, we get it," some of them cried out, "we know now what centrifugal force is, go on to something else, sir!"

"Well, the same thing happens with Earth," Krutohlav replied, "as it turns on its axis, assuming that it was originally soft and runny. But be none of you in any doubt that the views presented have long been proven, because piles of fossilised marine creatures can be seen not only in mines, but also on the highest peaks, which really does point to Earth's original surface."

Krutohlav wanted to go on telling his companions about Earth. Some, already quite convinced, didn't wish to hear any more arguments. And Krutohlav would have happily left it at that, but, at Zvedoš's request, he began proving its rotation on the basis of

g) how Earth is flattened.

"I won't offer you any more proof, I think you're satisfied now. But since Zvedoš has asked, I will at least present rotation on the basis of how Earth is flattened. I've already said that the Earth is a sphere, but that's not quite true, and why? Well, you could have gathered as much from the potter's wheel. But keep listening.

"As soon as students of nature became convinced that the Earth was spherical, they gave no further thought to any alternative possible shapes. Later, after improvements to telescopes, and other mathematical instruments, many set about investigating and describing this habitation of ours properly. Since then, such proper observations have been made everywhere, especially as regards Earth's size and shape. The results of all these enquiries confirm that Earth is a sphere, as had been believed up until then, but not a perfect sphere, because it is spinning, and, like the blob on the potter's wheel, it is compressed at the poles, while having a bulge at the Equator. The compression at the poles amounts to about three leagues, from which we may readily infer that our conjectures are guaranteed true, and that Earth does indeed spin about its axis!"

They reacted to Krutohlav's words as to an electric spark. Not one of them now harboured any doubts, and even Pochyba acknowledged the truth of the insights with which he had been presented. The thrill of being able to accept that Earth was a rotating sphere and so to rise above the commonplace views of the vulgar masses stirred their minds to such a flurry of merriment that they began acting quite the giddy-goat. Having rounded off that subject, Krutohlav was the first to climb back down the ladder into the corrie, then the others all followed in humility.

DIFFERENCES IN EARTH'S GRAVITATION

"What *is* gravitation? Is it something to do with the Earth's own weight? Except no one can ever have weighed it," said Pštros,[86] already near the top of the ladder. Just like ants, Krutohlav's companions were clambering back up the ladder to hear his latest lecture. He himself picked up a stone between finger and thumb

---

86   The name means ostrich.

and began to weigh it in the palms of his hands, meaning to speak about gravitation.

Once the hum and buzz, chatter and clatter had all subsided he took up his position on top of a boulder and, stick in hand, began:

"Pštros has tentatively proposed that we should find out what gravitation means. I hope neither Vadoš nor Jedoš[87] will hold it against me, and the rest of you, learn something about it," Krutohlav replied in a loud voice. "You know that any item – a rock, water, a piece of iron etc. – falls straight down to the ground, in other words, they are attracted by an unseen power towards the centre of the Earth. Throw a stone or anything and in the end it will drop straight back to Earth. Right?"

"Yes," his comrades yelped.

"This mysterious power by which all things are drawn towards the centre of the Earth is called an attractive force or gravitation."

Bystroš[88] wasn't at all keen on the notion that everywhere on Earth attracted falling objects in the same way. On the contrary, he thought that Krutohlav was taking things so fast that even Lenoš[89] had started taking note. "But why?" he hastily retorted.

"You will concede, Bystroš, that it is at the Equator, that is, half-way between the poles, that the Earth is whizzing fastest, won't you?"

"Indeed."

"Precisely because the centrifugal force acts as a brake on the rate of fall of a falling body, it is natural that one will fall less fast there. And conversely, the closer we approach the poles, the rate of Earth's rotation is slower and bodies – their speed

---

87 His name suggests venom or sarcasm.

88 'Quickwit'.

89 A name suggesting indolence or sluggishness.

unimpeded – will fall sooner and faster. It then goes without saying that at the poles things will fall sooner and faster."

"Hm," Bystroš muttered under his breath.

"So our two poles can be treated as matter, ground, that isn't rotating, but static. But even around the Equator Earth's movement is quite slight and barely appreciable by sight, so the outcome of it will be likewise. The difference is only 1/289 of gravitation. But if Earth were spinning faster, that's to say if our days were shorter, the centrifugal force would greatly outweigh gravitation. So, if our day were 17 times shorter, lasting only a quarter of an hour as we know it, then objects dropped below the Equator would float freely in the air and never fall to Earth; and if the force of rotation were even greater, all objects cast adrift would remain at liberty in the air forever. So the whizzing effect of the Earth is 1/289 weaker at the Equator than at the poles."

CONSTANT
EASTERLY WINDS

Although Krutohlav kept hammering away now at one topic, now at another in the course of his presentation, he, like Earth itself, kept going round and round the case for the Earth's rotation just like Earth going round and round its own axis. His inexhaustible supply of arguments and reasoning afforded him such diverse material that once he'd started yapping, there was no stopping his train of thought. His companions, but especially Zvedoš, Bystroš and Chtivoš,[90] finally came down hard on him and begged and pleaded, willed and pressed him into drawing yet more treasures

---

90   The name suggests greed or simply eagerness.

from the wellsprings of his wit and wisdom, the pith that was growing ever more important.

Having done something about his unruly hair and cleared his throat in stalwart style, he took up the request of those named and launched into the following expansive disquisition:

"I believe that you, Tvrdoň[91] and Mudroš, Hlasoň[92] and Sokol,[93] have all sailed to America."

"Yes," they all replied.

"What struck you most as regards the wind? You see, it's my belief that on such a long journey from Europe to America every seabird, fish or anything else will start observing it out of sheer boredom."

"You're telling me: the voyage is endless and you've got so much time on your hands you even start observing the spiders and their cobwebs," said Hlasoň in a loud voice.

"When we made that journey, we set out from Marseilles, passed Gibraltar and headed straight south towards the Equator. When we were about 20 degrees from it, we were picked up by an easterly wind, which then carried us all the way to America," Tvrdoň added entirely relevantly.

"What Tvrdoň says is quite true," the others acknowledged.

"Quite so," replied Krutohlav, "both above and below the Equator, in a band about 20 degrees wide, that easterly wind blows all the time. Sailors exploit it to get from Europe to America or from America to Asia and once caught in its orbit, they can reach their destination quickly. But let me tell you something about

---

91 Presumably an error for the previously named Tvrdoš.
92 This name probably implies resonance or assertiveness.
93 'Falcon', though across the dialects of Slovak the word may refer to certain other raptors.

where that wind comes from: its cause resides in how the Earth rotates around its own axis."

"Well I'll be damned – even winds are due to it!" said Pochyba.

"I don't want to go too deeply into such an important topic, and yet, to the extent that you might understand what I'm saying, I shall deal with it, especially for the benefit of Pochyba. So:

"Along the line of the Equator itself it's all peace and quiet. But up to 23 degrees in the northern hemisphere there is an incessant north-east wind, while in the southern hemisphere the wind comes from the south-east. Throughout this belt the inhabitants still have the Sun beating down from directly overhead. The very heat makes the air thinner or more rarefied and, lifted higher, it flows, or drifts, towards the poles and so, in the heights, constant winds hold sway. Cold air comes down in turn from the poles, sneaking into the thin air at the Equator, hence the permanency of the winds' rule. It's further aggravated by the Earth's rotation, slight at the poles, fastest at the Equator. So the air coming from the poles is set in motion by the Earth's rotation, which is what gives the winds their great vim and vigour. So, they, too, depend on the Earth's rotation."

"True, it's true," several responded, but Pochyba remained dubious.

HOW THE EARTH
CIRCLES ROUND THE SUN

"But this as well," Zvedoš chimed in, "is it not true that besides rotating round its own axis, Earth also whizzes round the Sun?"

"Just so," said Krutohlav. "I could give you endless evidence that, notwithstanding the deceptive appearance that the Sun moves round the Earth, in fact it's the other way round."

"Do, please, give us some of the proof," Zvedoš asked.

"Well, as you see," Krutohlav began, "the Sun is the source of light and heat not only for our Earth, but also for many other bodies, notably the planets and comets. For this very reason, and quite rightly so, the Sun is the focal point round which the entire system, including Earth, rotates. But that notion sounds more mythical or metaphysical, so although I've said it as a fact, it doesn't amount to much.

"Now, the Sun is a huge sphere, so huge, so gigantic, that you could knead one and a half million Earth-spheres out of it. Whatever the bond, power, force that reigns between the two bodies, it must be entirely natural, and at first sight perhaps rather flattering, that the Sun must have ascendancy over Earth, the lesser power being subordinate to the greater, the smaller body circling round the larger. If we tied two different stones to the end of a piece of string and threw them up into the air, then by the laws of mechanics the heavier one will be static while the smaller one spins round it. So what must it be like for Earth, when it's a million and a half times smaller than the Sun?"

"It's only natural," Hledoš[94] replied, "that power dominates weakness."

"And so, my friends, as I've told you a thousand and one times before, the planets are much closer to us than fixed stars. We see them as a disk, or the bottom side of something. Because of the sheer distance, we see other stars only as indivisible dots. The planets sometimes come up so close that, say, Venus and Mars distinguish themselves by features similar to the Moon. This is the evidence that both Earth and they belong to the same solar system.

---

94 The name suggests 'seeker'.

"The Sun moves with absolute precision – or rather our planet round it – which can't be said of the other planets when viewed from Earth. They may revolve now faster, now slower, or may even seem to be standing still. Their motion can be now eastwards, now westwards, while their orbit is uneven and sinuous. The same goes for comets, but even more so."

"Dearie me," said Mudroš with a sigh. "Such amazing things go on in Nature."

"Copernicus it was who laid down new principles in the science of the stars by telling the truth and insisting that the orbits of the planets be traced not from Earth, but from the centre, that is, the Sun, which would throw the best light on how the planets behave. And so darkness and shadow were taken over by brightness and light!

"And that is why the Earth should not be treated as a free-standing body, but as one part of the solar system. Just as Jupiter and its four moons rotate about themselves and around the Sun, so, too, do Earth and its Moon circle the Sun. An observer standing on Jupiter would see Jupiter as standing still with the Sun and Earth going round it, in just the same way as it seems to us. But that really is just an illusion.

"I've no desire to harass you further, just believe what I've told you. The annual circuiting of the Sun by Earth must be ascribed to the size of the Sun and the primal motion of the universe. It is faster than its daily rotation round its own axis. The motion of Earth round the Sun is 1,430 Paris leagues per second, or 64 times faster. If we could travel that fast in a boat, on board our balloon or the dragon, it would take us 22.5 minutes to encircle the Earth, a journey of 5,400 leagues, whereas Captain Cook needed three years and 14 days. A ship doing ten feet a second, would go round the Earth in 142 days and 18 hours, or four and half months."

Krutohlav's discourse on how the Sun, such an immense body, attracts the Earth to it and keeps it spinning round it, left them gasping.

THE WEATHER ON EARTH

Krutohlav having announced he was going to change the subject and tell them about the weather on Earth, Všetečkoš[95] chimed in to say that they'd all had experience of winter and spring, summer and autumn and knew jolly well what they were and what they were like!

Krutohlav looked at him, goggle-eyed, and raised a menacing finger at him. So he quickly drew in his horns and Krutohlav, as requested by all the others, began:

a) the conformities of the Earth's changing weather.

"What on earth's that, I don't understand," said Slaboš.[96] Without so much as a glance in his direction, Krutohlav began:

"So far I've been telling you all, and providing the evidence, that the Earth really does turn on its axis and rotate around the Sun. Now I want to explain the advantages, the benefit or, if you will, in short, the gain, the consequences of this rotation for us who on Earth do dwell.

"The core consequences of this twofold rotating are the facts that we have night and day, that winter is followed by spring, then summer and autumn. The Earth going round its own axis once in twenty-four hours is what gives us night and day; and its orbiting the Sun once a year is what gives us the changing seasons. What

---
95 Suggestive of Busybody or Fusspot.
96 Suggestive of Weakling.

an incalculable benefaction for us it is that when we get up in the morning we can enjoy sunlight; what an ineffable favour to us it is that in the spring the whole of nature attires itself anew, thanks to which we can live and survive! Who can put a price on such a boon?"

b) what would become of us if the Earth did not turn on its axis.

"To help you have a better grasp of this, try imagining that the Earth only rotates around the Sun, but not round its own axis. The way the Moon goes round the Earth, only ever showing us one of its faces. That's how it would be with Earth: the half of it turned away from the Sun would never enjoy its rays and remain in constant darkness. If we, I mean Europe, Asia and Africa, were so fated, things would look quite different for us, for nature, for all plants and animals. What would we do if it were dark all the time?"

"We'd be drowning by misery," Svedomoš[97] sighed.

"You have to understand: consider the Earth rotating round the Sun, but not round its own axis, how would things look for us?"

"Well, day and night would definitely have to change and every village would have to be turned to face the Sun," Vrtoš responded, frivolously.

"Just so, but what would day be like, and night – you haven't quite got it yet, Vrtoš. All over Earth, a day would last six months and a night likewise, as has been observed at the poles. How would you, Vrtoš, spend six months in the dark? You'd be freezing cold and have to keep making candles to survive."

c) what would become of us if the ecliptic merged with the Equator.

The moment he uttered these words he was assailed by voices demanding that he explain them.

---

97 Suggestive of 'conscience'.

"The Equator is that line in the middle between the poles, where Earth's belly projects furthest. The ecliptic is the line the Earth follows as it circles the Sun."

"So it doesn't circle the Sun in line with the Equator?"

"Indeed not, it twists this way and that around the Equator like a snake. The line it takes round the Sun is now above, now below the Equator, meaning it keeps crossing it. If there were no ecliptic – that zigzag line that the Earth follows as it circles the Sun, and if it went hand in hand with the Equator, what would it be like for the Earth?"

"We see the point, do go on."

"Listen up then. One consequence would be that our weather would be quite different and I'm sure none of you would like it. Everywhere would have the same day and the same night. People and plants living at the Equator would burn to death and those at the outer edges would freeze to death. Only a small section in the middle would be habitable, but not even there would any worthwhile fruit grow."

"God preserve us from constant cold and blazing heat!" Mudroš concluded. And the company broke up.

d) the oblique position of the Earth's axis vis-à-vis the ecliptic

"The Earth goes round the Sun in a near-circle. Not a perfect circle, being now slightly closer to, now slightly further from the Sun. It gets closest in winter, farthest away in summer. Don't be thinking that it is always in the same direct line from the Sun. Far from it. It stands at an angle to it and also rotates at an angle. That oblique position accounts for the different kinds of weather on Earth. I could easily get that across to you, but, in the absence of the requisite diagrams and a lot more talking, let's leave it at that. Just remember, and believe me unwaveringly, that that is how matters stand. Much as if I were to start telling you all about the alphabet, you'd soon get fed up, so I shall set this topic aside for now in order that you may learn about more important things and, so far as possible, get to know about Earth's surface. Because those more delicate matters belong to the realm of mathematics. There let them think what they want and argue to their hearts' content." Thus did Krutohlav bring that subject to a close.

e) the hot, cold and median orbit of the Earth

Zvedoš had long known that it's colder in Kamchatka than in Borneo, Java, Sumatra and elsewhere on the Equator, but he couldn't stop pestering Krutohlav into telling them more about that.

So Krutohlav began, thus:

"He's right," he said, confirming what Zvedoš had said, "heat and cold are by no means uniform across the Earth. If we bear in mind that the Earth is spherical, then

1. at the poles, or along the Earth's axis, at the north and south end, it is equally cold, so very cold that neither man nor beast, nor any flora can weather it. They are, technically speaking, frigid zones.

2. The Equator is the warmest region on Earth and because of the heat people turned black.

3. Between the poles and the Equator there are two separate regions: between the Equator and the middle belt is the hot zone. It is 47 degrees wide, each degree being calculated at 15 geographic leagues. The middle belt, which lies between the hot zone and the poles is 43 degrees wide. This is where we live. The circumpolar zone is 23 degrees wide."

"It really is odd that that's how things are on our Earth," Mudroš replied.

"That one can get both roasted and frozen to death," Hladoš added.

"Do stop chattering," Krutohlav responded. "People living in the hot zone see the Sun at noon directly overhead and it shines down on them almost vertically, which is why it's so blazing hot there. Besides that, days and nights there are equally long almost all year round, absolutely equal at the Equator itself. Where the hot and middle zones meet, the longest day or night lasts 13 hours and 28 minutes. At noon, the shadow of any object standing upright at the Equator can disappear completely, at different seasons it inclines to the south, and sometimes to the north, so 24 times a year the inhabitants of this zone have no shadow, and sometimes they have a double shadow."

"And what's it like there with how the stars rotate?" Zvedoš asked.

"Well they're obviously on the horizon at the poles, and the stars won't go round in circles over their heads as they do with us, but rise and set as we see the Sun rise and set."

"Strange that, but true," Zvedoš responded. "It can't really be otherwise. And how about the inhabitants of the central belt?"

"In the central belt, where we ourselves are living, things look quite different. The Sun is never vertically above our heads, but even at his highest stands to one side," Krutohlav replied. "The closer anyone lives to the frigid zone, the more oblique the angle at which they will see the Sun. That also explains the variability of night and day: the further away we are from the hot zone, the greater the inequality between night and day. At the limit of the frigid zone is the longest night and day, and the difference is exactly 24 hours. At the Equator it is summer all the time, with frequent rainfall. And, lest I forget to remind you: when we of the northern hemisphere are enjoying spring or summer, people in the southern hemisphere are having autumn and winter."

"And how is it with stars and their shadows?" asked Vadoš.

"Stars move at an angle in circles round the Pole Star. As for the shadow – we call it the umbra, it always points north from our perspective, but south in the southern hemisphere. We can't see their poles because we're too far away.

"Finally let me tell you something about the frigid zone. When, in the southern hemisphere, the Sun inclines beyond the Equator or close to it, in the northern hemisphere it will have set, that's to say stopped shining. But having crossed the Equator towards us, it does shine and doesn't set. Just think about it a moment and remember the ecliptic and you'll see and understand that what I'm saying is right. As for how the stars turn, most will turn steadily around the Pole Star and only some will rise and set. At the poles everything turns horizontally and no star either sets or rises.

"At the boundary of the central belt, as I've already said, a day and night (the longest) lasts 24 hours. The closer we move from here towards the poles, the greater will be the inconstancy of nights and days, so they will last between one and five months and at the poles there will be six months of uninterrupted darkness and for six months the Sun will shine non-stop.

"But don't go thinking that the Sun will gleam right over people's heads: from the instant it pokes up over the horizon, all its rays will fall at an angle across the entire region. Which is why, as the Sun is about to set again, the cold is so vicious that any flora and fauna are quite out of the question."

f) on the differences between night and day

"I trust you won't mind if I pick out a few examples to back up what I have been saying and throw more light on the subject."

"Please do, sir!"

"Listen up, then. In Vienna, the longest night, and day, lasts sixteen hours and twelve minutes. The shortest day in winter lasts only seven hours and forty-eight minutes. Whereas in Archangel the longest day lasts twenty hours and forty-two minutes and the shortest winter day a mere three hours and eighteen minutes. There are places where a day lasts twenty-three hours and thirty minutes, and the shortest only half an hour. I could give you countless more examples, if that didn't conflict with how I mean to go on. So let these suffice," Krutohlav concluded.

g) temperature differences on Earth

"Look at Hnevoš here, he would assume that wherever the Sun's rays fall at the same angle the temperature would be the same, or he might determine cold and hot on the basis of latitude," someone said.

"But he'd be wrong," Krutohlav replied, "it's not like that. Bear with me and I'll tell you about more of the Earth's properties."

"Please do!"

"Temperature is indeed dependent on the things we've been saying, but it also depends on an area's height above sea level, how far it is surrounded by hills, how close it is to the sea, rivers or mountains, and even on the quality of the soil. Heat isn't so much dependent on the steep angle at which the Sun's rays hit a region, but more on how long the Sun dithers above it. To give you a better idea: at the Equator, the Sun stands right overhead in March and September, but it never hangs about there for long and clears off after a few days. In mid-June and December it is far from being overhead, but since it moves slowly the temperature is constant. And since with days and nights being the same length the temperature drops perceptibly, it is natural that in those parts of the world where the Sun tarries longer, it will actually be warmer than at the Equator."

"Good to know, that," came Ludoš's[98] response.

"But Earth's temperature doesn't depend solely on these factors, but also on others of which we have no knowledge. So, for example, Germany and Kamchatka are at the same latitude, but look at the difference in temperature! In all likelihood there are certain local factors at play."

h) the snow line and isotherms

"A mountain or hill's height has a strange effect on a region's temperature. It is safe to say that at the Equator, or indeed elsewhere in the torrid zone, temperature does depend on elevation. At the summit of Chimborazo it's just as cold as at the poles; the further you descend, the warmer it gets until at the bottom it's very hot indeed. And so throughout the world we find, at the same altitude, points where the mercury drops to zero, and these points – even if they were in the air – are called snow lines. The snow line at the Equator is the highest above sea level, and the further we move towards the poles, the lower it drops, and at the poles proper the snow line is at sea level. But, lest I forget, I should also tell you that the southern hemisphere is cooler."

"Why's that, then?"

"No idea," came Krutohlav's reply.

"There's more I'd like to tell you about, but you have to pay close attention to what I say!

"If we compare the mean temperature of many different places, we observe that there's no consistency: northern Germany is

---

98 His name suggests 'importunate'.

warmer than Kamchatka, which is at the same latitude, and the same applies to most places on Earth. If we imagine lines drawn from place to place we get what are called isotherms that prove that they run parallel down at the Equator, but the closer they are to the poles, the more twisting and irregular they become. These lines recede eastwards at the meridian, pass through the centre of Germany to the west and at the western meridian incline again towards the Equator."

"What's a meridian?" asked Zvedoš.

"I'd almost forgotten to tell you about that," said Krutohlav. "What's the Equator?"

"That's the line that runs round the Earth where it sticks out the most and it lies exactly half-way between the poles," Mudroš replied.

"Right. A meridian is the line that, in contrast to that one, runs through the poles and goes all the way round the Earth. On our side it touches the Ferrari Islands,[99] and in America its western part," Krutohlav added.

"We've got that now," Mudroš replied and Krutohlav brought the matter to a close.

---

[99] I have failed completely to find what islands he means. Or indeed what meridian – not, apparently Greenwich, though if he does mean what is now the prime meridian, we can exclude both the **Faeroes** and the Isola de **Ferrari**, one of many past names of the Isola di Garda (though Wikipedia neglects to say what name applied when). If, however, he does mean the Greenwich meridian, there is one group of islands it does (almost) touch, namely the Balearics. These have never been known by any other names, but in central Minorca, at its highest point, is the municipality of Ferreries.

THE HEIGHT AND THE DENSITY
OF THE ATMOSPHERE

"Any one of us will acknowledge that what we breathe is air, and that air is the source of wind and gales, so I need to pass on to you something about the height and density of the atmosphere."

"Please do."

"Everywhere the Earth is completely surrounded by the air in which we live. It doesn't reach that high, because at the summit of high mountains, at an elevation of one German league, we have an acute sense of how rarefied it is because our ears and noses may start oozing blood.

"Like any other body, air has weight, with which it presses down on us. At sea level the pressure is such as to push mercury upwards by 28 Paris inches. So the weight of air in proportion to mercury is 1:10,462. If the Earth's atmosphere were uniformly dense, its height above the Earth would scarcely reach one league. But as we are taught by pressure gauges, that isn't the way things are, for the higher we go, the more rarefied the air becomes, so it is down at ground level that it is densest. How high it actually reaches, no one has yet determined, but it can be reckoned that if it stretches 17 leagues above the Earth, it will be so rarefied by then that no earthly creature could survive there. We can observe with certainty that at a height of even two leagues its density is already one eighth of what it is at sea level. So air becomes rare in proportion to how high we move upwards."

The reflection of rays

"Like any transparent body, air, too, has the facility to reflect and deflect the rays of the Sun. The natural consequence of this is that the Sun or the stars are actually hanging about up there in a different place from how it seems to us. The reflection of rays in the sky often causes the Sun and Moon to appear other than as they ought to. Their disk is already up, but flattened on the underside. We can already see half of the rising Sun or Moon, yet it is actually still beneath the horizon. The reason is in how their rays are reflected. This also accounts for how we can look into the rising Sun without damaging our eyes, though not at mid-day.

"You mustn't think that this law applies only to the Sun and Moon, no, it applies to all physical bodies. For example, we don't see the tip of a spire or the top of a hill where they actually are, but somewhere quite other, and it's all down to refraction. The same also applies at dusk. We still see the Sun on the horizon, but in fact it has already set, thus making our day longer. Even after it has set completely, its rays are still reflected in the air and we get twilight. If the Earth had no air, we'd only be able to see such things as would be lit up by the Sun, and everything else would be in utter darkness. Even the slightest cloud would cast us into darkness. The skies would have ferreted out darkness, and even our living rooms would be dark if the Sun didn't shine into them. Dawn wouldn't earn a mention and thereafter we'd be lit up by rays, or, at sunrise and sunset, immersed in a dense darkness."

THE CONSTANCY OF THE EARTH'S AXIAL TILT

"We've known for a long time that the greatest depth of the ocean gives us very little. It seems likely that the depth of the ocean will not exceed the height of the mountains that rear up over the surface of the sea and that it will be of the order of 30,000 feet. Despite that, in far distant days, the Earth was covered (though not entirely, just parts of it) by a flood, of which we have excellent evidence in the shape of marine fossils. In 1771, on the sandy bank of the River Viltna[100] in Siberia, a complete rhinoceros carcass was dug up; even its skin was complete. In 1799, an elephant[101] of extraordinary size was dug out of the ice in the Lena delta, also so complete that the Yakuts could feed its flesh to their dogs.[102] All this has led some to conclude that the Earth's axial tilt changed and caused these animals to be cast suddenly up from the Equator towards the poles. On this important matter I shall merely remind you that those worthies completely overlooked the fact that, having been tossed up there, the animals would have immediately frozen to death.

"But consider certain other arguments about or explanations for these things," said Krutohlav, "and rest assured as to the constancy of the Earth's axis.

"If any such sudden change had indeed come to pass, it could only have happened through the agency of some exterior force. But what kind? You'll see in due course that it could not have come about. Or only in the event that some unknown comet had bashed into the Earth and wrought havoc. But then how could a limpid comet so humble our Terra firma?

"Isn't it possible that Siberia was once inhabited by elephants? The one they found by the Lena may have looked a bit like an Indian elephant, but it was black, with a long, thick, black coat. And the rhino was endowed similarly. So couldn't they have easily

---
100 The real name of the river is Vilyuy. Whether this is a misreading on the part of Reuss, or one by readers of his manuscript is impossible to say. It is the longest tributary of the Lena.

101 I.e. mammoth.

102 Other sources suggest that before the finder could return, the beast, after thawing out, had been largely eaten by bears.

lived in Siberia given they had such nice thick windjammers? If you don't like this argument, then another possibility is that beasts such as tigers, lions and others, might have wandered into Siberia quite often, only to freeze in the marshes, get caught in landslides or simply, chilled to the marrow, to succumb. Once frozen, they could last for thousands and thousands of years, so why should we give credence to those geographers who maintain that the Earth must have shifted its axis? Another argument in defence of the fixity of the Earth's axial tilt is this," Krutohlav went on, having paused for breath. "Originally the Earth was spherical; after its first dig in the ribs it started to spin about its axis. With the sheer speed, it grew oblate, flattened at the poles, but its axis remained the same. And precisely because the Earth is an oblate spheroid it cannot change its axis. Even if some foreign body jolted into it, the flattening at the poles would immediately correct the axis and keep the Earth from moving out of orbit. If it were a perfect sphere, then there would be more chance of the axis changing.

THE INVARIABILITY OF THE AXIS OF ORBITAL PATHS

"The orbital paths of all the planets circulating round the Sun are constant and invariable. Were that to change, that would be the end of all harmony and sooner or later one planet would inevitably ram into another, or even into the Sun. It follows from this that our Earth's orbit round the Sun is constant.

"And while the ocean that has wound round our patch of earth since time immemorial may seem ever the same and stay ever within its shores, it is a mass that does rise and fall every single day. To the observer standing on the shore it is rather odd to observe how the frenzied waves contemplate smashing up and flooding rocky coasts, then, as if talked out of it, calm down again.

"Twice a day, regular as clockwork, the ocean's waves rise and sink back. In the first six hours of the day they always rise, flood low shorelines or islands and thrust their way deep in the mouths of rivers. This is called the flux. And when they reach their maximum height, that is called high tide. Then the sea begins to recede until it has receded completely, which takes another six hours. When it is at its lowest, that is called low tide. But you mustn't no one be thinking that these movements of the sea are caused by winds; oh no, for even at the most profound calm, the motions are the same."

"So there must be another cause," Bdeloš[103] interrupted Krutohlav's flow.

"Indeed so," the latter replied. "If we seek the causes, they shall indeed manifest themselves, but only to genuine observers. These motions of the sea depend on the New Moon and the half-moon, that's to say how the Moon is positioned vis-à-vis the Earth. So over the course of twenty-four hours, two rising and two falling tides can be observed, day after day the same. Sometimes the rise or fall may be delayed by the odd minute or come slightly early, but that is due to the unsteady speed of the Moon.

"But once we acknowledge the Moon as the main cause of tidal motion, it will, after all, be now greater, now lesser, and that depends not only on the proximity of the Moon, but also on that of the Sun, especially at its closest to Earth.

"These strange phenomena apply only to the oceans, not to lakes or harbours, where local obstacles get in their way. So at

---

103 The underlying *bdelý* means 'vigilant'.

Dunkirk the tide only begins to fall or rise twelve hours after the culmination of the Moon, but at the Cape of Good Hope it's only ninety minutes.

"The same sort of thing goes for the air: as the sea gets tossed about, so does the air, but even more so because it is lighter. The movements of the air are revealed to us daily by the barometer. With the aid of other instruments it has been ascertained that air rises most in the morning, between nine and ten o'clock, and least around four in the afternoon. It rises to its highest again at eleven at night, and drops back to its lowest at four in the morning. That's how it all changes in an orderly fashion."

With these words Krutohlav concluded his disquisition on the Earth. His incredulous audience couldn't get over the surprise at all the things Krutohlav had been telling them, much of it entirely new to them. His presentation had been so cogent that none of them harboured any further doubts. They had heard much about various terrestrial phenomena, what place the Earth occupies, how it stands in relation to the Moon and Sun and other planets, but they cherished the hope that Krutohlav would think of more things to tell them about and at some future date make his wide circle of listeners even better informed.

Sitting about at home, moping, he tried really hard to think what to do next. Since he had had his fill of Earth, he began, in a transport of higher thoughts and ideas, to focus so hard on a new subject that it nearly drove him mad.

"I don't want to hang about here," he snorted, tossing aside his pipe and pen. "I want to move on, come what may. True, here I am, but I shall move on and leave these rapscallions to an eternity here on Earth, where they can do whatever they want – but nothing will deflect me from my resolution!"

At which point Krutohlav's entire house shuddered so violently that neither Thekla nor Vesuvius bear any comparison.

And when he thumped his fist on his desk, the bang was so loud that it echoed back from Mokrá luka[104] in one direction and Revúca's St Quirinus[105] in the other.

And when he suddenly sneezed, the tip of Kohút hill came crumbling down along with its topknot of fir trees.

And when he stamped his foot, Lisbon collapsed.

And when he scratched his nose, all the forests about Telgárt[106] were laid flat.

THE END

---

104 Presumably, in light of the second echo, it pinged off the bells in the tower of the Church of the Visitation in Mokrá Lúka, a village bordering Revúca on the south-east.

105 The Catholic parish church of Revúca is dedicated to St Lawrence, though previously to St Quirinus of Neuss. One of its three bells is called 'St Quirinus' (sv. Kvirín), the others being 'St Joseph' and 'Our Lady of the Seven Sorrows'. Reuss's notes on the Quirinus bell were edited and published in the 1858 *Svētozor* supplement ('for leisure and literature') of *Slovenské noviny*, the shortlived (1849–61) journal of the Mekhitarist (Armenian Benedictine) congregation in Vienna.

106 Telgárt is c. 25 km as the crow flies ENE of Revúca. In Reuss's day a remote hunting area, today it is a popular ski resort, linked to the outside world by what must count as one of Slovakia's most impressive railway lines (tunnels, viaducts and the Telgárt Loop).

FROM THE GENERAL GEOGRAPHY OF THE WORLD WITH WHICH REUSS'S BOOK ENDS

appended here for the benefit/amusement of the Anglophone reader.

England[107]

"All I can see here is two large islands and innumerable ships buzzing about on the sea. What country is that? Could it possibly be England?"

"Indeed so," Krutohlav replied. "The country only has mountains in the north, otherwise it's bare, and with few trees. Its mountains rise to 4,000 feet. Its rivers are more like streams and the longest, the Thames, is only thirty leagues long. But, as you can see, it has innumerable canals, which have a total length of four hundred and seventy leagues. You'll find plenty of lakes and marshlands, though they're fairly insignificant.

"Like its inhabitants, the climate in these parts of the globe is mild, awash with mists coming in off the sea and usually quite overcast, changeable, but otherwise salubrious. But look, you can hardly make it out. And why? Because of the mists, rain and snow. In the northern half of the larger island (Scotland) the mountain tops are permanently covered in snow, with mists predominating in the valleys. The smaller island (Hibernia) is wet and cold, so unhealthy. England also has metals, especially lead, tin, copper and iron. There's coal everywhere, with annual sales of ten million pounds sterling. There are no green crops worth mentioning, but they do have excellent horses, sheep and herrings. There are no longer any wolves."

"But the islands are obviously densely populated, with one settlement next to another," said Hledoš.

"True. It has a population of twenty-seven million. They are a mixture of Germans and Celts. Most (seventeen million) speak

---

107 Then, as Slovaks and Czechs today, he means Britain.

English, others German, Celtic or even other languages. The English language is closely related to German."

"These Celts, you keep mentioning them. What sort of people are they?" asked Zvedoš.

"The Celts were a mighty race, and, especially at the time around the birth of Christ, they covered the whole of Europe. They were even in Slovakia – under the name of Wallachians. They are of Indo-European stock, just like the Slavs and the Greeks. Today they have mostly died out or merged with other peoples.

"In no other country in the world are there so many factories as on this small plot of land. And their sea power is so great as to outweigh all others in Europe and the entire world. If someone took their sea power away, they would, because of the density of settlement, starve to death very quickly. Bonaparte knew that very well, but luck wasn't on his side. At some time in the future, North America and Russia will have their say.

"The English are a remarkable nation and often ridiculous. They make excellent soldiers and they're very good at thievery. Advantage and profit are their driving force, or, as the saying goes, if there were money in it, they'd whip a wasp all the way to Jelšava.[108] Which is why they are also cheats, sycophants and double-dealers. Thus, for example, they took control of Gibraltar and, as profit-seekers, made themselves masters of other countries as well."

"I really wouldn't fancy living there, unless all I wanted was to get rich," said Miloš.

[...]

---

108 One of the towns within the district of Revúca.

America

This is a massive region of Earth, which can be reckoned at 700,000 square leagues.

Stretching the whole length of America, from north to south, is a gigantic chain of huge, and volcanic, mountains. Their names are many and various, but the highest is Sorata, at 23,640 feet,[109] Jenimani at 22,7000 feet,[110] Chimborazo at 20,148 ft and others. America's interior consists of endless mountains, so the whole is covered in trees. The mountains are inaccessible. In addition, there are here the most elevated plains, overgrown with long grass. Gigantic rivers rise among the mountains and some are among the largest on Earth. Otherwise, America is very fertile and has almost no deserts. They are not short of lakes either. These range in size from 1,400 to 100 square leagues. It is also very rich in metals, flora and fauna.

Its climate is cooler than Europe's at comparable latitudes, which is down to all the trees and mountains. It has a population of forty-six million. These are Indians, Europeans and Negros,[111] all speaking different languages.

[...]

---

[109] I cannot trace any hint of the oronym Sorata; today Sorata is just a small town in the Bolivian Andes. The reference can hardly be to Aconcagua, for all it is the highest, because it is way to the south in Argentina. If we knew how long a foot was to Reuss, we might work out which mountain he really meant.

[110] Perhaps today's Illimani, the highest mountain in the Cordillera Real (part of the Cordillera Oriental, a sub-range of the Andes), in western Bolivia.

[111] Any other term than this would be a gross anachronism.

Canada

Canada is very mountainous, afforested, but also fertile. It is a beautiful, water-filled land, with the largest lakes and the most memorable waterfall on Earth. The water drops from a height of one hundred and forty-two feet, and the River Niagara is three thousand six hundred feet wide. There is neither gold nor silver here. The population is approaching one million. Of New Alisa,[112] Nova Scotia, Newfoundland, Labrador and New Brunswick we know very little and there's nothing about them deserving of any further attention on our part.

The Republic of North America

This is truly a fine stretch of land, consisting of twenty-seven regions. It is mountainous, afforested and fertile. The mountains rise to 23,000 feet. It has many lakes and rivers, of which the Mississippi is six hundred and fifty leagues long. The whole country is starting to be crisscrossed by canals. The population will rise.

---

[112] Untraced: no such place is mentioned even in the detailed history of the evolution of Canada's provinces and territories (https://en.wikipedia.org/wiki/Provinces_and_territories_of_Canada#Territorial_evolution, accessed 08.08.2022). In light of the rest of the list, it could refer to Prince Edward Island, or the Province of Canada, the colony that existed from 1841 to 1867.

Australia[113]

Krutohlav, having taken an age to whiz across the Pacific Ocean, stopped above Australia and began to describe it:

"This section of Earth consists of nothing but islands, most of which are mountainous, with some peaks rising to 15,000 feet. New Holland[114] is a bare and barren stretch of coastline. However, the other islands are fertile and beautiful. They have a superabundance of metals, flora and fauna. The inhabitants are Papuans and Malays and there are about three million of them."

---

113 Clearly meaning Australasia.
114 Australia proper, or what little was known of it.